The Tree

Matt Lany

ISBN 978-0-692-53796-1

For Nancy and Eloise

The Tree

Part I

Rise

1

The tree comes at night. No person sees. It's always this way.

No one sees me, either.

I am not bad. I would not call myself good. I used to feel different. Sometimes you are swept into a situation, and the man, woman, boy, or girl you were is erased. Who you were doesn't matter.

Days ago, at the rim of this forest, the tree arrived. Days ago, where the tree now stands, there was nothing except a damp layer of dead leaves. Now roots have fastened as if sunk for 100 years. Branches, like enormous antlers, rise from the thick trunk. Where branches meet the trunk are smooth knots. The leaves are diamond-shaped—olive green and small—and few. They look hard, pointy. Old. The trunk has a black gap, a lure. The opening is big enough for a person to enter.

I know. I have seen. Year after year, boy after boy, I have watched them. I know their names. Birthdays. Favorite flavors. Secrets. Everything.

They enter, and none return.

Who have I become? Sometimes I ask myself. The answer is difficult to accept. I am the keeper of this madness.

How I came to be is a story I will tell, but not now.

Three new boys have arrived.

They are so near I can smell them.

Two are together, the other alone. They exit the forest from opposite ends, and a gust of wind shakes their hair. It is late afternoon, wrapped in gloom and tense chill.

In the clearing they see each other and begin walking through knee-high grass towards the tree, which juts from the unusually straight edge of the forest.

The lone boy, named Phillip, carries a stick, tapping the ground as he steps. Earlier, he found the stick bridged across a narrow stream. It is firm and glossed and as high as his armpit. Phillip is tall for his age, but his slouch makes him appear shorter. Stringy hair falls over his eyes, which rarely rest. He has been walking in the woods for hours. Every day after school he walks these woods.

At home his dad, an Army soldier, cannot stop his hands from shaking. He is back from war, but the war has not left him. In four years he was deployed three times. Mostly, Phillip's father sits near a cracked kitchen window and stares into the small backyard, overgrown with smutty weeds and shrubs that need hacking. When Phillip watches his father, he is always drawn to the spastic hands, and he gulps breaths that sting his chest. His mother is seldom home. When she is she sleeps. She hasn't spoken to Phillip for months. Phillip's toes are scrunched in his sneakers, but he doesn't tell anyone. He makes dinner for himself—ham sandwiches, chips. Sometimes he is pushed at school. He stays quiet, looks down. His teachers ask if things are okay. He's smart, one of the smartest in his grade. Why hasn't he been doing his homework? Phillip shrugs.

The other boys, Cole and Adam, are best friends. They live in a gated neighborhood miles away from Phillip. There are bike paths, parks, and a pool with a snack bar. Cole and

Adam play on the same football team, the Knights. Last summer the two families flew to a giant waterpark in Florida and stayed at a hotel with an elaborate display in the lobby: concrete, stones, logs, and fake plants fashioned to resemble a swamp. Baby alligators, as still as stones, floated atop the murky water. There was a sign that said, "Do Not Feed the Alligators," which the boys disregarded. They tossed orange crackers and laughed at the little creatures scurrying for treats—snapping their jaws, pulverizing the crackers.

Cole and Adam rarely walk into the forest adjacent to their backyards. They've never roamed this deep. They were bored, looking for something to do, so they started hiking.

The wind stirs again, but the tree does not move. Not a branch, not a leaf. The opening in its trunk is black, so black the color seems to swirl.

The best friends and the lone boy meet.

"Where did you get that?" Cole points to the stick.

"Somewhere," Phillip says.

"Let me see." Adam has always been the biggest, the one who can reach the high shelf. On the football team he plays lineman and pushes aside smaller kids for Cole, the quarterback.

Hesitant, Phillip hands Adam the stick. He knows he won't get it back.

"What class are you in?" Cole says.

They have seen each other at school.

"Mrs. Phillips."

"What's your name?" Adam twirls the stick. He drops it, picks it up.

It's my stick, Phillip wants to say. "Phillip," he says.

Adam looks at Cole, and they burst into laughter.

"Phillip. Mrs. Phillips. What, are you two related or something?!" Cole snatches the stick from Adam.

"Hey!" Adam says.

Cole runs and sweeps the stick high into the air.

All three boys watch its arc, now turning downward. The stick bounces when it hits the ground. It lands at the base of the tree.

Adam arrives first. "Look at this." He places his hand into the opening. When he does, his hand vanishes. He yanks it back, still there. He laughs as he fans his fingers, which tingle.

Cole's bright blond hair is dulled by the overcast. "That's," he says, smiling, forgetting his thought.

"Phillip, come here," Adam says.

Phillip hears the two boys whispering as he approaches. He stops, staring ahead.

"I dare you to walk in."

Phillip doesn't know which boy speaks. He isn't paying attention. "I dare you," he vaguely hears again, but he is already walking forward, taking the dare, not for them. He knows they plan to push him. He doesn't care. He doesn't give them a chance. The dark grows as he nears, calling him, engulfing him.

Then he is gone.

"What?" Adam says. He looks at Cole.

They peer into the tree.

"Where'd he go?"

Cole is laughing nervously. "I don't know!"

Cole and Adam should run. They should run. But they are confused and fearful. Instead, Cole grabs Adam. They start wrestling, trying to push each other into the tree.

They totter. The stick is by their feet. Their muscles are taut as they struggle—grunts and strained breathing. Their hands grip the sleeves of each other's jackets, and there is a moment when they both want to stop, know to stop, and they share this knowledge, say it with their eyes: *stop*.

But it is too late. They are falling, and neither wants to go in alone.

It is impossible to know who enters first.

I sigh, partly out of acceptance, partly out of sadness.

2

"Oy, newbies! Newbies!"

Cole adjusts his groggy eyes. He wipes slick, gritty sweat from his forehead. There is a jumping boy whose shadows dance around him.

"Oy!"

The boy seems close to his age, but it is difficult to see because of the dark. A soft pink glow in the corner is the only light.

Phillip stands in the glow and stares at the light's origin, but Cole does not see Adam. "Adam!"

"Newbies have arrived! Ha! Adam has arrived!"

The jumping boy is covered in grime, his face a gaunt brown mask with white eyeballs bulging. He is so lean that his bones stretch his skin like the skin of a drum. His ribcage, shoulder blades: he is skeletal. A leather pouch bounces on his hip. His bare feet squish.

There is mud, deep and heavy. Cole feels himself sinking. Alarmed, he lifts his knees while the floor sucks at his feet, which are sopping. He almost loses a shoe. "Adam!" he says.

"Oy, newbies!" The jumping boy stops jumping. Breathing heavily, he bends at the waist, hands on his sides. "Hey, your friend's right there." He points.

Cole discovers Adam in a corner, a few feet away. Adam sits, rocking, arms wrapped around his knees. His eyes blink rapidly.

"Adam," Cole says. "Hey, Adam."

Adam's lips move, and Cole leans close to listen. He must lean closer. He waits for a familiar word, but he soon realizes that Adam's frail mumbling is nothing more than gibberish.

"He's lost it a bit. That happens to newbies sometimes. They get over. He'll get over."

The boy kneels beside Cole. He is wearing filthy and cracked underwear, the elastic shredded. Because of this the underwear droops. His hand is extended. "Name's Tony."

Cole shakes his hand, as dirty as the rest of him.

"What's your name?" Tony says.

"Huh?' Cole says.

"Your name?"

"Cole."

"Cole, I know what you're thinking."

"Where are we?"

"That's what I knew you were thinking."

Cole grabs the boy by the shoulders. He opens his mouth, but he has no words. His breathing hurtles.

"Calm down calm down."

Cole relents and lets go with a push.

"Explore the wonder about you," Tony says, enhanced by the sweeping flourish of a scrawny arm.

Cautious, Cole closely scans the dim enclosure. Above, a low ceiling drips as if from a hundred slow leaks. He reaches up, digs his fingers into the loam, and rips free a warm clump of mud. A fat waterdrop splashes on his head. Suddenly, the heat presses into him. It is crippling, foreign heat that sheens him with sweat. Earthen walls surround. The room, or whatever this is, is small, just enough space for the four of them.

Pit, he thinks. *Rot*. He ingests the piercing and heavy smell, which he can't describe, the smell of fungus, muck—words like this. Then he sees how the cylinder of pink light carves a circle in the wall.

It is the opening to a narrow tunnel, the source of the light beaming from somewhere within. The tunnel leads up at a steep angle. It is the only path.

"Is this a cave?" Cole says.

"What do you remember last?" Tony says.

Cole closes his eyes. He recalls plunging into the dark. As he was falling, he glanced outwards, beyond Adam's shoulder, at the approaching dusk, and saw a flurry of black birds lift into the sky. "We went into the tree," he says.

"Oy, you did, and your friends, too," Tony says.

"What is this place?"

"This place." Tony clicks his tongue. "Well, there's no way to know certain, but the boys here, we think we're under the tree."

"Boys?" Cole looks around.

"That's right, many boys, just like you, like me."

There is something about Tony's voice, and Cole speaks aloud his observation. "Your accent."

"Oy. From Gloucester."

"Gloucester," Cole says.

"Indeed."

"I don't know where that is."

"In England." The boy's eyes protrude like a gecko's. "The tree travels," Tony says.

"But—"

"It will be okay."

"How are you here?"

The question hangs in the stagnant air, lingering, and what follows is a crazed laugh, a quick and high-pitched cackle as cruel as any witch's. "Same as you," Tony says, "same as all of us. Was walking about. Went into the tree. Been here since."

3

Phillip studies his arms. They are becoming covered just like Tony's. It is a continuous process. A cycle of mud and sweat coats patches of skin in a thick paint. *Armor.* He is transforming.

He smiles.

They sit in the sludge.

"There's levels," Tony says. "Up the tunnel, see. Three of 'em. That light's from the first, Level 1 boys. Never been beyond Level 2 myself. Been told about three, the kings up there you know, but got no inclination. I'm a first leveler all the way. You go up the tunnel, find your level, your home. That's what you do here."

Tony reaches into his pouch and pulls out a grimy handkerchief. Any colors that did exist have blanched into shades of brown. He looks up, gauging the random drips of water. He then carefully lays the handkerchief on the ground.

Phillip thinks he understands, but before he can ask Tony about the handkerchief, Adam grunts.

Adam saws back and forth. Trying to speak, he looks desperately at Tony, but can only moan and spit.

Cole rubs his friend's back.

Phillip considers the concern on Cole's face. They are real friends, he realizes. He, though, feels nothing. Listening to

Adam struggle, Phillip has no empathy for the arrogant boy who took his stick and plotted to push him.

"It's okay," Cole says, encouraging. "What is it?"

"Go on," Tony says. "Out with it."

"H—." Adam rocks with every syllable. "How."

Philip thinks, *Ha.*

"How. Good. How what, Adam?" Cole says.

"How." Adam winces, as if the word causes pain. "Long." He exhales. "Long!"

Tony claps his hands. His broad smile shows surprisingly white teeth. "How long have I been here? That's what you're asking, right?"

Adam nods and nods.

"Well, exact time is hard to say. There's no sunlight. No day or night. You're awake, sleep when you feel like it."

"4:37," Phillip says.

It is odd: all their eyes swiveling onto him. The chance to be the center of attention compelled Phillip to speak, but now he is angry for wanting attention. "October 12," he adds. There is just enough light to see the white hands of his wristwatch and the date below. He taps the glass face. "It's stopped."

"They won't work here," Tony says. "The clock stops, as you say."

Watches track small increments—seconds, minutes, and hours. They often mark the day and month. Phillip has never seen a wristwatch that displays the year. His eyes, owning a still and weighty focus new to him, glom onto Tony. He stares at this boy who knows the mysteries of this place, mysteries he wants to know.

"Never got your name," Tony says.

Phillip looks away. The pink light is constant, never flickering. "Phillip."

"A stately name," Tony says.

Phillip shrugs, habit.

"No? You don't think?"

His eyes return to Tony. "No."

"Well then," Tony says, recovering, "you were saying. The time. Date. Anything to add?" He cannot hide his irritation.

This time Phillip maintains his stare. He thinks of the tree, its high branches and sparse leaves, the way these few leaves and branches connected to form spidery constellations. He answers Tony's question.

Phillip tells him the year.

Tony stiffens, his spine lengthening; he rises an inch. But after a moment when his entire being seems concentrated into a dense bead of recognition, he thaws, relaxing into what looks like bliss.

Is he recalling a happy time? Phillip does not want to know. Such memories do not belong to him. A memory has one owner.

Then, like a towel-snap, Tony returns to his chatty, busy demeanor. "Well, I was eleven when I stepped into the tree." He scratches his cheek and picks up his handkerchief. "And that was 31 years ago."

A thrill, not of surprise, bites Phillip. The excitement derives from an expectation that has been met. He expected this place to be magical, and it is. He watches Tony bundle the now saturated handkerchief into a ball, which he then squeezes, drinking dirty water that drips from the fabric.

Just as he thought.

"What?" Cole says. He keeps saying this.

The math has perplexed Cole. Phillip sees Cole lost in numbers that do not make sense. The larger realization has yet to penetrate Cole's notions of what is and is not possible.

"You're 42-years-old," Phillip says matter-of-factly.

"As are my underwear, just about," Tony says. He wrings the handkerchief again. A final drop of water dawdles, gravity lengthening it, before it separates and falls onto his tongue. "Here in the tree you stay as you are. The clock stops, in more ways than one. But there's more. Lots more. It's best I just show you, rather than try to explain. We've got to go up the tunnel. Climb. Go to the levels. Find your home. I'm a Level 1 as I was saying…"

Tony's jabbering fades as Phillip recalls walking into the tree. Steps before he entered, he felt the slow heartbeat of a different world. Knowing he was leaving did not scare him. This world is better than the world he left. Right now, the unknown future is better than his past, when he was a ghost. A ghost waiting for his mother. A ghost watching his father's lost eyes. A ghost in school. A ghost roving the forest.

A ghost isn't seen, except by other ghosts, and ghosts don't like to talk.

He does not feel like a ghost here.

Looking down he sees, nestled in the mud, as if placed there for him, the stick. His stick. He bends down, pulls it from the muck. He shakes off the mud and stakes it into the soft ground. He looks towards the pink light, towards what must, he thinks, be better.

4

"Take off your shoes," Tony says.

Sitting upright, Adam's back sinks into the soft wall. His legs stretch across the width of the tunnel. He wiggles his toes.

It's as hot and wet as steam. His guess is they have crawled for about an hour.

His sneakers are coated with globs of mud. The weight is like cement. He yanks them off, one then the other. Immediately, he feels lighter.

He slaps the shoes together.

"Socks, too."

His socks have become blubber affixed to his skin. Everything is slippery, and he must pull with great effort. The same malady that makes it difficult to speak also impacts his hands and limbs. Shakes rumble through and exhaust him. It is fear. He knows this. He strains to yank a muddy sock over his ankle, stretches it past his heel, but it becomes stuck. His shoulder begins to twitch.

His mind booms. Unfinished questions send shards of lightning through him. The questions are like the mean formations of storms.

Adam tries to create a noise in his head to scramble the fear. A bell. A howl. The louder the noise, the easier it is to move his hands and legs and concentrate.

There, the sock peels free.

He begins on the other.

I am so scared.

He starts to cry.

Scramble. He imagines static, crackling in his eardrums, full volume.

The other sock is off.

"Tie the shoelaces and put them around your neck. Or put the shoes on your hands."

His hands, Adam sees, are swollen. They are red in the pink light, which glows gradually brighter the higher they slog. His hands sting. They are buzzing. His hands are hives of bees. The mud has irritated the skin, and he stuffs his swollen hands into his shoes.

Far away is the bright pink pinhead, like a distant star. Remnants of light diffuse towards them. Their breath mixes with this pink haze and envelops them in a fleshy hue.

"All right, ready?" Tony says.

Tony, Phillip, Adam, and, lastly, Cole: this is the order. From behind, Cole tells him he is doing well, lying to him.

"Good job, Adam," he says, like a father to a child.

Cole is his friend.

They trudge single file, on their hands and knees, up the tunnel towards Level 1. There is never enough air. Adam is always huffing for more oxygen, on the verge of suffocation. Heat glows within him. The narrow tunnel swelters. The mud slurries as they drag a path, liquefying in places into black puddles, and he envisions his body merging into the walls of the tunnel until he is an indistinguishable part of it.

Their jackets are bundled into a boulder, tied together by the sleeves of Adam's jacket. Tony pushes the bundle, thick with accumulated muck. He is strong and agile. He is used to this place. He has been here for 31 years.

The tree travels.

Right hand, left. There is nothing to grab onto. Even if there was, Adam could not because of the shoes on his hands. His knees dig in the mud.

Sometimes he feels movement beneath. It is like a creature slithers under him, and his hand or knee will drop. When this happens, the shock makes him trap his breath. He stops breathing for a few seconds then urgently inhales. Do the others sense the creatures?

He can't ask. He can't form the words.

This tunnel is alive.

Concentrate.

Right hand, left.

Get to the light.

5

After adding the newbies' shirts and pants into the clothes ball, Tony uses the legs of Adam's jeans to start a tight, secure knot.

They are taking another break, having traveled a significant distance. At last the tunnel has slightly widened and become less cramped. Tony is thankful for the extra space. One more long push and they will reach Level 1.

Adam, he sees, stares vacantly down the tunnel. Eventually, the light disappears into stark, solid black.

Mumble-mouth. Tony clicks his tongue.

He gets back to the knot.

Finished, he deliberates. Yes, the knot will hold. The clothes bundle came undone at one point during their climb, and he had to rewrap the entire mess as the newbies looked on, useless, and he does not want to repeat that debacle.

He lifts the clothes, like a medicine ball now, and heaves them as far up the tunnel as he can, which isn't very far.

He sits down with a plop, lays out his handkerchief.

The newbies are desperate for water.

They sit across from him. They may not look new, slathered in grime, having slunk through mud for hours, but they're still newbies. They are because they do not yet know what is waiting for them and how it will obliterate any sense of understanding they had about the world. They will tremble.

He knows. He trembled.

But he has survived. He has accepted and, therefore, learned to cope. Few do. Most don't last. That is why *he* belongs with the kings up in the cleaner, cooler air.

Level 3.

He has a plan.

These kids, he stifles a chuckle as he looks at them. They hope they are climbing towards escape. That makes sense. It's basic. Down here. Get up there. Open the hatch or crawl out the hole. Their motivations stem from wanting to go back home. Of course the requirement here—to change the motivations that govern action—is a process that eventually crushes most.

Admittedly, he was the same. He remembers waking disoriented in the pit. He remembers that first climb. He was worse than Adam. What a weak, pathetic kid he was then, not the strong boy he is now. In the tree they are all boys, even a 42-year-old.

He has had this debate with himself, what it means for a boy to become a man. He has thought deeply about this idea.

He studies the newbies across from him, sizes them up. It is brighter here, so he sees them clearly.

Adam, right now, is wasted and weak. He still can't even speak for goodness sakes. His bet is Adam is not a laster. He will not be able to change. He will go away. He will make that choice.

Some boys choose to go away.

Tony considers Cole. He checks his eyes because they reveal. Cole's eyes are not Adam's numb orbs. Plutos, Tony calls them. When you've got Plutos for eyes, you're done for. There is still swimming in Cole's eyes, and swimming equals mechanically sound thinking. 2+2=4. Cole has not let emotion overwhelm logic, even if his logic does not apply to this place. At least Cole is trying to understand and anticipate, which means not looking back to the pit from where they came—or even further back, to the tree and its black fold—or even further, to home, to Mum and Dad.

That home is gone. This is home now.

He will continue to watch Cole, to see how he develops.

Phillip, though, is beguiling, the one difficult to figure. His eyes are calm. They are lakes. He has barely spoken since leaving the pit, and his words are measured. Below, whenever Adam crumbled, Phillip would move aside, preserving his energy, to let Tony and Cole help. Then Phillip would retake his position and plod mechanically on, saying nothing. Obviously, Phillip is not a friend of Cole or Adam. He sits apart.

How did they enter the tree together?

It is rare for a boy to so quickly shed both past and future and resign himself to now, as Phillip seems to have done. It is hard to understand his motivations. In a certain way, such a person has no motivations. Motivations are built on wanting a certain future or protecting the past. Phillip doesn't seem to care about either. This makes him harmless or dangerous. Tony is not certain which.

There are times when, looking back to make sure the newbies haven't fallen behind, he swears he sees Phillip smiling.

What is this boy?

And he has the stick. No one has a stick like that. There isn't anything comparable inside the tree, not at any level. It has value. It could change a boy's status. It could make a boy's status.

Kings want a stick like that.

*   *   *

He senses Phillip watching him.

"Nice stick," Tony says. He tries to appear nonchalant as he looks up.

Phillip's eyes remain still.

"Can I see it?" Tony says.

A small smile, definitely a smile, cracks the mud at the corners of Phillip's mouth.

For a moment Tony is unnerved, but then he, too, grins. *He doesn't know what is waiting for him.*

Phillip slowly extends the stick.

There is an interlude when they are both holding the stick. Tony feels the pressure of Phillip's grasp. Phillip gives a short tug, which pulls Tony's arm, before he opens his hand and lets go.

Tony balances the stick in upturned hands. The wood is smooth, the weight evenly distributed across its length. Despite the wet, it is light and maneuverable. There is a round knob at one end. An image of a pool table flashes within Tony's mind, from his past life. The knot is the shape and size of a cue ball.

He leans, handing the stick back to Phillip. He nods his thanks. "You don't say much."

Phillip rests the stick in his lap, his hands on his knees. He shrugs.

Tony checks the handkerchief: soaked. He lifts it from the mud by one corner and shapes it into a ball.

"Here," he says. "Go ahead." An offering.

Phillips shakes his head, no.

"Wa—."

Mumbles. He'd forgotten Adam was here.

Tony turns, and Adam reaches. "Water?" Tony says. Instead, he hands the water bun to Cole. To do so it must pass Adam, whose frantic eyes follow.

To Tony's disappointment Cole gives the handkerchief to Adam, who shakily squeezes the bun. Water splashes around his mouth. He swallows, coughs. The gritty water, Tony knows, takes getting used to. Despite this, Adam squeezes and squeezes, full of mania, until there is nothing left, trying to wring water when none remains.

Tony snatches the handkerchief from him. He spreads it in the mud between them. "You have to wait," he says.

Water drips all around them.

A plop catches an edge of the handkerchief. Another just misses.

Adam looks above. A drop hits him in the forehead.

"Don't do it," Tony says.

Adam doesn't listen. He gapes his mouth. He moves left, right.

"It doesn't work, mate. You just have to wait."

Adam is like a baby bird, his beak craned, hopeful for a drop of water to fall into his mouth.

"Adam," Cole says. He reaches to try to settle him, but Adam won't stop. He pushes Cole aside and dives pitifully, scrambling up, wild-eyed.

"Adam, stop it!" Cole says.

Then Cole attacks his friend. He dips his shoulder and tackles Adam to the ground.

Tony lets it happen. He knew it would.

In seconds Cole is on his knees, over the much bigger Adam, curled on his side. Adam's arms are up, but Cole's precise punch plows through Adam's guard. "Stop it," Cole says. He punches again. "Stop," he says. Each punch becomes more labored as he tires, getting weaker.

Eventually, Cole is so exhausted he can no longer lift his arms. They hang loose at his sides. Slight shoulders slope lengthily down to fists, still clenched. The wide fists don't seem to belong to a boy. Cole's entire body is lost in a quiet tremor. On his knees, in repose, he stares with ferocity up the tunnel and away from his friend. He crawls off Adam and rests against the wall.

The only sound is Adam's sobbing and the scattered plop of water.

Tony adopts a look of concern, attempting to hide his exhilaration, but he feels a smile twittering on his mouth, which he tamps into a frown. "Okay, okay," he says. "Just a little dustup. It happens. The stress gets to everyone." He takes the handkerchief, the start of all this, and wipes Adam's face. There is a nasty cut, which Tony plugs with mud.

When Tony finally gets the wound cleansed and Adam sitting up, he is genuinely surprised. A swollen and nicked patch of skin seems to have been placed under Adam's eye.

Tony turns away, towards an imaginary task, so he can camouflage his laughter with coughing. When he composes himself, he looks to Cole, who is staring forward. His fists have unclenched. What Tony sees past Cole, up the tunnel, surprises him. He thinks of how rare and pleasant it is to be surprised.

Phillip has left them.

When did he leave? At the start of Adam's drubbing?

Phillip is maybe fifty yards ahead, quite a way to travel in this muck. The light illuminates the tunnel, so Phillip's silhouette is clear. He is on his knees, the stick raised over his head. He waits, then explodes into a swing. The knob of the stick bashes the ground.

"That won't work!" Tony says. His laughter grows until it becomes rousing, shaking him. "Hey, that won't work!"

Still, Phillip continues. He lifts the stick again.

"Come on, you two." Tony grabs Adam's forearm and urges him forward.

Cole follows.

Neither looks at the other, Tony notices. The friends have parted. Matter of time.

He dips his jaw and sets off, talking to himself as much as anyone else because he likes the sound of his voice reverberating in the tunnel. "See, his approach is all wrong," Tony says. "He's all brawn. It's not like hunting, oy. You can't chase them and whack. You got to *lure* them in. It's more like fishing, except you're not using worms for bait. No, sir, not worms!"

6

Tony whispers. "The key is staying still. Play dead. Let them nuzzle you. Wait for one to start suckling. It won't harm you. Their teeth are nubby, not sharp. When they start, they won't let go. This is when you strike. Pull hard and hold with two hands. It's got to be two hands, or you'll lose it."

Adam had no idea such creatures might exist. It is horror, seeing them corkscrew from the ground.

Tony lays still in the mud, and two worms have emerged. One squirms near his thigh, another by his side.

"Watch me." His eyes close. "Just watch."

The worms are two feet long and thicker than most snakes. They are translucent brown, and a bright red interior vein runs the length of their bodies. The vein gives each worm a slight glow. Their mouths, which seem to sniff blindly, are the size of quarters and shaped like suction cups curled at the edges. The edges are lined with tiny, barely discernable teeth.

A worm coils on Tony's stomach.

The other, with a quickness that surprises, slaps its mouth onto Tony's thigh and begins gnawing, pulling the skin taught.

Tony strikes, snapping to his feet. The worm on his stomach is flung and merges back into the mud like a ripple of water. He grabs the other, two-handed, yanking the sucker from his thigh, and holds it up for display.

The worm is twisting fiercely, trying to escape, but Tony has a strong hold.

"Now, boys, watch!" Tony says.

His arms extend, which straightens and weakens the worm into submission. And then Tony begins to eat. With each bite he rips away a chunk of rubbery flesh. He chews and swallows quickly, gobbling it down. When most of the outer layer is stripped away, he bites through the red vein, and a spurt of blood dots his cheek. Soon his mouth is ringed with a red smear, like sloppy clown makeup. His chews intersperse with licking blood from his lips and off the limp worm.

I can't do that. Adam is sapped. He had been feeling stronger, better able to speak and whispering words to himself like "fight" and "push," readying for a moment when he could show the others his regained voice. But now this. Fight. Push. These are words Coach uses at football practice. They are words Adam repeats through his mouth guard when breaking from the huddle. He recognizes the irony: the strongest kid showing himself to be weakest.

He is overwhelmed by nausea and woozily crumbles into the wall and retches gritty water into the mud. He keeps throwing up until his stomach is empty and the bitter taste of bile heats his throat. When he finally stops gagging, he looks up, first to Cole then to Phillip, who pay no attention to him. Instead, they intently watch Tony.

"Blood is essential. It's the minerals," Tony says. "The worms are it, the lone cuisine. One worm can feed you for an entire day. Either you eat them or you starve, and if you starve the worms eat you. Oy."

All Adam must do is stay down and still. Beneath him they will come. They will rise from the mud and slide onto him and stick him and feed. Thousands of them. If he wants, they will do more: they will take him away.

He closes his eyes and begins to build a wind in his brain. It will be a hurricane stretching hundreds of miles, so jarring that it will paralyze his fear. He wants away from fear. His thoughts relax. He begins to feel free, to feel escape. A band of dark, low clouds appears on a horizon, and he expands the storm within him. He is the creator. Fueled by warmth, the storm collects balmy air and spreads, consuming every wind and water touched. Squalls flock and shriek and form a spinning eye. It is happening. The edges of its borders sharpen, and a final shape begins to set: a circular saw blade. But this storm, at the point when all is ready to explode and hurl salvos of wind and rain, somehow, unexpectedly, sputters. The wind relents. The rains reduce. The bottom falls out. A cloud and nothing more. Calm.

No, he decides.

Adam places his palms on the ground. He thinks of football, settling into his stance across from his opponent. He revives that moment: the smash of helmets and shoulder pads and the caged view through his facemask. He thinks of how good he was at that game. The way he, just by himself, was like a storm. The way he moved aside what was blocking him. The way he cleared a path. He pushes himself up, away from his retchings.

"Fight," he whispers.

7

Progress occurs in inches. Cole's hand stamps the mud, sinks, and slides back as his other arm reaches forward. All the while his toes scrape, and he attempts to keep his knees stable. The knees are key.

His tongue is thick with the taste of worm, and he has started to wheeze—as if moth wings flutter in his lungs.

Tony, Phillip, and Adam pull ahead. Cole lets them. He needs a minute alone.

We are four big babies crawling. Towards what?

He thinks of a tart, pulpy glass of orange juice.

The yellow yolk of an egg.

The colors burst before him like dollops of paint dropped on a window, through which he views the world.

But these bright colors are quickly overrun by the surrounding mud, this single shade of burnt brown, and Cole has the sick thought that they are in the hot womb of a beast. Soon the tunnel will become a maze. His friends will become separated and lost.

He crawls quickly, gasping, and catches up. In this flurry he thinks of his mom.

Her name is Helena.

He has not thought of her since falling into the tree. He imagines her walking into his bedroom at home. He is awake, but he pretends to sleep. It is early morning, just past sunrise, awash in yellow and orange light, and she sits on the edge of his bed. She places her hand on his shoulder. "Time to wake," she whispers.

Mom. He is of an age when he says, "Mom." When did he stop saying, "Mommy"?

Whenever he worries about a test or a game, she knows, and she appears beside him, and her hand finds his, and her fingers weave his and she tells him, gently, with assurance, so that only he will hear, "Whatever happens will be alright."

She is a great mom, but she is not beside him now, no matter how hard he thinks of her.

But if she were to appear ahead (and he envisions her there), and if she called to him, the lilt of her voice filled with love, he would rip through this mud, and nestled within her hug he would be instantly cleansed. He would say "Mom," and he would say "I love you" again and again until the words lifted them, away from this place, taking them home.

Still, she is not here. She stays a memory.

8

Ahead, the bright bones of a large animal skeleton block the tunnel. The group stops. There is confusion. Awe. The pink light is so penetrating Phillip visors his hand to shield his eyes. Pearly flecks shimmer in the air, and the bones appear bleached. Light pours from the left side of the tunnel, just past the skeleton, the entrance to Level 1.

Without stopping Tony twists his neck. "This is The Bear," he says. He speaks loudly because the light emits a sustained hum that cottons their ears.

It could not be stranger. To have travelled here and slogged through mud and eaten a giant worm and been led by a 42-year-old boy and then encounter this fossil that seems so random and out-of-place: it is almost extraterrestrial.

They plod towards the bones.

Phillip would sleep if he could. He would sleep without concern of waking up, and he is sure Adam and Cole would as well. They are all drained and skinny. The crazy light darkens their mud-slathered bodies, so they look like shadows or tar scarecrows. Phillip feels his bones pushing from beneath his skin. Even Adam, burly not long ago, is slim. The tunnel still bakes them, but the heat seems lesser by a degree or two.

Phillip evaluates their physical deterioration. As much as they have changed, they do not match Tony. Tony carries a toughened, starved layer that Philip, Adam, and Cole do not yet possess. Tony is like a piece of cured meat. Jerky. With sharper angles.

He has not trusted Tony from the beginning. He knows Tony will steal his stick if he has the chance. But Tony has survived here for 31 years. Phillip has no doubt this is true. How he knows, he cannot say. He just does. This longevity compels him to listen to Tony.

Even when Phillip acts like he is not listening, he is, and as Tony crawls to the skeleton, stops, turns, and prepares to speak to the three new boys at the cusp of exiting the tunnel and entering Level 1, Phillip readies himself to listen.

But his attention wanders. It settles on The Bear—what is left. The bright bones are brighter than the extraordinary light itself, and Phillip has the dreamy thought that they comprise the brightest object in the universe. In this dreamstate he begins to see not just bones.

Muscles wrapped tightly in tendons and ligaments weld onto the bones. Organs—lungs, a thumping heart—fill the ribcage. Sheets of thick skin layer overtop. Fur and claws and teeth sprout. Before him, he sees the bear reanimate into what it was, into a magnificent creature.

Long ago, a bear fell into the tree.

I see this.

Phillip understands that the bear never had a chance. Entering the tree was an accident.

A mistake brought it here.

Tony announces, "No one disturbs The Bear. That's a rule. Anyone who disturbs The Bear will go away." He places his back to the wall of the tunnel and carefully shuffles past the skeleton.

Cole and Adam quickly follow. Cole first. Then Adam.

Go away?

When it is his turn, Phillip studies the bear skull. It is massive, and an uneasy heat fills his neck. The skull is a reminder sent from the world he left. When he entered the tree, he was swallowed by the comforting dark. But here at the entrance of Level 1 there is only exploding light like from the thrusters of a rocket, and it exposes every detail: every sculpted tooth of the bear and the curve of its eye sockets and jawbone.

And the light shines on the faces of Adam and Cole and Tony. And this light, he knows, shines on his face as well. For the first time since entering the tree Phillip is self-conscious. He can feel his neck blushing just as it does in school. He blushes because he knows others can see him and maybe notice what he fights to keep hidden inside, what he does not want to tell anybody, what he came here to escape.

Go away?

For the first time since entering the tree Phillip feels fear. His belief that this place is better than what he left is made uncertain. He is not sure whether he wants to know all its mysteries. Maybe, he thinks, he was wrong.

Past the bear the light is blinding—loud—a soft solid that he pushes through. He must shut his eyes. Tony yells to them to keep a hand on the wall and follow his voice. They are close and about to turn.

As Phillip leans forward, stabbing the stick into the ground with each deliberate step, he thinks of the worm he ate. Catching it was easy once the shock wore off: a gigantic worm cupped to his shoulder. He yanked it free as Tony had. But keeping the worm outstretched fatigued his arms to the point they started to shake. He was not prepared for the worm's strength, and tearing his teeth into it did not come naturally. He was able to puncture the vein, but when the hot blood squirted on his lips he saw Tony recognize his anxiety, which angered him, and now he follows Tony with fear grating within his stomach, like some pit he has accidentally swallowed.

He is a blushing boy, feeling weak, unsure.

9

The time spent confined in the tunnel makes the new expanse around him even more dramatic, and as his equilibrium adjusts his legs become shaky, and Cole begins to lean. He almost falls, but manages to steady himself.

It is quiet, holy.

They have entered a cavern. It feels huge, like being inside a stadium. Cole's eyes travel up rock walls, wet and shimmering, and up to ledges higher still and beyond to a cloudy darkness that offers no answer as to what is above—except for one magnificent fact: there is no water dripping on him. It is still hot, but the heat is dispersed and not constantly attacking him. Mud remains underfoot, but it is mixed with sand. He feels the wonderful grit. Sand. This field of mud, big enough for a football game, extends to a narrow shore that encircles a vast pond, perhaps a mile around. The water shines like a luminous pink pearl, but it is not water. Water is the convenient word. It is a thick, undulating soup. This is the source of the powerful light.

Boys surround the pond. There are maybe a hundred, spaced as if for privacy. Their poses are ramshackle. Some lie on their side. Others rest on both knees. Unmoving and quiet, they stare into the water.

Cole thinks of his almanac at home, the back pages filled with numerous flags representing the world's nations and how the boys of Level 1 are as diverse as these flags.

The tree travels the world, and it takes.

Every so often a soft laugh is heard. Is that crying? The sounds have no discernable origin. They echo off the cavern walls.

And then there is the square white rock. The sides are flat and shiny, as if the stone has been cut and polished. It is the size of a treasure chest. It waits at the outer edge of the shore and acts as a gateway to the pond. Is it granite? Marble? How did it get there? It must weigh a thousand pounds. Anyone who approaches the pond must pass it. The rock is embedded with silver flecks of quartz, and glittering reflections of light strobe from the stone like musical notes. Atop the rock is a brilliant gold bell. Cole squints. The gold gleams in concert with the hyper sparkling of the rock. The handle of the bell is a deep, dark wood.

"Whaddya got? Whaddya got?"

Cole's attention is drawn downward to a boy who, like an aggressive beggar, stands by his knee with his arms lifted and hands open. The boy is barely taller than his waist.

"Feldstein, away!" Tony says, as if shooing a dog. "He's got nothing!" He drops the clothes ball and jab steps towards the boy.

Feldstein's quick retreat is matched by an equally quick return. He has a small animal's darting energy. "Whaddya got? Whaddya got?" He crowds Cole again. Feldstein then notices Phillip. He rushes him and tries to grab the stick, which Phillip lifts overhead, out of reach.

"Let me see! Let me see!"

The boy wears thick glasses and hobbles. One leg is no-ticeably deformed; below the knee, a shortened and curved shin leads to a lumpy foot lacking any contour. The foot's shape resembles a ball of dough.

"Leave us be, Feldstein!" Tony lifts the clothes ball above his head and hurls it at the boy. It hits him in the chest with a loud thump and sends Feldstein flying.

Swiftly back up, the boy keeps his distance. "You're a jerk, Tony! A big jerk!" He scurries away with an awkward gait, headed toward an area of the cavern shaded by an outcropping of rock.

"Don't let Feldstein bother you. He's a pest, an intolerable parasite obsessed with relics. A pest! Do you hear me, Feldstein?!"

From afar, they barely hear Feldstein: "Big jerk."

"He is not typical of Level 1. Most here are gentlemen who prescribe to the tenants of considerate behavior," Tony says.

With difficulty Cole turns away from the pond's hypnotic glow. Boys, significantly lesser in number than those surrounding the pond, are scattered around him in the mud. One sits cross-legged, eating a ragged worm. Others are passed out on their backs, curled on sides, or lying face up—sleeping. No worms emerge and slide onto them.

The worms stay in the tunnel.

At the edge of the cavern a boy pees. Additional boys shuffle about, looking up and down, their eyes stuck in a daze that says they are thinking of elsewhere. Cole hears soft voices. Foreign languages. Are they are talking to themselves?

There are loose groups of three or four, but most seem content existing in their own orbit, and Cole does not observe any boy speaking to another. The overall impression is of disorganization and apathy. The slow, haphazard movements of individuals not linked to some larger purpose makes Cole think of wayward cows or zombies who are not hungry.

Meanwhile, no one besides Feldstein has acknowledged their arrival. Some trade brief eye contact with him but then disengage, uninterested.

When he turns back to the pond, another observation becomes clear, especially when he contrasts Adam with the boys of Level 1. Adam has always been the biggest and strongest, but here Adam is more: he is a giant.

Many of the boys are small, slight. They do not appear younger, just weaker. Narrow-shouldered. Short. In terms of size, Cole has always thought of himself as average, but here he feels different. He sticks out, too.

And he, Adam, Phillip, and Tony are covered in mud. They resemble members of a lost tribe from another world. The boys of Level 1, except the one still chewing on the gristly remnants of his worm, appear mostly clean, and their skin is chalky from lack of sunlight. The pale skin exposes purple veins beneath.

The pond. It grips him. His sight funnels forward until all he sees is the gooey texture of the water. He is captivated. Earlier, he thought of a pearl, but he now realizes he was wrong.

On special occasions, his mother wore a pair of dangling opal earrings. They were light pink with dazzling, darker striations. The water is like liquid opal. It is as if a precious stone has somehow liquefied, and the water is "opalescent," a word his mother taught him.

He remembers sitting on his parents' bed and watching his mom. A babysitter was coming. A wedding anniversary dinner. She clasped an earring over one lobe, then the other. "Opalescent," she said. She told him to say the word slowly. "Speak the word and you will remember it," she said.

Now Cole becomes aware of his legs. They move without his input or permission. Something else has decided they will walk. He senses Adam and Phillip beside him, also headed to the pond. An invisible force is pulling them. Through some weird instance of telepathy, he is aware that Adam and Phillip know this as well. This is not scary. They willingly let themselves be taken. There is something in the water.

It wants them to see.

Beside him Tony is waving his hands. It appears he is yelling.

Cole sees his mouth move, but he doesn't hear a word. The pond is closer. Keep walking. Tony disappears. The white rock nears, and its silver flecks fling pinpricks of light onto his skin.

The gold bell.

But his legs are knocked out from beneath him. He falls, and he hits the ground hard, which dislodges him from the charm of the pond.

Lying on his side, with a mild headache, Cole watches Tony tackle Adam, then Phillip. In each instance Tony dives into the backs of their knees, and they crumble.

They all slowly recover—groggy, regaining their senses, until each is sitting up.

Tony has placed himself between them and the pond. His arms are outstretched, as if to block them if need be. "Listen to me! Are you awake? Oy? I have one thing to tell you. Whatever you do, do not go into the water. I repeat. Do not go into the water."

Tony says this as if doing so would cause great harm.

10

Tony remains behind. Phillip has shed the group and chosen to hike to a far shore.

The hairs on Adam's arms tingle. Cole is beside him. Adrenaline wards off the sleepy effect of the pond looming before them. The closer they get the wider it seems to spread. They walk slowly, like going is something unpleasant they have to do.

"I'm sorry I hit you," Cole says.

"It's okay." The cut below his eye no longer stings. There is just a dull ache.

"How did you stop your fear?" Cole stares ahead.

"It's not gone," Adam says. "I feel it less. It's spread around, not just in my head anymore."

Cole says, "I'm afraid of what's there."

They stop and scan the congregation of boys arranged around the pond like flexible statues placed in various poses.

"Maybe we're dead," Cole says.

"We would know."

"Why?"

"Are you dead?"

The mud on their skin has dried and become brittle in the less humid air. Cole cracks off a piece from his forearm. "No, I'm not dead," he says.

"Me neither. I know I'm not."

"Maybe this is punishment then."

"For what?" Adam says.

"For what we did to Phillip. Taking his stick. Teasing him."

"Then why would Phillip get punished, too? Who's punishing us?"

Their families belong to the same church, though Cole's mother rarely attends. She comes on holidays. She smiles warmly and offers hellos and small talk, but she doesn't say the prayers or sing. She is very pretty with long, shiny hair so black it seems dyed and combed straight down her back. Whenever she is there, Adam likes to watch her. He knows she does not believe in God or heaven or hell, and he has wanted to ask why, but he has never had the courage.

"Nobody's punishing us," Adam says.

"We never went that deep into the woods," Cole says.

"Why did we?"

"I saw birds."

"You did?"

"Blacks birds in the sky," Cole says. "Right before we began walking. That's the direction I followed, towards them. I saw them again when we fell inside."

"I saw them too." Adam remembers now.

"Think of everything that had to happen for us to meet Phillip there, at that moment."

They resume walking.

"Do you remember?" Adam says.

"What?"

"When Phillip went in the tree."

It is haunting: Adam's memory. There was a moment when Phillip stopped walking and, levitating, drifted into the opening, but Adam doesn't share this with Cole. He is not sure Cole saw the same thing.

"It was like he knew," Cole says.

"No one would choose to come here," Adam says.

"We could have left after he was gone. We could have run home and never told anyone. But I grabbed you. I tried to push you in. I don't know why."

"I'm the one who took his stick. We were both wrong."

"We could be home," Cole says.

Adam imagines a search that must be taking place. Police and volunteers combing the woods, their names and photos on television. What are the chances they will find the tree? Is the tree still there?

"Cole, what do you think this place is?"

Cole takes a deep breath. "This place," he says. He shakes his head.

"We won't wake up, will we?"

"We're not sleeping."

"Like we're not dead."

"No, we're not."

Not yet, Adam stops himself from saying. He has to keep from smiling. It sounds like some ridiculous line from a movie.

The pond is close. It feels alive, possessing a great and roiling power.

They reach the edge of the shore, which begins a gentle slant to the water. They stop. Carefully, Adam steps onto the sand, which is noticeably cooler. He trades smiles with Cole. Dry granules of fine white sand. Adam digs with his toes. Cole reaches down and scoops a handful and lets it sift through his fingers.

They walk. Just a little longer now. There is a wide space for them to approach unimpeded. They begin to diverge;

Adam feels the distance lengthen between them. They become spaced just like the other boys surrounding the pond.

Adam reaches the end, where sand meets water. There are no small lapping waves. Rather, the entire pond shimmers in one repeating undulation that has no beginning or end. It should be lovely. It should be. His eyes travel along the shore's edge, from boy to boy, and what he sees, what has been hidden until now, jolts him.

In the pond, just a few feet in front of each boy, is a black shape, the same shape replicated in the water.

"Cole," Adam says.

"I see them, Adam."

The shape has a wavy border and is relentlessly black. The color swirls. Each seems part of the pond, not separate forms overlaid on top. They are like the unnerving shadows of sea creatures or watery pieces of night itself, one after another.

Adam knows.

They are entrances, just like the opening of the tree, like the one they fell into.

Falling is not what is happening now. It is something more peculiar.

11

A vampire cape.

A puddle of ink.

So black it is almost blue, but the color does not change. It is as black as black can be.

A pupil.

Cole made the discovery about one year earlier, and before bed every night since he has leaned forward until inches away from his bathroom mirror, and he stares into the reflection of one eye, into the round black center. The pupil always holds within it a miniaturized reflection of himself. He sees his entire being housed in his eye.

Portal.

A portal is like a door, a way to go from one place to another. Room to room. In to out. You enter. Or exit. An entrance is also an exit; it just depends on where someone is headed.

He leans towards the water. The next step is to kneel, which he does, resting his hands on his knees. It is not the same as staring into his pupil. Cole sees himself, but it is not his reflection. This is different.

"Help me," he whispers. He does not know to whom.

12

He split from the group to be alone and calm himself. He has reached the edge of the pond, and a flame—a blush unlike anything he has felt before—throbs around his neck.

The pond is filled.

Before Phillip the same black shape begins to materialize in the water. It starts small, a flapping circle, and expands evenly outward.

The tree.

It is the exact same entrance. Phillip is not moving. The stick is staked into the mud, and he is not moving. He tightly grips the stick, yet he is leaving. He feels it. He went through the entrance once before, and he is going through it again.

Night.

The street is empty.

His house. A low chain link fence borders the small yard, gone to weed and dirt. Grimy brown siding. The roof is patched with a piece of tarp.

No sound, just an image. Sometimes the image distorts, like looking through water.

Frost shines the leaves of a tall oak.

Peering down, Phillip floats in the moonlight.

At the end of their driveway, in the yellow glow of the street-lamp, stands The Boy.

That is me, Phillip thinks.

The Boy is a replica. Each hair, each fingernail. And inside The Boy, Phillip senses, is anger. He sometimes recognizes anger in himself.

Are they the same? What waits at this late hour?

The Boy bends and picks up a rock, and without warning he throws it hard at the streetlamp.

It misses, barely. The rock travels through moonlight, through Phillip, before landing in a neighbor's yard.

I would never do that, throw a rock like that.

In his other hand The Boy has a stick, a short and thick club.

Across the street is the svelte black stray that roams the neighborhood. Phillip calls her Midnight. She has yellow eyes and purrs whenever he pets her. She lays in the middle of Ms. Gains' driveway. Ms. Gains is an elderly widow.

The Boy bends to one knee and taps the ground with his stick, like he is saying, Come here, Midnight. Come here.

Stay, Phillip thinks. He tries to find his mouth. He has none. He cannot speak.

Do not trust The Boy. He is not me, Midnight.

Midnight lazily arches her back to squeeze out the sleep. She walks with her tail straight up.

She is halfway to The Boy when she stops.

The Boy taps the ground again.

Here, Midnight.

Phillip reads his lips.

How does he know her name?

She lowers, sensing something wrong. Her tail flattens.

Tap tap.

Lower.

Midnight.

52

Lower.

Belly flat on the ground. Paws kneading.

The Boy lunges forward with the stick raised.

Midnight flees.

He doesn't get to swing. Instead the stick is hurled uselessly towards the black shape that skitters behind an unkempt hedge.

The Boy turns, glares into the moonlight.

A moment of panic: there is nowhere to hide. Phillip has no sense of how he appears or whether he will be discovered.

Then he learns how it feels to have wind go through him. It is like being wind, which is like being a god, and it soothes him. He settles his sight, the image.

The Boy. Him.

Phillip sees his own eyes. They are his eyes. He looks at his own eyes. And for a moment he swears they stare back. Not at moonlight, but at him.

The Boy walks towards their house, his long and thin shadow. He crosses under the big oak. He opens the unlocked door and enters. When the door closes, Phillip waits, but no light clicks on. The windows are large eyes that reveal nothing.

Phillip stays in the moonlight. He watches until the image shudders and changes.

Morning. At school. The Boy reaches into his backpack.

Phillip understands: he has been replaced.

13

The nametag sticker reads "Lily." Her writing is neat, straight lines and near perfect loops. It slants evenly, unlike his rough handwriting.

The Boy sits next to her.

Adam drifts by the door of Mrs. Kruse's art class.

Normally, he feels so large. He towers above other kids and knows how much heavier he is than their lighter bodies, but here he has no weight or height. It is like he is nothing.

He watches The Boy and her.

Lily must be a new student. The nametag is so everyone learns her name.

How many times has she written her name?

Adam sees his group at the other table. Colin. Jacob. But Cole isn't there. Where's Cole?

She draws with strict attention. She has a gray pencil. Placing the pencil on the table, she rummages through the bowl until she finds black.

He rises above the door to view her drawing. He cannot solve the image; she has sketched on different sections of the paper. The shapes do not yet connect.

He descends, back to his place by the door.

The Boy crouches towards her.

She notices him and offers the black pencil.

Thanks.

What is it? The Boy asks.

He turns to see her response.

Surprise. Her drawing will be a surprise.

The Boy smiles, but then his eyes cut across the room to the other table.

Adam follows.

Colin and Jacob make kissing gestures. They stop when Mrs. Kruse approaches.

Adam is embarrassed at having been teased, but The Boy seems unfazed. He is back to his project, coloring intently with the pencil Lily gave him.

Adam rises again. When the drawing comes into focus, it seems foreign, because it is a product of himself—this other self—and he did not know he was capable of creating it.

I drew that?

Mrs. Kruse appears behind The Boy. Her hands rest on his shoulders, and her face is quirked with pleasant surprise. She leans over and whispers into his ear. She pats him on the back and continues to the next student.

Whatever Mrs. Kruse said has made The Boy feel proud.

It is a series of lines, from straight to wavy. A man's bottom half is embedded in the ground. The legs lead to feet and toes that extend into deep and wide-spreading roots. Above ground, from his trunk, long arms lift toward the sky, hands open, and the fingers split to form the loftiest branches. In one corner a yellow sun sprays lines of light towards the green canopy. Blue stick birds swoop and veer. The treeman has a coy smile, as if he knows a secret.

Lily speaks to The Boy.

Adam doesn't catch what she says. Their mouths move too quickly for him to understand.

They stop, the brief conversation over.

Lily returns to her drawing.

He closely watches The Boy, who is thinking, preparing. Adam knows this part of himself, how he sometimes must pause to gather confidence.

The decision is made. Adam sees it.

The Boy leans towards Lily.

Adam leans forward, too, focusing. He watches The Boy, and the words form within him as The Boy speaks: Your name is pretty.

When she smiles, her long eyelashes lift.

The Boy goes back to work. He picks out a green pencil from the bowl.

Adam feels the floating and leftover numbness of bravery. He knows he would never have said this; he would not have had the courage.

Your name is pretty.

He is smiling. He watches himself, this other boy.

14

All the familiar pennants are tacked to the walls. There are 15 total. 9 football. 4 baseball. 2 hockey.

They are his father's, not his. Some of the teams no longer exist.

A piece of moon scallops the corner of the window. The shadow of a tree limb shakes in the light, which fills the room with blue glow.

Cole knows the body in his bed, covered only by a thin sheet. A hidden face is curled into a shoulder.

A blanket lies bundled on the floor.

Did it fall, or was it pushed off?

The Boy beneath the sheet trembles as if a chill plows through him, this other Cole.

Normally, he is wrapped tightly in the blanket and leaves a small opening to breathe through.

The sheet is so thin.

The moonlight is sharp.

The book on the bedside table is the same one he left. He reads every night, sometimes with his mom. They visit the library, and he roams the aisles while she seeks out books for him. They always leave with an unsteady stack that he carries to the car. He often stays up later than he should, lost in a story. Sometimes during school or practice all he can think about is the book on his bedside table.

He talks about the stories with his mom. They like to sit on the porch, in the shade—

The body twists beneath the sheet, and The Boy jolts upright.

Sweat gleams on his forehead. His expression is the grimace of fever. Ache has stiffened his neck and shoulders and back.

Cole doesn't feel sick, though.

The Boy struggles sideways out of bed. He takes careful steps in the dark.

The bathroom light clicks on.

Cole follows. He does not know how. He has no thrusters or fins. His thoughts steer him as he glides with perfect control to the bathroom. He settles behind The Boy, just above his head.

Looking at the mirror, he sees The Boy's reflection but not his own. Where his reflection should be is nothing.

The Boy, his hair slick with sweat, bends forward. Fitful sleep has left his eyes shaky with fatigue.

Is he looking into his pupil for his miniature reflection?

No. Something else.

The Boy squints and wipes his nose with the back of his hand. A smear of blood. The Boy looks at his hand, then back to the mirror. A gush from both nostrils spills down his mouth, his chin. Blood bowls the sink. Vivid red. Drops splash on the tile floor.

Skittering, Cole floats backwards, not knowing what to do.

They are like little water balloons that burst on the ground and leave a trail. The Boy rips off a strand of toilet paper, which he balls up and presses to his nose. The paper quickly becomes heavy and dark red.

Leaning his head back, he sits on the floor.

The Boy should call for his mom.

Call for Mom.

Cole wants to help, but he can't. He can only watch himself bleed.

15

"You didn't have to throw it, Tony. That was mean. It was mean to do."

"Feldstein, shut up."

"That's mean, Tony. Mean words."

"You're right, Feldstein. I'm sorry. Please forgive me. I request that you please not speak because your voice, which resembles the squeaking of a small rodent, is driving me insane."

"Not nice, Tony. Not nice at all."

Tony sighs, leans against his boulder. It is his boulder, which he has earned. A German named Helmut tried sitting on it one day and, well, Helmut hasn't tried that again. Tony bit off the tip of Helmut's nose. He is known for this; he has bitten off the tips of three noses. No, Helmut doesn't come anywhere near the boulder anymore.

Oy.

Over the years, Tony's body had adapted to the rock. Scrunched up, he can comfortably fall asleep atop it, which he chooses over sleeping in the mud. He will not sleep in the mud like an animal, like these pond addicts scattered about him. They are like drunks, sleeping off a binge, or pigs wallowing in a sty.

They have no discipline.

From the shaded, rocky area that serves as his base of operations, Tony scans for and finds Phillip, lying on his side and staring. At the other end of the pond sits Adam, who, surprisingly, has shown himself to be mentally stronger than Tony thought. Next to Adam is Cole.

The newbies have been watching for hours, and they will watch for hours more before their bodies tire to the point of collapse, and the black shape will fade, and they will shuffle away from the pond in a daze and crumble in the mud and sleep.

And that is what most here do, every day. Or they do something similar to this. That is their pathetic routine: sleep, have a worm, shower, and head back to the pond—to lives that are not theirs anymore. They view these lost lives as if they still own them.

Not Tony.

He hasn't stared into a pond for more than 10 years, not since being booted from Level 2 and becoming a free agent, a mover of relics, a traveler of the tunnel, a tradesman.

He is a boy with a profession. He has purpose. He has a goal.

Phillip's stick will earn him a home at Level 3. Geiger will not pass up a relic like that. It is a stick meant for a king. He grins at the thought of presenting the stick to Geiger: "A stick meant for a king," he will say.

He dreams of cool air, the tart berries—all that is rumored to be at Level 3.

He could try to grab Phillip's stick right now and push him into the pond, but he runs the risk that Phillip, in his semi-comatose state, might grip the stick with inhuman strength. He doesn't want to try and fail. It would only make the next attempt more difficult.

No, he will wait for the perfect opportunity and then take possession of the stick. He will do whatever he needs to do. This willingness—to lie, steal, or kill if need be—has only recently steeled within him. It was always loosely part, but now he feels this resolve like a metal rod in his spine.

He knows that his substitute—the other Tony—is aging. In the alternate world, the world beyond the tree, the other Tony is getting older. This Tony will not live forever. Illness will overwhelm. A flood will drown. Or on a bright morning in Gloucester, on his way to the bakery, the other Tony might attempt to cross a cobblestone street, and a car will speed from nowhere and crush him. Eventually, mortality will win.

And when the other Tony dies, he dies.

I will not die at Level 1.

It is an odd and impermanent relationship: a boy whose world does not allow him to age will die when another world determines so.

He stands, ready to shower and scrub free the muck acquired from the tunnel. Nearby, Feldstein soaks Cole's shirt in the water trickling down the cavern wall and rings it out. He lays the shirt next to the remaining clothes drying on the plot of small, jagged rocks that mark a corner of their hovel. Earlier, they rifled through the pockets. The only relic found was in Adam's jeans: an old cough drop, lemon-flavored, a very valuable commodity. Anything edible with a taste other than worm will draw much interest. It is a relic Tony will keep hidden in his pouch, a secret, until the proper moment arrives.

Truthfully, it takes every fiber within him to restrain from tossing the cough drop in his mouth. But this is what separates himself from the pondheads.

Discipline.

Tony takes a mental inventory of the relics. They are always displayed for current and potential customers. He does

61

not worry about theft; his reputation for biting off the tips of noses is an effective form of security. Tony immediately notices that in his absence Feldstein has taken it upon himself to reorganize.

"Feldstein."

"Yes."

"What have you done?"

Feldstein smiles hopefully. "It's a new system."

"A new system."

"Yes. New."

"I told you to leave everything alone."

"This is better, a better system."

"'Leave alone,' Feldstein. What don't you understand about that?"

"It's helpful."

"Feldstein, I gather the relics. I loan the relics. I trade the relics. I allow you near these relics only because you follow my orders. I am the boss, and you are my assistant. When you stop following orders, no more relics."

"Please, Tony." Feldstein hobbles towards him. He removes his glasses, tearing up. "I only—"

Tony holds up his hand. Stop. "Why, for instance, place a drumstick next to Batman? It makes no sense."

"Please, Tony. It's better. I was just rearranging. I thought—"

"Don't think, Feldstein! These are my relics. My toys, my book, my drumstick. *Mine.* The compass. Keys. Everything. All mine. I arrange them how I want to view them. You are the assistant. You assist me."

Tony feels a presence behind him. He quickly turns, on guard.

"Mr. Tony." A small boy, eyes down, nods. He is embarrassed at having arrived during the middle of a quarrel. "*Essalamualeku.*"

"Mr. Tayib." Tony transforms into a suave and courteous salesman. "Hello to you as well. How are you today?"

"I am fine."

"That's some worm."

Tayib tightly holds a thick, long worm around his neck. There is still a fresh red welt on his stomach. "Yes. Thank you. It is a good worm."

"I'm certain it is. Loan?"

"Yes, I would like to loan."

"Excellent. It saves me a trip back into the tunnel. Just picked up some newbies, you know. Three of them. There, there, and there." Tony points to Phillip, Adam, and then Cole.

Tayib regards the new arrivals. "It is good to see," he says. "New people." He takes the worm from around his neck and drops it into Tony's makeshift cage made from piled rocks and the threaded strips of old clothes. Layers of denim form the floor.

Tony watches the worm briefly rear up like a cobra, before it descends and begins searching for a way out. *There is no escape. You're dinner.*

"So, Mr. Tayib, what interests you today?"

Tony steps aside and cuts his eyes at Feldstein to do the same. Feldstein scampers into the darkest corner, where the shade is so deep he is not visible.

Tayib moves closer to the relics. He wrings his hands as he considers them, eyes darting.

"A new system," Tony says. "Sorry if things have moved around. Unfortunately, my assistant exercised unrequested initiative. In other words, he buggered everything up." He speaks the last part loudly so Feldstein can hear.

"No, Mr. Tony, it is fine."

Tony is always struck by Tayib's skin, which somehow has retained a golden tone in this sunless place. He is ten-years-old, 27 if you count his time in-tree, and he is from Egypt, a place that for Tony still inspires exotic thoughts of pyramids and pharaohs and mummies. He understands, though, that this is a child's perception.

What little he knows about Egypt was learned before he entered the tree, and that knowledge has not expanded. The only significant means of access to the larger world is the pond, and the pond does not teach. It does not educate. Its virtual alternative does not match real experience, and it only offers incomplete snippets of life. Viewers, over time, learn the language of adulthood but never live adulthood. It creates childmen.

The pond only numbs.

Tayib scans the relics.

A bit embarrassed, Tony knows he needs some fresh items.

"Can I interest you in a flashlight?" Tony picks up the black and yellow flashlight brought in-tree by an Australian boy, long since gone. He unscrews the bottom, and out pops a battery caked with leaked acid. The flashlight, of course, does not work.

Tayib is too polite to say no, but Tony recognizes his disinterest. They have a long-established business relationship. The first time they met Tayib spoke little English. That was long ago. Now they communicate easily.

"The book then? The only book known for three levels," Tony says.

"No, thank you. I will again loan the book, perhaps later."

This is the first time Tayib has ever declined the book. Tony thinks about revealing the cough drop, but he would need fifty worms for such a rare item and fifty willing traders for those fifty worms. Tayib is a customer, not a friend, he reminds himself. Friendship only gets in the way.

"Have you considered the bouncy ball? It is wonderful enjoyment. All I ask is that you be careful. It is small and easily misplaced."

"Yes, I enjoy the ball, but not today."

"Well, hmm. Let me think." Of course, Tony isn't thinking. He has already picked the relic he is going to suggest next, and he knows Tayib is going to say yes. He knows this because he knows his clients. He smacks his forehead, as if he's experienced an epiphany. "How could I forget?"

It is irritating that Feldstein has moved the relic from its normal place, but Tony quickly finds it—next to, of all things, the Velcro wallet of Hank Hawkins. "Hawk," as Tony used to call him, was a Canadian who disintegrated right before his eyes, a mere few feet away. Hawk had brought him two worms, and they were settling the terms of a loan when... It is the sound that Tony never forgets: the sizzling and popping.

"Tayib, I have what you want." Tony holds up the comb. "You will feel luxurious. Merely be patient, and go slow at first. There is nothing like running a comb cleanly through your hair. I could do it all day."

Tayib smiles. "Yes, I would like the comb, Tony."

"I knew you would."

Lightly turning the relic in his hands, his eyes alight with anticipation, Tayib seems very much a child. It is the look of a boy who has received a present. For a respectful customer like Tayib, it gives Tony a sense of gratitude to see his hard work benefit another. The comb is in excellent condition. None of the teeth have snapped. The black plastic has remained shiny but for a few scratches.

Tayib turns to the pond. He positions the comb at his hairline and begins the process of slicking back hair that has not grown for 17 years. "Tony, these new boys, what are they?" he says.

Tony finds Adam and Cole. He sees Phillip, still engrossed. "Americans."

"America," Tayib says. "They always bring stuff. The new boy, he brings a…how do you say it?"

"A stick. It's marvelous."

"No, not 'stick'. A, you call it…"

Tony searches for another word. "A staff?"

"Yes, staff."

Tony nods, smiling. "You're right. That is a more appropriate word."

"Tony, these boys. Their arrival is as three. Three is a special number. I think these are special boys, bringing special things."

Tony responds to Tayib's intuition with neutrality. He shrugs, trying to be calm and dismissive. He doesn't want Tayib to know that he agrees or let on that he has a plan. Adam, Cole, and Phillip *are* special. Their arrival is special because he has been waiting for it. Waiting for the right object, one that will provide the means for his departure. He has always believed that he would find a way to Level 3.

Now he knows it.

Later that day or night (there is no way to know which), after hours, perhaps, have passed (there is no way to know how long), Tony stops his rearrangement of the relics. He looks towards the pond.

Phillip is first to rise. Cole soon follows. Last is Adam.

They drag forward, their feet barely lifting from the ground, away from the pond. Their blank eyes are stunned wide. The three mindlessly congregate towards a remote corner of the cavern and crumple in the mud. Phillip's staff is wedged under his body.

They sleep.

Tony returns to the relics. He moves them like chess pieces, each a reminder of his time spent here. He will work until order is restored and a path to victory made clear. He will work until the relics form a map that shows the beginnings of his journey and where it is destined to end.

16

The comb rakes smoothly. His hair feels thick and slick-ened—rejuvenated.

Tayib thinks.

He is married.

He does not separate himself from the older Tayib he views in the pond. They are the same person. They have to be. This is his belief, his faith.

He is father to a son now ten years old. They live in the same small house where he was born, where his parents passed years ago, after he left.

He is worried.

He is not worried about caring for and feeding his young son. His wife is a loving mother and homemaker; he is a hard worker. They will provide. No, he is concerned about the stars and how at night they have been waking the child—as Father and Mother sleep, unknowing.

This is what the pond has been showing him lately, these night scenes.

They make him think.

And whenever he thinks his mind travels to the same place and moment.

He is transported to the dusty and poor rim of Cairo, the capital city. This is where he trod barefoot and kicked a flat and tattered soccer ball. Where, long ago, in the middle of a starry night, he woke. It was the light that stirred him, starlight so strong he felt its pulse through the walls. He stepped carefully over his calico cat sleeping on the floor, and after sliding a small, rusted latch, then silently saying goodbye to his family, because he sensed that he might not return, he departed into the nightworld.

He walked for miles, away from the city, down narrow streets he had never been, through alleyways and iron gates he quietly pulled open, just enough to slip through, until reaching the edge of a vast desert.

It was where the city ended and the desert began.

Here, a strong, ceaseless wind blew. It cleansed him. The wind removed the city's smells and discordant sounds, its dizzy crowds and struggle, and there, like a mirage, its shape looming against a backdrop of sand sculpted into colossal dunes, was the tree.

Tayib is worried.

Will the tree return for his son? Is that what the night scenes mean? Will the boy wake, just as he did, and be drawn to the same path that leads to the desert's edge?

The wind behind, steering.

He combs, long and meditative strokes, a lone image forming in his mind: he and his son, the same age, sitting beside one another, staring into the pond.

What type of mutant would they see? What monster?

Is the tree speaking, asking him to make a choice?

He has not seen his mother and father in so long. He has so much to tell them.

Question after question, he thinks, troubled.

17

Cole's head keeps bobbing. He doesn't want it to, which is frustrating. Now it falls forward. He flexes his neck and lifts, ripping open his eyes, trying to keep them wide and awake. Sleepy, though. His chin slips to his chest again.

He wipes away drool with a floppy hand.

His thoughts get mixed up.

He sees Phillip.

Not anymore.

The sound of water makes him thirsty, and he opens his mouth in the hope water will somehow find him, stopping his thirst, but that doesn't work.

This goes on for some while.

Until it does not.

He awakens with his eyes already open. The second of adjustment, processing an image that is already there, is jarring.

Adam and Phillip sit across from him.

They seem equally startled.

Awake now.

18

"Did you see?" Adam says quickly to Cole. "What did you see?" he asks Phillip.

The three glance to one another in a loop. They all want verification, but no one wants to speak.

They have reached a bridge, Adam imagines. The bridge is made of rope and shaky planks of wood. Far below is a fast river that rushes over jagged rocks, and if they are going to continue, there has to be a volunteer. In order to cross, some-one has to be first.

"I'll go," Adam says. "I'll tell."

Once he begins, the words come easy, as if relayed to him by another person. There was a girl, Lily. They sat close to one another. It was art class. She made him feel hidden, like no one saw him but her. "I hope I see her again," he says. He describes his drawing—The Boy's drawing—of the treeman, each arm, each branch, and how they were divided into long, bent fingers. Below the tree were deep roots, thick ones that thinned into tough string. "When we look at a tree, we don't see the roots, how far they go." They're roadways, he recog-nizes now, reaching for water, not wanting to die. Surprising himself, Adam says, "The tree is a man, and we're roots."

He stares at the mud like it is an imaginary campfire. Imaginary flames lick his thoughts. In the tree, all you do is think about important things. You cross bridges.

"We're trying to survive," he says.

19

"The blood was the color of candy."

Cole thinks of cherry lollipops, round and bright red.

He has never liked sweets. On Halloween his big bag of treats is thrown into the pantry. He leaves it alone. For months his mom and dad pilfer pieces while he's happy with frozen raspberries or thin slices of salami. His parents end up eating all the candy.

In his veins swims the blood of his parents. There is Mom, and there is Dad. But their blood is not his. Their blood is a veil.

There are other people. These people could not or did not want to care for him. They gave him away. He has never seen or spoken to them. He does not know who they are or where they live or even if they are still alive. He only knows that when he was a newborn, just days old, he was left outside a fire station, and weeks later a man, Dad, took him home to Mom.

Cole is their only child. Adam is an only child. Phillip, he assumes, is too, as is every boy inside the tree.

A lone son, taken and replaced.

"I thought it was a dream at first. I thought it was me bleeding," he says. "I thought it was make believe."

Within a drop of blood is the past: the past is a mystery that will never be solved. Mystery is in him, in every move and word. If he could see all that was in his blood, would he see The Boy? Those people who left him?

He should see God.

But he thinks all he would see is red.

He will never know parts of himself. Never know certain parts of this world.

He decides that what is known matters most, and that has to be good enough.

20

Phillip does not doubt the truth of what Adam and Cole have recounted. What they described is real. They have all visited home, and in their places other boys have been inserted, or these boys have inserted themselves, somehow.

A void has been filled.

Now Cole and Adam wait.

It is his turn.

Phillip feels the blush on his neck rising. The pond fills the cavern with light, and he knows they will see his stress and embarrassment. What has happened to his confidence, his brash beliefs about this world and its possibilities?

He has been diminished, turned back into a ghost.

As if aware of his discomfort, Cole speaks. "Phillip, we're sorry. It's our fault. We shouldn't have treated you like we did."

Adam softly punches the ground—then again, harder, so his fist makes a thud. "Now that we're here, we need to help each other."

Phillip sees that Adam wants to say more, but he can't. There is nothing else to say.

Adam reaches and places a heavy hand on Phillip's shoulder. Phillip feels himself relax. He didn't expect that. The blush recedes. If he was a ghost, Adam's hand would fall through him

Phillip has never had a real friend. He hasn't known how to foster friendship. Rather, he has only known anxiety. For others friends seem to arrive and depart naturally like the coming and going of seasons. For Phillip the seasons are his companions. Fall and winter come, say nothing, and leave. He says nothing. Summer is the same, and so is spring. Instead of seeking friendship, he has chosen to roam the woods and calm his loneliness with squirrels and leaves and the feeling of firm ground underfoot.

He sighs.

What can he tell them, really? That he saw himself try to kill a cat? That nestled at the bottom of his backpack is his father's handgun? A weapon nicked and worn from use, carried through years of war.

Should he tell them that in an empty school hallway, in the early morning quiet, The Boy reached into the backpack, and before the image shuddered and disappeared, Phillip had tried to scream? He tried, but it was like he had no mouth.

Instead, he asks, "Do they know we're watching?"

This is a question he already knows the answer to, but he asks it anyway. Anything to not tell the truth.

21

Maybe he did not want to remember and accept what he saw. Phillip's question, though, forces Cole to go back. He closes his eyes. In his mind, it is not like a memory, a copy of what already occurred. The moment he sees is like being there again.

He hovers near the ceiling. The Boy, bent at the sink, turns on the faucet. The gush of water mixes with blood, forming a pale red pool, when—
a slight cut of the eyes, as if to check behind him, to look at Cole. The Boy's quick glance to the side of the mirror is like an animal scouting an enemy.

"They know," Cole says. "They sense us."
"Yeah," Phillip says. "They do."
Adam leans forward, his eyes glassed from not blinking. He is more eager, because he is less convinced. "How do you know?"
Cole considers his words. He wants to be clear. "There was a mirror. I saw him recognize me. He knew I was there."
He is certain.

22

"They're not us," Adam says to himself.

"They're versions," Phillip says. "What we could be."

"I could be him, but I'm not?"

Phillip scrapes mud from the stick with his fingernails. "That's what I feel. I feel that."

Water trickles down smooth ribbed walls. Adam listens. The sound urges surrender. Mud. Stick. Skin. Bone. It's all the same, braided together. He is so tired. Are mountains above, a rainforest? Maybe, directly overhead, beyond the dark, is home.

"Where did they come from?" Adam says.

"Inside," Phillip says. "From us."

The Boy is his creation. "How?"

"I don't know."

"I felt it," Cole says. He stares at the pond. His voice is composed. "Right before I entered the tree, there was a moment. It was like I was in two worlds. I was being pulled and holding on. When I finally fell, a part of me...shed. It came off, like a piece of clothing. I think each of us left behind something, with the same knowledge, the same body, the same chance. There was an empty spot. They walked back to our homes. They sat in our seats."

"But they're different," Adam says.

Cole faces Adam. "They make their own decisions. They can."

"You're sure?"

"I saw it, at the center of his eyes. He had my face, but what's beneath, that's theirs. The more we accept that the better off we'll be."

"We might not be best friends anymore, back home," Adam says.

Cole says, "No, maybe not."

Adam leans back. Above him is a sky of sorts, of shadows. If he were here freely, able to leave, would he find the cavern beautiful? Probably, at first. It is easy to be tricked. Eventually, though, there would be the feeling that something was wrong—a sixth sense, whatever you want to call it, recognizing the ugliness of something that, on the surface, is pretty.

"I saw you," Adam says. He looks at Phillip.

"What?" Phillip says.

"In school. The other you."

"What was I doing?"

"You were in the hall. You walked past the room."

"Oh," Phillip says.

"You don't remember?"

"No."

"But we were looking at the pond, at the same time."

"The pond might only show each of us what it wants," Cole says. "It gives scenes. Not everything, just scenes."

A brown-skinned boy enters the cavern. He is streaked with mud. With two hands he holds a hostile worm by its tail. When the worm twists, its teeth click, and the boy hops back, arms outstretched. He shuffles slowly backward. He reaches the wall. They watch the boy swing the worm, smacking it against rock until it goes limp. It takes many swings. Then the boy plops down in the mud to eat. He tears into his meal with gusto. Bright blood blots his chin and chest.

Adam says, "If the other Phillip saw the boy, the one who looks like me, do you think he would recognize him, as the same?"

"You mean, would he know he was a replacement?" Cole says.

"Yes."

"I think he would. Phillip?"

"I do too."

"It would be like having a secret," Cole says, "and you don't want anyone to know. Then you meet someone, a stranger, who knows, because they have the same secret."

"I wouldn't like that," Adam says. He notices Phillip turn his face. His neck has flushed red. "Phillip, you alright?"

Phillip nods. "It's just hard, to understand," he says. "Everything, I mean."

Cole crosses his arms and tucks his hands in his armpits. Adam thinks he sees him shiver, and he's about to ask Cole if he's okay, but before he can Cole speaks. "All we can do is watch. Our lives are theirs now, and we have this place. That's what we have."

Adam scans Level 1. The tree brought them here, and this place is part of the tree, and the boys are part of the place, just like the pond, mud, and shore. He notices the bell, waiting. He catches the red glow of a worm, and as his eyes continue their tour, a thought stops him: the tree needs boys, like the boys need worms.

Adam's attention settles on the middle of the mud field, where he has noticed, off and on, boys gathering. He counts. There are eleven now, and together they slink from the pond's light towards semi-dark. He hears tendrils of their voices, the frayed ends of phrases. It is nothing he can understand. They are like a team breaking huddle, readying to run a play.

Keep an eye on them, he says to himself.

23

Cole watches a crawling boy cross from sand to mud. His expression is round with delight. What did he see? What is occurring in his life, or is it his life anymore? Tomorrow, the same face might be lined with fright.

Beyond the boy, the gold bell shines just as radiantly from a distance. "I wonder what the bell is for," Cole says.

"Maybe it's for dinner," says Adam. "Come get your worms."

They laugh.

"It's awful, but I'm hungry," Adam says.

"Me too," says Phillip.

For the first time Cole notices the stench of Level 1. "They don't seem to care where they go to the bathroom," he says.

"Just as long as it's near a wall." Phillip points his chin across the cavern to a boy squatting.

"That doesn't seem like a good policy," Adam says.

"I can't accept that we're stuck here forever," Cole says. A surge of anger hardens within him. "We have to leave. This is a dead place."

"Where do we go?" Adam says. "Level 2?"

"We climb," Cole says. "We go to the top. We try to find a way out."

"I don't want to stay here," Adam says.

"What do you think, Phillip?" Cole says.

"Tony will want to come."

Cole softly bites his lip. "You're right." His confidence undercut, he notices himself slouching, so he sits up straight, placing his palms on his thighs. "I don't trust him. He wants the stick, Phillip."

"I know," Phillip says. The stick lays near him.

"It has value here."

"We need to protect it," Adam says.

"But it might help to have him along, for a little," Cole says. "There's so much we don't know. We just have to work together, and make sure we watch him."

"What if it's worse, above us?" Adam says.

"It doesn't matter. We go to the top," Cole says, "as far as we can."

As if on cue, Tony emerges from a low crop of rocks. He heads towards them, whistling. It doesn't take long for Cole to recognize the tune: "Happy Birthday." The unusual choice of song strikes him as sick, and he resolves to fully analyze why at a later time. For now he files it away.

"As far as we can," Cole repeats. "Together."

"No matter what," says Adam.

Cole looks to Phillip.

Phillip nods. "Okay," he says. "No matter what."

24

When Tony arrives, he knows they have been speaking of him. He sees they have decided to make a break from Level 1 and slog up the tunnel in some misguided delusion that they can escape this hell, do what no one has ever done.

Idiots.

"Oy, friends," he says.

Tony sits cross-legged, wedging himself between Adam and Cole. They must scoot to make room.

"So you have seen," he says, "the hard truth."

He lets the statement sink, like a stone, to the bottom of a deep lake.

"The world you left has passed you by, and each of you has been replaced. It is not a good feeling, is it? It is an empty feeling."

The blunt assessment immediately reasserts Tony's authority. Whatever scheming has gone on is now in disarray. Whatever recreated sense of self or pact forged or plan crafted has turned flimsy. *I am the master. I know things they do not. I am in control.* How easy it is to put the newbies in their proper place.

"This is difficult, I know. But it is the truth, oy?"

There are shy nods of concession, mumbling affirmations.

"But do you know what?" He leans forward, the move of a practiced salesman. "Not all is lost, boys. That truth, as hurtful as it may be, does not disqualify other truths, for I have a secret."

They are toys to be arranged.

"I have not viewed the pond for ten years."

He lets this profound fact settle.

"Ask anybody. They will tell you. I choose not to. When I made my decision, it was because I chose *this* world, and I have studied this place, all its parts, because I have been searching. Year upon year, I have searched. And at last I have found. Do you know what I have found? Oy? I'll tell you. I know a way out."

Cole, angry, says, "You lie."

"I expect you to say that. I do, Cole. If I were you, I would say the same."

"And I said it," Cole says. "And."

"I need help," Tony says. "One can't escape this place alone. It's a four boy job, and you're the boys I've been waiting for."

There is, in each of them, Tony knows, the allure of possibility, the chance, however slim, that what he says is true. That chance keeps them from getting up and leaving. It keeps them from pushing him down and dispensing with him in a flurry of kicks.

"I cannot tell you, of course, exactly how we will escape, because I cannot risk you using that knowledge on your own—"

Adam abruptly stands, looking at something in the distance. "Someone's coming," he says.

Irritated at the interruption, Tony sighs in frustration. He is fairly sure who it is. When he turns around, he chuckles.

What he sees is no surprise.

25

"The stick," Adam says to Phillip. "Give it to me."

A gang of boys approaches. The synchronized plodding of their feet forms a march.

Without hesitation Phillip hands the stick to Adam, who adopts a wide, intimidating stance. He holds the stick across his chest with both hands.

The march loudens to a stop. A boy with shaggy hair and tiny round eyes leads; he is tall for Level 1. At first Phillip assumes the boy has a small, upturned nose—a dainty nose—but the further he inspects he sees that, in fact, the nose has no tip. Gnarly, scarred flesh has closed over the wound. The others fan out behind to form a triangle. Phillip notices two others with similar half noses.

"Be gone, Helmut," Tony says, still sitting, his back to them.

"Stay out of this, runt." Because of the nose, Helmut's voice is nasally.

"Runt?" Tony says. He turns around, remaining sat. "Really, Helmut, you can do better. I'll chew off the rest of that nose if you're not careful."

"We want the stick," Helmut says.

"Always wanting," Tony says, "without deserving anything."

"It's not yours," Adam says.

"It's no ones." Helmut glares at him. "Everything here is no ones. Everything is for the taking."

This is the point, Phillip thinks, where there will be pause. All will silently agree that no one wants to fight, and clumsy conversation will entail. Some type of compromise will be reached. Adam might show Helmut the stick, might even let him hold it. After some time, the stick will be handed back. The boys will leave. No one will feel bested. No one will get hurt.

But Adam does not allow for any stalemate. Instead, without warning, he rolls the stick overhead in a great oval that seems to hypnotize his eleven foes and, stepping forward, swings the stick downward like a jet into the side of Helmut's knee. The sound is equivalent to a smashed light bulb. The joint cracks and buckles into a tangle, leaving Helmut dazed and on the ground, with his lower leg angled in reverse.

Then Adam charges. The rest of Helmut's gang is not prepared. Eyes big, they stand frozen and begin falling. Phillip thinks of bowling pins. Adam does not attack knee joints. Instead he aims for the meatiest muscle: the thigh. One after the other, he connects. Each *smack* sends a boy reaching for his leg and falling over, groaning and rubbing the place where the knob of the stick met flesh. Dark, round bruises form. This dispatching of the entire crew takes about a minute.

Adam stands above those writhing below him. Plates of dried mud have shed from his skin during the melee, and shiny patches of sweat glisten. He breathes deeply, his broad chest inflating and deflating. He is an image of victory. He reaches and hands the stick back to Phillip.

When the bell rings, Phillip associates the sound with what he has just witnessed. It is a bell signifying the end of a match, the announcing of a winner. But he quickly realizes this is not so.

The bell rings again. It is the gold bell, the one he saw walking to the pond.

Level 1 is abuzz. Even the boys viewing the pond have awakened and left their spots and are rushing. Everyone is rushing, even the boys with damaged thighs. They have risen and are limping towards the bell. Even Feldstein, with his crippled gait, hurries as best he can. Helmut, Phillip watches, crawls forward, dragging his damaged knee towards the source of the sound.

A boy with golden skin stands by the rock and rings the bell, ringing and ringing and announcing loudly and with conviction, "I choose to go away!"

26

The bell's final chime extends to the perimeters of the cavern. As the sound stretches, it thins into gauze, tearing, becoming spotty, until there is silence.

"I am Tayib, and I choose to go away!" Tayib places the bell back on the rock.

There is immediate and coordinated action by the boys of Level 1. Initially confused, Phillip, Cole, and Adam are sucked into the practiced movements of the others. Intuition tells them what to do. A straight and wide path is formed, which leads directly to the pond. Neat rows of boys line each side. Shoulder to shoulder, they look like a well-trained regiment, an army.

Nothing is said. Water sluices down the cavern walls.

Tayib faces the pond and begins his walk across the shore.

There are somber nods as he passes, nods of understanding, nods meant to mean goodbye. One brief smile arises from Tayib, when he stops to hand the comb back to Tony.

It is a long short walk.

When he reaches the edge of the pond, Tayib does not wait for a black shape to appear. Instead he steps without pause into the soup. The undulation remains steady. His legs disappear to the knees.

Phillip thinks that if Tayib were to lift his legs, one then the other, there would be nothing except nubs, everything below the knee taken by the pond.

The water forms a tight mold around Tayib. He moves forward and descends. Soon he is waist deep. All this time his expression has not changed: stoic and accepting. There is no indication of whether the water is warm or cold.

But the pond begins to stir. The undulation quickens and rises. It's as if the soft beginning of a storm churns the waters.

The pond globs to his chest.

It touches his chin.

His brow furrows. There is fear now.

Lifting his arms, draped in pink slime, Tayib tries to turn around, but it is as if a strong, unseen hand pulls him downward, and he leans helplessly.

A grimace. His eyes close.

He is swallowed.

Gone.

All that remains is a quickly diminishing memory: a boy once named Tayib. A boy who viewed the pond, ate the worms, and rang the bell.

The boys stand in their staunch lines.

Soon after, the pond reshapes. Phillip watches in amazement. It is as if a trowel is pressed and dragged over the middle, creating a shallow, unmoving canal six feet across. This splits the pond into halves. Beneath the water, from the far shore, a shadow moves evenly down the canal towards them.

Phillip feels the beginning of fear. It starts as a dot in the middle of his chest that expands into the folds of his lungs, making his limbs heavy. It squeezes his heart.

The shadow accelerates and darkens to pitch black. Whatever is beneath is rising to the surface. There is a bulge.

The outermost layer of the pond stretches, like the skin of a pregnant belly, until the skin starts to rip.

A large capsule is slickly ejected. It sleds over the route Tayib followed earlier, erasing his footprints. Sand fountains from its bottom, slowing and eventually coming to rest in the mud.

The boys gather around.

The capsule is rectangular and rounded at the edges. It is sheathed in the same wet opalescent shine as the pond. But as it remains exposed to the air, the luster dries and flattens until becoming dull and leathered. Pink turns to rusty red.

Phillip reaches, but his hand is pushed away.

It is a coffin, he realizes.

From the crowd two boys emerge. They could be brothers. Their features are rough, like log sculptures hewn from chainsaws. They have wide, short torsos and messy mops of black hair. Their large hands—more like claws—are what most distinguish them. Phillip cannot identify their place in the world. Mongolia? Samoa? Steppe dwellers. Pacific islanders. Some place relegated to the confines of his imagination.

Wherever their home, their hands, Phillip can tell, are strong.

The boys take positions on opposite sides of the capsule. They raise their arms and proceed to tear into it. Long fingers easily pierce the material. Their hands dig to the wrists and pull back. Strips of dry pond, like strips of bark, are flung and form a loose pile.

A small piece lands next to Philip. He picks it up and flattens the waxy substance between two fingers. When he does, it turns to sand.

In little time the top of the capsule is torn away, and Phillip sees inside.

Tayib lays on his back, his arms crossed over his chest, his skin as white as a stick of chalk. His eyes and mouth are wide open, shock etched on his face.

He is dead.

The two boys reach inside and carefully lift Tayib from his coffin. One holds Tayib's wrists, the other his ankles. This is how they carry him to the tunnel, walking with measured steps. No one follows.

Despite the attention shown to the body, Phillip notices something wrong about Tayib. There is something inhuman—the way his neck and legs loll, the way his elbows twist. It takes a while for him to understand: Tayib sags like a ragdoll. His limbs contort as if stuffed with sawdust. His body bends in places where it should not bend.

His bones have been removed.

He knows this.

Phillip turns back to the pond, which shines anew as if revived. Barely perceptible is its electric hum.

The pond has taken his bones.

Then a sound seizes his attention. It is unlike anything he has ever heard—a screeching, a grating scraping of teeth that makes him flinch. Minor at first, it expands and then erupts from the tunnel. Phillip faces the horrible, frenzied chorus of thousands of hungry worms.

The boys, with their cargo, have reached the mouth of the tunnel. They must close their eyes to concentrate and withstand the wail. Phillip watches the boys swing Tayib. Once. Twice. On three they let go, releasing Tayib to the feast, and the body lands with a plop in the mud.

The worms swarm.

Phillip understands.

The pond takes the bones.

The worms take the flesh.

In return, the worms leave the cavern alone.
For bones, the pond shows boys the homes they have left.

27

While worms devour what remains of Tayib, the sullen boys of Level 1 trudge to the pond. Some cover their ears with their hands. Others sniff away tears. Every boy goes, including the newbies, their eyes fixed ahead.

They go to escape confusion and sorrow: a boy chose to leave. They go to find affirmation: I am still alive on the other side, where I am loved. I am still here. They go, ultimately, because they are filled with fear. One after another they kneel before the opalescent waters, and the black shapes come and take them away. A peace settles over the cavern.

Tony heads back to his relic shop.

He has no time to mourn. A quest awaits, and he must prepare. He takes stock of his items and deduces which contain value, which can be used as bribes. One would think the pocket tool, with its dull blade and corkscrew, as useful, but in fact it arouses little interest and has proven irrelevant to the requirements of this world. The same goes for money. The coins and paper bills are only painful reminders that there is nothing to buy. On the other hand, leather gloves, worn in the tunnel, help keep the hands from swelling and provide a firm grip on twisty worms. There is the cough drop, the comb. These are definite. The bouncy ball. Oddly, a key-chain that he hasn't pondered seriously for ages catches his eye;

attached by a small chain to a gold ring is a small blue-eyed lizard, covered in green sequin scales. There is something about the colors, how they remain vibrant, that stokes the senses. Such a wild card can sometimes be the item that most speaks to the soul. Colors in this world are in short supply. The lizard, Tony decides, is coming along.

And there is the small pocket mirror, his mirror, the one he took from a sniveling, collapsed newbie who never made it out of the pit. Couldn't deal. It happens sometimes. Tony has devotedly kept the mirror hidden in the pouch and only dares remove it when he knows no one might see. A glint of light could lead to its discovery. For him the glass replaces the pond, which offers no reflection. The glass allows him to see himself as he is.

No boy he knows has seen his own reflection since stepping into the tree.

He must be efficient because he can only carry so much. He grabs the backpack from beside the worm cage. The worms stir. He checks them, a bit sluggish from their captivity. Three left. He resolves to eat them all before leaving. He will need the energy.

The book? Should be bring the book?

It is valuable, but heavy. The book, too, sometimes causes too much interest. Instead of a trade or bribe, a normally sensible person can lose their mind and try to take. They attack. That is what often happens with items that possess immense allure.

Like the stick, for instance.

He decides that the book will stay. Besides, Feldstein has always adored the book. Tony will leave it for his assistant.

Surprised by this sentimentality, he skims the shore and finds Feldstein lying on his stomach, with his hands supporting his chin—a particularly boyish pose. The fact is that

Feldstein has endeared himself to Tony. Yes, he will gift him the book for years of loyal if uneven service. In the end he considers this generosity a good sign, confirmation that he is leaving for good, never to return.

Level 3. That is where he is going, and that is where he will stay. For a brief instant he allows himself to dream.

Plants.

Meat.

Fire.

The faintest glow of sunlight.

And then there is the wildest rumor, whispered once to him years ago and never heard again. A separate pond. The Pond of Lost Girls. What it means, he does not know. That is sometimes the naked, purely batty state of gossip, a mere collection of words without any explanation or mild proof, yet the words are still spread like they contain truth.

The lemon cough drop will be kept in a secret compartment of his trusty waist-pouch along with the mirror. The comb he slides into a side section of the backpack.

He has heard Geiger has long hair that travels well down his back, wild hair that shines black like a crow's feathers. The king will like the comb and the mirror and, of course, the stick.

When he zips up the backpack, he pauses for a moment: *Tayib*. In his excitement he almost forgot tradition. A good boy is no longer, and respects should be paid. Tony closes his eyes, takes a deep, calming breath, and whispers, "Goodbye, Tayib" to his departed customer. Then he begins a prayer, one beginning with "Our Father."

Somehow, over all these years, the prayer has stayed with him. He recites it only after one has chosen to go away. It possesses no significance to him; the words now form a relic no different than a set of keys, but he still says them. Tayib prayed loyally to his own god, Tony knows, but here in the tree such differences do not matter. They are the same. So Tony offers some final words, in his own way, in the case that heaven is as real as suffering.

28

There are candy bar wrappers. A water bottle lies on its side. A red notebook holds an uncapped pen in the metal spiral. At the back of the tent the backpack sits on the edge of a quilt.

Light blue with white stitching. Phillip reaches down to touch the quilt, which he has had for as long as he can remember.

His hand is useless; it moves through the material without response.

The Boy yanks open the tent flap. Phillip moves to a corner, becoming the corner.

The Boy is dressed for cold. His body is made bigger by the layers beneath his jacket, and this gives him an imposing size. He wears a black knit cap, and a gray scarf covers his face up to his nose.

It is Phillip's father's scarf.

He unzips the jacket, revealing a bulky brown sweater.

His father's sweater.

A grocery bag drops to the floor: a loaf of bread, peanut butter, oatmeal cookies.

He must have run away.

The Boy sits, his profile to Phillip, and searches the inside pocket of his jacket. He finds a pocket knife, a Christmas present from years ago. He blows warmth into his hands and begins making a sandwich, spreading peanut butter with the small blade. Done, he licks the blade clean.

The Boy chews, thinking.

What has led him here?

Heat rises off The Boy as he eats. The steam becomes a shroud. He reaches and slightly pulls back the tent flap, just an inch or two, enough to peek out.

From his corner Phillip is able to see.

The Boy has camped at the edge of the woods, back about fifty feet. The tent is camouflage. No one will notice unless they are looking.

The spot allows The Boy to watch people entering the park. A clearing containing play structures and athletic fields waits at the end of the mulched path, bordered by the high woods and those opposite. It is a lonely area, heavily shaded, where playing children can be heard but not seen.

Some parents warn their kids to only walk the path with a friend.

A family, a father and mother along with their daughter, pass. The father carries a scooter flung over his back. The girl runs ahead.

Wait, the mother says.

The Boy tears off another bite of sandwich.

In this confined space, so close to him, Phillip's breathing begins to quicken.

Relax. Be a ghost.

He settles down.

His attention goes toward the backpack, then the notebook and what it might reveal. If he could only open the notebook.

Eventually, the cold forces The Boy to zip his jacket. He rewraps his scarf.

It must get so cold at night.

He is a part of me, Phillip thinks.

I should know what is happening.

29

What's wrong? The Boy says.

The girl twists a blade of grass. She ties it into a knot, which she doubles.

They sit in a gazebo that overlooks a pond, empty in wintertime. In spring it will fill with ducks and fuzzy ducklings.

She hands him the knotted grass.

Thanks.

She flips up the furred collar of her jacket.

My parents asked about you.

Yeah?

Someone told them.

Told them what?

That we're friends.

We are friends.

I know.

What's wrong?

My parents.

Is it wrong that we're friends? We talk.

I know.

Ride bikes.

I know. She starts to tear up.

Lily, what?

They say I can't talk to you anymore.

He turns the blade of grass in his hands. They said that?

Yes.

Why?

They don't want me to.

But why?

Adam knows.

You're black, she says.

The Boy finds a rock on the bench. He tosses it into the pond. It barely ripples the cold water.

They look at the pond. They look at it for a long while.

It doesn't matter to me, she says.

It doesn't matter to me either, The Boy says.

They laugh.

She stands.

The Boy stays seated, watches her face him.

Standing, she is as tall as he is sitting.

The winter pond is still. Bare, dormant trees are still. The sky is still.

They share one soft and quick kiss. Their lips touch then part. Their eyes open as they tilt away from each other, smiling. It seems like the silliest thing ever done.

Let's run, says Lily.

What?

I want to run.

Where?

Anywhere. Chase me. You have to give me a head start.

Okay. How long?

Ten seconds.

Okay.

Adam watches her run. Lily runs as fast as she can. The Boy counts silently, slowly, letting the distance between them gather so he can sprint after her.

30

His mother smiles at The Boy. Her hand reaches and brushes back his sweaty bangs. Her eyes are heavy with concern.

The doctor sits on a stool, which he wheels forward. He pats The Boy's thigh.

"We're going to fix you up, Cole," he says.

"Okay." The Boy stays slumped, his hands curled over the edge of the exam table. His right hand is badly swollen. The skin is pink and stretched.

"You're going to stay here for a few days," his mother says, "I called your dad. He's coming."

"Okay."

Now Cole is confused.

His mom looks to the doctor.

"Cole," the doctor says, "you don't have the flu."

She rubs The Boy's back.

"We're taking a look at your blood. That hand has me concerned. You've got an infection, and we're going to check it out."

Cole descends, sits beside The Boy.

"We thought you had the flu. It's going around." The doctor scratches his head. "How did you get that cut on your hand again?"

The Boy's breaths are labored. "I think in the woods," he says.

"When were you in the woods?" his mom says.

"I don't know. A few days ago."

"Well," the doctor says, "we're checking it out."

The Boy shrugs.

The doctor tries to enlist his mom for help, some encouragement, but she is too lost in worry. Cole sees her mind spinning.

"So I hear you're a quarterback."

Cole hates when people say this, like playing quarterback gives him special powers. He sees the Boy's irritation, too, and that's when The Boy turns and looks right at him.

He wonders what The Boy sees.

"What we're going to do next is see what that blood tells us. We'll know soon."

But they aren't listening.

They stare at each other, The Boy and him.

31

Though they are tired, the aftereffects of the pond are less pronounced this time. It's as if their bodies have adapted. They gather in the same place where they met after their first viewing.

If they were to stay, this is where they would talk about The Boys living their lives. This would be their routine, year upon year.

Each is silent about what they saw in the pond, and there is no inquiry. Cole senses that no one wants to share, and it is a silent, joint decision to afford each other privacy.

Beyond this, there is no conversation to be had, no packing or planning for the next stage of the voyage. There is only the decision to leave, and leaving.

They will depart Level 1 changed.

Physically, they have toughened into whips, their bodies rendered free of any flab by the heat, climb, and diet of worms. Cole has the thought that each of them is being reduced into the person he really is—or whom he is destined to be inside the tree.

Phillip, holder of the stick.

Adam, their warrior.

And what is he? What is his role?

Cole knows he will always be quarterback, the one picked to call the play, the one to throw the pass. He has always known this. His reluctance doesn't matter.

And they will leave Level I altered in other ways. Much of their fear has been replaced by knowledge.

They know the pond's power.

They know the purpose of the gold bell.

They know why worms stay in the tunnel.

And they are friends—the three—who have made a pledge.

"Ready?" Cole says. He looks to Adam, to Phillip.

There are no objections. They stand, stretch.

Before they leave, they shower. They find a clean space near the cavern wall next to Tony's relic business and press themselves against rock, letting the thin pane of falling water splash over and soak into them. The water is clear, fresh. The water is cold, bracing. They place their lips on rock and drink, slurping until their bellies distend. The grime does not easily wash off. They must scrape with their fingernails until they find skin.

They finish, and viewing each other provokes laughter because without mud masking and hardening their features they appear, Cole thinks, youthful, as they should. Looking normal inside the tree is funny looking.

It is time to leave.

Tony is waiting by the tunnel. A full backpack is slung over one shoulder.

They walk, heads bowed, to mud and dark.

As they near the tunnel, Cole looks back one last time. Boys plod to the pond. Boys sluggishly leave. Some sleep. Some wake hungry. All have distant, glazed eyes. No one says goodbye. No one speaks, except in whispers.

The bell waits.

Nothing will ever change here, not unless the tree changes.

They move towards some unknown, the three of them—and Tony. Tony has told them they need to pick up an item at Level 2, for their escape, but he will not tell them what.

He is lying, Cole is certain, but he plays along.

No one knows that at home he is sick, and Cole senses that Adam and Phillip's recent quiet about what they last saw hides secrets they, too, are not ready to share.

Sometimes secrets make one strong, other times weak.

He hopes they are made strong, because they have promised to climb to the end, past Level 2 and past 3, and Cole senses that what looms will not be mere obstacles. What awaits, he suspects, will be terror—and its test of the heart and mind.

Keep your heart. Keep your mind.

They lower to their hands and knees.

"Onward!" Tony says. "Oy!"

His cackle shudders through Cole.

Again, a new crawl begins.

Part II

Run

32

When Cole walked from the forest, I whispered to myself, "Cole." I whispered "Adam" and "Phillip" without ever having seen them before.

I was right there, next to them, but they didn't notice.

When one becomes Keeper, one has immediate gifts. I am invisible to those who must not see me. I know everything about those whom I help keep.

I say "keep" because it is the best word. There are others: preserve, imprison, possess, watch. But sometimes there is no word to truly describe something. The word hasn't been created, or it can't be because no suitable definition could ever be constructed. That's the case, I think, for what I do and what happens to the boys inside the tree.

Li used the term "Keeper," and that's why I use it.

Li had the job before me.

I guess you could say I'm an assistant. I help the tree. I do not do anything, really. I help because I am here. I am a witness. It's my choice. You might ask why.

I'll get to that.

By the way, I'm not invisible to myself. How others do not see me, therefore, is a mystery.

If The Invisible Man were to remove his gloves, he would seem to have no hands. I see mine fine; they are right here. I hold them up, turn my wrists so that my palms face me, wiggle my fingers.

I used to wear a wedding ring, but years ago the tree was near a rocky coast in Ireland. Here, sheer cliffs hundreds of feet high sunk straight into the Atlantic Ocean. Below, heavy waves detonated into the cliffs, sending up sprays of water. The tree was close enough to the coast that I could walk to the edge.

I threw my ring into the churning waters.

I did this because of a great sadness. My husband had passed away from illness, and I was not there to console him in his last moments.

I do not age, just like the boys inside. I am 39-years-old. 11 years have passed since I left my family, which would make me 50, half a century.

One stays Keeper until it is time to go away. I will know when it is time; at least that's what I was told. I will go away differently than a boy inside the tree. There will be no worms for me.

When the tree travels, I travel with it. It is like being snatched up by a tornado and then, after a minute or so, gently landing on the other side of the world.

I never know where the tree will go.

I am tired. To think I enjoy this would be wrong. It used to be torture. See, I was once a parent, but I have merely become numb. I know that my own child was given a chance by my decision.

That's the choice: become Keeper and save your child or watch other children suffer.

This is what happens: someone knocks on your door. You answer it. The person standing there tells you that you have a choice. If you look down you'll notice that this person is levitating, the way I levitate now. In the yard is a tree you've never seen before. It stands there as if it has stood for a hundred years. The choice is explained. You can either leave your child, or your child will go into the tree, and you will never see him again.

The woman who came to my door in Arizona was Asian. She was shorter than me by an inch or two. She looked exhausted. Her name was Li. She spoke in a language I had no knowledge of, but I understood every word she said.

I am a woman, a mother. Do you know what's funny? My first name is Lee Ann, but everyone called me Lee, pronounced just like Li.

When I understood that I had to leave, when I made that decision, Li walked past me into my house. As she did I watched her change, from an Asian woman into me. She became another version of me. I became her.

"Goodbye. I will do my best," she said in her strange language.

Then the tree left, and I was taken along with it.

The Keeper of the tree, I sense, has always been a mother.

It is interesting to consider why. I have my theories.

My son is now 23-years-old. He loves airplanes. He is learning to fly. Maybe he will fly over me one day. Li has done a good job it seems. Whenever the tree settles near a pond or puddle, I am usually able to view my son. Water provides me a window to view the life I left. Sometimes I see my mother or, more rarely, Li. Li likes to drink coffee. She always has a steaming cup near her. So much time has passed. The ocean shows me nothing, which is okay, because the ocean is so large, and if my son's image were the size of an ocean my heart might break.

One day, when I am ready to go away, I will knock on someone's door, and I will be levitating.

The door will open. She will see me. That person always does. Just like I see the boys.

Someone else will take charge, exchanging their life for this.

33

Soon after leaving Level 1 the light behind them begins to fade. Later, there is surprise when they are plunged into absolute dark.

It is as if they become the dark.

Phillip holds his hand in front of his face, and he sees nothing. Having his eyes closed is no different than having them open.

"There's a curve ahead," Tony says. "It blocks out the light from Level 2. After a ways there will be a glow. Just trust me, oy? Follow my voice, and don't freak out."

With no light to climb towards, no pink pinhead, no distant star, the tunnel is a black void. Phillip had not realized the comfort provided by the pink haze and how it was a source of calm. In the sudden absence of sight paranoia erupts. Each time he is about to sink his hand in the mud, Phillip worries that nothing will be there, and he will topple forward off some endless cliff, and he will fall, forever.

Stress radiates from the group. This tension causes small, hidden fractures in the dark, making the infinite gloom feel rickety and about to collapse around them.

To help keep track of each other and relax their hammering hearts, Tony starts a game. "Foods. I'm first. Mashed potatoes and gravy."

Phillip tries to recall the smell of gravy.

"Steak," Adam says, "with ketchup."

"Your turn, Cole," Tony says.

"Carrot cake."

"Mm. Good one. Phillip."

He wants to choose the first thing that comes to mind, but cannot. He scrolls through choices. What would he like to eat? "Cheeseburger," he says, "and onion rings."

"My turn again. A nectarine."

They soon adopt a regimented order that includes no commentary, only food.

They climb.

It is an effective, torturous distraction. It is impossible, given their starved bellies and limited menu options, not to think of food. Food takes precedence over the dark. Hunger is more powerful than fear.

Next they list colors.

Lime.

Purple.

Tony says, "Periwinkle blue."

They have a brief argument about magenta. Is it closer to pink or red?

They move to animals.

"Porcupine."

"Goat."

"Pelican," Cole says.

This causes a silent and playful moment of rumination. Phillip senses them all smiling, remembering the wonderful creature and its somewhat comical appearance. The long beak and throat pouch. The big wings flapping.

Then countries.

The games go on. The tunnel remains pitch black.

Phillip observes that everything they list is not inside the tree. He wants to say this but does not.

At times a slow but steady descending flow of water makes traction difficult. They slide backwards, grabbing at the sides of the tunnel and each other. Even Tony expresses frustration, describing the conditions as "slop."

"Iceland," says Adam.

When Phillip is almost to the point of screaming, of raving, he sees it ahead: a faint pink glow, as small as a dot made by the slender tip of a paintbrush.

Level 2.

"Land ho!" Tony says, followed by a cackle.

The water, too, returns to its normal dripping. Mud below them clumps, becoming sturdier. The boys find their groove and grind upwards, the tunnel slowly filling with light.

They stop to eat. They catch worms and consume them.

The worms are bigger here—longer, thicker, and much stronger, with sharper teeth. Phillip must wrestle and chew as his squirms vigorously in his arms. While he eats, the worm still tries to bite him. Only after half its flesh is gone does the worm finally wilt. He sucks down every last drop of bright blood he can. The welt on Phillip's shoulder is sore and ringed with teeth marks.

They rest, letting the warm worm blood course through them, energizing their exhausted bodies.

Tony uses his collapsed worm vein as dental floss. He meticulously cleans between every tooth. He massages his gums. When he is done, he yanks back the rubbery vein and slingshots it at Adam.

The vein dings Adam in the forehead. For a second it stays there, sticking to skin and dangling past his chin, before falling into Adam's lap.

Infectious laughter skips over them. Phillip cannot stop laughing.

A smiling Adam picks up the worm vein and shoots it at Phillip.

Phillip ducks, and the vein flies overhead into the tunnel wall. He reaches behind him, grabs it.

He has a thought.

He knots the two ends together and laces the vein around his fingers. The boys watch. He starts, reverses himself, and continues, as he tries to remember the proper moves and order. At last he is done. He smiles. The smile is unlike anything he has ever felt before. His eyes proudly rest on his creation.

He has made a Cat's Cradle.

The boys break into applause and more laughter.

Ahead, the tunnel curves and appears to level off.

They stop.

An actual curve. It bewilders.

"This is halfway to 2," Tony says.

He renews the climb.

The closer Phillip gets to the curve, the more he feels the dense light around the bend. He hears its steady drone.

The sharp turn means that for a moment Tony disappears, and when Phillip rounds the corner he bumps into Tony, who has stopped. The air is crisper, still warm but no longer balmy. The light is made a brighter, deeper pink—almost neon—by the lower temperature.

Adam and Cole arrive. The four of them stay ganged together and staring.

There is a boy in front of them. He sits, legs outstretched, leaning against the wall. His body is lined in light. It appears that he has made the choice to never move again.

"Peter?" Tony says. There is shock in his voice, and concern. He rushes to the boy and is quick to offer water.

The boy drinks the few drops Tony is able to squeeze from the handkerchief.

"Thank you," Peter says. His voice is gravelly.

"I hadn't seen you. I wondered—"

"I left. Time to go." The boy grins.

Tony directs them all to sit.

"Hello," Peter says.

They nod hello.

"Why?" Tony says.

"He is very old."

Phillip realizes the boy means his other self, in the other world.

All around is the presence of worms.

"I came here to be alone," his voice a trace stronger now, "but I am glad I am not. You will be my witnesses."

Witness. Phillip ponders the word. An observer. A bystander.

"I was named after St. Petersburg. Did you know that, Tony?"

"No, I didn't."

Peter leans his head back. "My grandfather, he lived near the city. That's where I was, visiting him, when I came here. I was walking through snow. I breathed into my scarf. The warm breath on my face and cold wind. A white storm fell all around me. It did." His eyes dance with the vitality of remembrance, but they quickly turn sad and plead for confirmation: is the memory real or imagined?

"I believe you," Tony says. He takes Peter's hand, holds it.

"It snows where we come from," Adam says.

"Then you know. It is so beautiful."

"It is," Cole says.

There is the pain of recalling something beautiful, which is now far away.

"Peter."

"Yes, Tony?"

"You brought me from the pit."

Tony's concern for Peter now explained, Phillip studies the boy more closely; he has a deep scar over one eyebrow that shines through the mud.

"Long ago," says Peter.

"And then, after I came back to Level 1, you asked me to take your place."

"Yes, you're right."

"Why? I know why I went to the pit, but why did you? Why did you choose me?"

There is Peter's uneven breathing. His chest moves up, suspends, crashes down. For a moment Phillip does not think Peter will respond.

A long silence passes.

"Tony," Peter says. He clears his throat. "If we can help someone, then we must. Why I asked you, of all?" A fit of coughing interrupts, until settling. "I asked because no one else would go."

A witness means that no one should be made to suffer alone.

Peter winces, and his face furrows with alarm. Something has occurred within him. The boys instinctively scoot back. He winces again, this time crying out, his back arching, and

117

his entire body freezes into a flex. "It's starting," Peter gasps. His begins to pant.

"Go," Tony says. "Go!" He drops Peter's hand.

Tony corrals them back down the tunnel, rushing, pushing them to where the tunnel curves.

"What's happening?!" Adam says.

"Get down!" Tony orders.

Phillip crouches, turns, and peers around the corner.

It begins with small blinking dots of white light. What starts as a few multiply until, it seems, hundreds cover Peter, then thousands, then millions, a growing number impossible to estimate of bright lights as if from all the world's cities combined. Pieces of Peter—his eyes, mouth, fingers—begin to slough off.

Intense heat flushes the tunnel.

There is a moment, a flash, when Peter's face reverts to that of an infant. In this instant Phillip sees Peter when he was a baby, and Phillip sees the dark, round birthmark that was removed, the scar above his eye.

Peter's boy face returns, without eyes. There are deep sockets where eyes should be.

And now there is a sound: sizzling and the pop of oil. But it is not oil. They are cells, Phillip understands. The basic building blocks of life are being torn down. Each light is a cell. Each pop is a cell gone, and parts of Peter disappear. The sound strengthens until rapidly reaching a whine that takes the place of Peter's evaporating body, which evaporates in no discernible order. A portion of his forehead is erased, some of his torso. One foot disintegrates. Shins vanish.

Soon there is just vapor, an eerie presence of something that is no more, followed by a final and loudest *pop* that deletes even the vapor.

The Boy has died. The boy is dead.

Phillip counts as his breathing slows, his heartbeat returning to normal. He counts to 22, then stops. He is crying.

Cole, too.

And Adam.

Even Tony wipes his eyes.

They cry because of death and its resolve. What they have witnessed is that death, in the other world, will make its way inside the tree, and when it does the light within will be revved so that a boy will shine his very brightest, just so that bright light will burst and perish.

They will die here if they don't get out.

34

Since the erasing of Peter, they have not moved or spoken.

Adam thinks of snow. Snow, he decides, does not fall. It steps down from the sky. Snow uses air like stairs. Or snow is in a race and missiles to the ground. First to the ground wins. Snow does not fall.

People fall.

Everyone will.

He hauls off and punches the wall of the tunnel as hard as he can. His hand disappears to the wrist. He must twist his fist from the mud.

"When the boy walked into the pond, what happened to his other version?" Adam says.

"Nothing," Tony says. "We can't hurt them." He speaks blandly, without his normal pomp.

"How do you know?"

"You three are not the first multiples. A twin once watched his identical walk into the pond. The next time he viewed he saw his brother, but it wasn't him. It was the other one, still there. The world above," Tony looks up, "the world we left, that's what determines when our lives end. Not the other way around."

"What about heaven?" Adam says. "Maybe the boys who go into the pond enter heaven."

"Or maybe they don't," Tony says. "Or maybe you can escape and see your family again. The pond has never had anything to say about an afterlife. It only shows an alternate life."

This is the first time Tony has mentioned escape since leaving Level 1. He then reshapes into the old Tony, the ringmaster. He claims that at Level 2 there are four identical keys, silver keys (which he knows intimately), mixed amongst similar relics, that have the proper shape and depth. They are *the* keys. There is a door, he says, only he knows where, a secret door he found during his explorations, with locks oddly placed at the bottom and top corners, and the keys will fit. And the keys must be turned in unison or else the door won't open.

It is a grand, pathetic performance.

"It's a four-boy job," Tony says.

"What's behind the door? Adam says. "Santa Claus?"

"Freedom."

Cole laughs. "Freedom, huh? How do you know?"

"I know. That's how I know."

"Why do the keys have to be turned at the same time?" Adam says.

"Because they always have to be turned at the same time. For the same reason that the house is haunted. And the paintings are alive. And the pirates are ghosts. And the drink is cursed. And the gypsy with tarot cards won't say diddly! And the bloody genius kid is the one who knows all this while the adults blunder about like hippos! That's the way adventures work."

"This is an *adventure*?" Cole says.

"What else would you call it?"

The tunnel abruptly rumbles, a tremor.

"What—?" Adam says.

"Uh oh. Hold on," Tony says.

121

Before they can prepare, the tunnel rolls. The boys flip and fall. They are shaken from the ground and lifted and thrown down again. Their shoulders ram into the mud. Their faces slam into mud. They crash into one another, becoming tangled, then are flung apart.

Adam is flat on his back and digging in with his fingertips and heels. The tunnel continues to shudder. His fingers dislodge. He is airborne again. He wraps his arms around his head for protection. Splat.

In a few more seconds it is over, the ground still.

They lay scattered, in disarray.

Adam is shaking.

"Nothing to worry about!" Tony says. He is up and laughing hysterically as if having just exited a rollicking rollercoaster. He scoops away mud from beneath his eyes with his thumb. "The tree moved. Let's hope somewhere cool and dry."

"Argentina," Adam mutters to himself, not that he knows anything about Argentina's climate. Rather, he knows the country is at the bottom of South America, which is one of seven continents. Staring at the dripping ceiling above, he says, "Continents."

"Europe," Tony says. "Oy!"

"Asia," Cole adds.

Phillip: "Africa,"

"South America and North America," Adam says.

"Oy, Australia."

"We're missing one," Cole says.

Adam sits up. "Antarctica." The frozen land. Snow does not fall. People fall. Be snow, he thinks. Be snow. "I wonder what continent we're on now?" he says.

35

Feldstein hopes for a different outcome, but he is a realist. He always has been.

Tony is gone; the rumor has spread.

He hides the book behind a rock.

He showers, pats down his curly brown hair, wipes clean his fogged glasses, adopts his best smile. He will give it one try. Just one.

"Hello, how may I help you? Would you like to loan or trade?"

The brutes don't even speak. They just ignore. Helmut, limping terribly on his damaged leg, pushes him aside, and Feldstein trips and falls. Pulling himself from the mud, he watches them raze the shop, toppling and snatching.

A boy takes a toy car and smashes it against a rock.

Stacks of intricately arranged shoelaces become a messy pile of noodles.

Years' worth of work is destroyed in a minute.

When they are gone, Feldstein holds back his tears. He brushes off as much mud as he can, but it smears.

Checking to make sure no one is watching, he retrieves the book. He holds it securely under one arm. As silently as he can, using shadows, sticking close to the cavern walls, he makes his way to the tunnel.

He steps inside. The heat and wet and dark are never consoling, never friendly. He takes a moment to look toward Level 2.

But he does not go up.

He always knew Tony would leave, and he will not follow like some starved fan.

No, he is not headed upward.

He is a realist. Did an unlucky draw make him different, or was he chosen? Was it fate? He looks down to his foot, his lump, and the grotesque shin as curved as a bow. Being born with a deformity forces one to be a realist. Never knowing anything but a limp is real. Being stared at is real. Teased. Bullied. These are realities.

He would never make it at Level 2. He would be dog food at Level 3.

There is only one direction left.

With the book held underarm, Feldstein begins his descent to the pit, to where his time here began.

36

"Travelers!"

Two boys stand guard outside Level 2. The entryway is tall and arched like the dramatic entrance to a cathedral. Vicious pink light floods the tunnel, more intensely than at Level 1.

Phillips stays upright, but the light seems to atomize through him as he climbs. It is almost paralyzing.

"Announce yourselves!"

More guards appear. They are shadows, black shapes gathering.

This is all Phillip can see between the obsessive blinking needed to protect his eyes. He uses both hands as visors.

"Announce yourselves!"

"Tony. Level 1."

The guards leap down the tunnel and grab them, herding them towards the entrance. They are shoved and kicked.

"It's Tony you numbskulls! With newbies! Unhand me!"

"Back off!" Adam takes a blind swing that misses.

"Watch out for the big one!"

"Hey!" Cole says.

Phillip surrenders to the momentum of the bodies as they are led to the entryway. He takes short steps to guard against tripping. He merely wants to escape the powerful light that pummels them.

Passing the threshold into Level 2, Phillip looks up. The throbbing tunnel flips to a loose darkness above, just like at Level 1. They are dumped into a cavern. The size dwarfs him. Mild heat, unlike anything he has felt since being inside the tree, raises goosebumps on his arms; he is used to the sweltering temperatures of the tunnel and below. He is pushed some more, stumbling as his eyesight returns to normal.

Underfoot, the same mud with granules of gritty sand. Another undulating pond seduces.

He sees Adam's hands tied behind his back, wrists bound with a rope of woven shoelaces.

And then, before him, there appears the blurry image of a boy, his face covered in shadow. He speaks with a strange reedy drawl.

"Brother Red, move them to holding."

They are steered to a corner of the cavern. Waist high rocks form a square pen. They stagger single file through an opening.

"Stay here. Don't be stupid heroes." A heavily muscled boy wearing a red winter cap motions for a group of guards to fan out and surround the pen. They all wear armbands, torn strips of clothing tied around their right biceps.

"Here." Tony unzips his backpack and starts tossing out shorts and t-shirts. "Before our stuff gets confiscated. It's cooler here. You'll need it. Phillip, they're going to take the stick. Let them. You'll get it back. Trust me. If I'm right and things haven't changed, Swan will be arriving any moment. He's the gent who talks like he's got a wad of peanut butter in his mouth. He'll wax about brotherhood and family, but don't buy it. He's a maniac, and the Armbands are nothing but hyenas."

Phillip pulls a stiff t-shirt down over his head. He steps into a pair of weathered orange swim trunks patterned with hibiscus flowers.

Cole quickly unties Adam's wrists. They dress—similar outfits to Phillip's. The clothes, even Adam's, fit well.

They look ridiculous, like they're dressed for a beach party.

"Thanks, Tony," Adam says.

"Yeah," Cole says.

"Think nothing of it. Just listen to me, oy? I know this place. Used to call it home."

"You used to be at Level 2?" Adam says.

"I did."

"What happened?" Cole says.

"Let's say it didn't work out. Leave it at that."

It isn't that Level 2 is packed with more boys, though it might seem that way. What is so different is the activity, which fills the cavern with a type of bustle one associates with city life, a place teeming with work and commerce. This gives the illusion that twice as many boys inhabit Level 2 than 1, when in reality the ratio is much less severe. Boys move from one end to another, to the pond and back. A team washes clothes. The wet clothes slap against a patch of rocks, and dirty water is rung out. Another group, arranged in a neat row, is practicing karate. A pair of boys grapples. In an area designated for sleep, boys lay atop blue tarps; shirts have been stuffed and made into pillows. No boy roams randomly about—or individually. They walk in groups, in lines, navigating the cavern as if on roads. Four muddy boys return with worms. They pass four others who head for the tunnel. There is a shower area. Old shirts are handed out to dry off with. A patient line of approx-imately ten boys waits for the pond. A boy flips an hourglass, directs the next in line to an open spot. An attendant leads a boy away from the pond towards the tarps. A boy is awakened on a tarp and led to the showers. Boys are spaced evenly around the pond, but in lesser number than in Level 1.

The viewing is controlled. Phillip surmises that a static number—about fifteen—view the pond at one time, and they do so for shorter, pre-arranged periods. Meanwhile, more boys with armbands form a perimeter around the pond. They face outward, at attention.

Phillip considers the arrangement. They are positioned as if to dissuade interlopers. Are they protecting the pond or something else?

Then, as he scans the shoreline, he sees it. The sight leaves him gutted. It feels as if all his insides are removed at once and dumped at his feet.

It is not déjà vu. Déjà vu is a trick of the mind that makes one believe he or she experiences something previously fore-seen, as if possessing the ability to access the future. No, it is not déjà vu. There is no trick in what Phillip discovers, but the supernatural burst—the brief feeling of perplexed wonder-ment—is the same.

Those who wish to go to the pond must pass a square white monolith with flecks of quartz shimmering in the pond's light. Atop it, waiting, rests a gold bell with a handle of the darkest, polished wood.

37

Tony is about to tell one of the guards, an oafish-looking bloke with a unibrow, that he is as ugly as a catfish, when he notices his fellow prisoners gawking.

He looks to where they stare.

He sidles beside Cole. He checks Adam and Phillip. All three are lost in the web of an unsolvable mystery.

"See the bell, eh?"

"How?" Cole says.

"Well, to be honest, no one knows. It's no relic. All I can gather is that the rocks and bells were here before the first boy arrived. Been here since the beginning I suppose. Placed by the gods or Dr. Frankenstein or alien spacemen with ten hands and giant brains."

Tony sits down.

The boys follow, forming a circle.

"I'll tell you a story. Saw it with my own eyes. Happened many years ago. A Level 1 boy...can't remember his name, not around anymore. Anyway, one day he gets mad at something he sees in the pond. Afterwards, he goes and grabs the bell, rings and rings, says, 'My name is'—can't recall his name, had red hair, I think—says something like, 'I choose to throw the bloody bell into the bloody pond!' So he hurls it into the pond, chucks it a good ways. The bell sinks. Glub, glub, gone.

But when he turns around, when we look to where he's looking, there's the bell, back on the rock. It's the same bell. Like it never left.

"Some things," Tony says, "got no explanation. Some things are so spooky that you worry if you talk about them you might get cursed. I'm not worried about that, though. This place is a curse all by itself. Oy, Lord Swan approaches."

As Brother Swan robustly walks towards them, with an assured sense of purpose that governs his every action, Tony sees little has changed. The stamina is still bottomless. The charisma remains. His ridiculous hairdo bounces atop his head as if connected by springs. But there is one interesting difference: four Armbands cover Swan's flanks and rear. It used to be two.

Did someone try to strangle him, or is it just paranoia?

"Good to see you, Tony."

"Likewise, Swan. Well, not really."

"Still with the wit, I see."

"Still trying I suppose."

"Are you staying with us for a while?"

"A day or two, enough time to get my strength back, maybe do a few trades."

"Sounds acceptable. What have you brought us?"

"Cole, Adam, and Phillip. Thought they might belong here."

"I see."

Swan inspects the newbies like they are livestock. Tony gets a kick out of his rehearsed repertoire: expressions of mild disgust balanced with subtle poses meant to provide hope. It is rude and narcissistic. He never says a word. This is all about Swan.

When he does finally speak, Swan clasps his hands behind his back. He thrusts his chest out, chin up. His mane of yellowish hair is styled into a wavy pompadour. Mud is used like styling gel. He wears a purple short-sleeve shirt, with the collar up, and a shiny gold chain around his neck—ten or so chains braided into a thick one. He is thin-armed and plump around the stomach.

"My name's Brother Swan. We're all brothers here. We are because we're a family. I am the leader of the family. The elected leader." He smiles at Tony, then turns his attention back to the new boys. "Everyone works, and we work together, as a family should. This is our farm, so to speak, and we tend to it, from sun up to sun down, so to speak. I love my brothers. They love me. We work for each other. We also understand the need for rest and escape, but such diversion must be earned and not come before work. You'll each be given jobs. You'll get to know us. We'll get to know you. You'll be asked to leave, or you'll be offered a chance to stay. Right now you're Travelers. That's how we'll refer to each of you, as 'Traveler.' No disrespect is meant. We only want to stress that, at this time, you're not a member of our family, of Level 2."

Tony must hold back laughter. *What a bunch of crap.*

Brother Swan turns to the red-capped boy. "Brother Red, store these boys' possessions, except for that stick. For now, place it with my personal relics, for safe keeping of course. I'll provide you assignments shortly."

Tony is last in line as they are led from the holding pen. He has surrendered his backpack and pouch. Phillip has relinquished the stick. Tony watches the three newbies split for the first time since their arrival; each is steered by Armbands to a separate part of the cavern.

Phillip goes to washing.

Adam to grappling.

Cole, interestingly, is guided to the far empty shore of the pond.

Tony, meanwhile, is sent to latrine duty. This is no surprise. He is always given latrine duty whenever making an appearance at Level 2. He will scoop mud onto poop and splash water over pee.

He doesn't mind this time. His focus lies elsewhere.

He watches the backpack and pouch get carried over to Relics, an operation five times the size of his Level 1 shop. He sees a boy he knows, Fuentes, working the rental counter. Brazilian, if he remembers correctly. Other boys he recalls only vaguely. Shane or Sean. Something like that. Ellison.

Tony knows that the stick, for now, is Swan's.

In the interim his plan will continue. Stage one is already complete: Phillip is separated from the stick and his friends. Now for stage two: taking possession of the stick and reaching Level 3.

Tony lightly taps the stiff, muddy cap of hair that houses the lemon cough drop. No one, not Shane or Sean or anybody, including an Armband, will be able to refuse such a bribe. They'll look the other way.

Now it's just a matter of timing, patiently waiting for the proper moment and not hesitating when it comes.

38

Behind him sits a chest-high pile of clothes.

Each piece is weighted with water and remnants of mud. His back aching, Phillip bends his knees and propels his body upwards. Then, with his arms extended above, he arrests this momentum and slaps the piece of clothing—shirt, shorts, or pants—down against the rock. With each slap he envisions a sledgehammer driving spikes into railroad ties, him working as part of some exploited child chain gang. The clothes spray him with dirty water.

He is one of four boys performing the same task. They stand in a line. No one has spoken. No one has told him how long he must continue without rest. No one has rested.

After three or four slaps, he tosses a pair of shorts into a done pile, which two other boys sift through. They separate and hang. A clothesline, spun from shoelaces, is set up in a well-lit area of the cavern.

The boy with the red cap announces, "Break!"

Phillip's workmates drag themselves to a nearby wall where a steady trickle of water beckons. Phillip follows.

They cup their hands and drink.

Then they sit. The entire cavern is at rest, except when a spot by the pond opens up.

A boy with a mini afro says, "I'm Mash. Short for Mashburn. That's Browning and Satori. He's Japanese. Got a bit of a language barrier. We go by last names when it's just us three."

Nods are exchanged.

Phillip notices that Mashburn's bottom lip is split. Satori, meanwhile, has a black eye. Both injuries look fresh.

"What about 'Brother'"? Phillip says.

Mashburn stretches his back. "Brother? Shoot."

"Brother," Satori says. He spits into the mud.

Mashburn laughs. "Satori's right. Swan talks a good game, but ever wonder why us three do the most washing? Why Swan always gets a second helping of worm? Because Swan chooses favorites. And Swan's favorite is Swan. His second favorite is Red Cap. His third favorite is an Armband. He doesn't have any other favorites. That's why. He talks about family, like that means equal, but talk is all it is. It's alright, though. Just as long as we get our pond time. We get our pond time, some steady worm, we're good. Right, Browning?"

"You know it," Browning says. He low-fives Mashburn.

Satori, understanding, joins in the hand slaps.

"What's your name?" Browning says.

"Phillip."

"Your last name."

But before Phillip can tell them, Red Cap announces, "Break's over!"

And Phillip goes back to the clothes pile. His back is sore. He wonders when he will move to a new station. He thinks about what Mash said, that this is how it is.

There's always someone who gets chosen last, the least favorite, the weakest, people lower on the totem pole.

39

"You fight good."

This is how they talk. Sometimes they grunt.

They have taken a break from wrestling and are eating. A group of muddy boys just dropped off ten freshly dead worms.

"You become an Armband, you get the best worms," a boy says, his mouth full.

"We run place," another says in broken English.

"Yeah?" Adam says. His worm is enormous, the biggest he's seen. He has gotten used to the taste.

All the Armbands eat the same way. Heads down, they attack their rotating worms like sawmills. They focus on one section, then another. The veins are sucked dry. The extra calories coupled with training have made each Armband thick. They possess the fatty muscles of sumo wrestlers.

"They got to listen to us. Not the other way around."

"What about him? The one with the red cap?" Adam says.

"That's Red," a boys says. "We listen to him and Swan. That's it."

"Just them. We get more pond time than anyone."

"The others get their time, but we get more."

"We get the best of everything."

"We train."

"Someone steps outta line, we bash 'em."

"That's what we do."

"Bash 'em," a boy says.

"Bash," a boy adds.

"Become one of us, you get to bash 'em."

"And you get the best worms."

40

Swan unfolds the board. The plastic checkers are the size of buttons. It is a travel set, Cole knows. He had one at home. His mother would pack it for trips, and it would never get used. On the other side, he bets, is backgammon, a game he's never wanted to learn.

He sits cross-legged in the sand across from Swan.

Swan has chosen red.

Cole is black.

They have hiked to a remote area of the cavern, near the pond, and they are practically alone. Two Armbands stand posted on both sides of the pond. They block anyone wanting to gain access to Swan. The rock and bell, the field of mud, the workstations and viewing area: all rest on the opposite shore. Across the way the cavern bustles.

Here, though, it is serene. They are bathed in soft light. The sand is an undisturbed plane except for their footprints. The pink glow and comfortable temperature and his clothes lead Cole to think of a tropical island.

"This is my area," Swan says, "where I view. No one is allowed here except me, or those I invite."

From faraway Cole watches the boys viewing the pond. They seem to stare with greater fervor than at Level 1. They want to notice everything they can, to bring back and keep with them.

"Guests first," Swan says.

They play slowly and in silence. Both take time reviewing the board. After many safe moves, they trade pieces. Then again. The board opens up.

"Why did Tony leave Level 2?"

Swan stops his arm mid-reach. He grins. "An interesting question to begin our conversation." He resumes and slides a checker forward. "Tony lost by two votes. Instead, I was elected leader. It became unsafe for him."

Cole runs through the options. The board has tipped to Swan's favor.

"Why was it unsafe?" He sacrifices a checker.

"Because Tony made it unsafe."

"How?"

"When you lose, you have to accept that loss. Tony had a hard time accepting his role."

"What was his role?"

"His role, which is everyone's, was to work for the family, because we are all brothers here. King me."

Cole stares at the board without focusing on the board. "Why did you bring me here?"

"You know why."

"No, I don't," Cole says. He moves.

"Shouldn't have done that." Attacking from behind, Swan palms two more checkers with his king.

"I'm going to lose this game."

"Yes, you are."

"Unless you make a mistake."

"Don't bet on it."

"Well, I won't forfeit."

"I know you won't."

"Why? Because I play to the end?"

"Because you're a leader, Cole, like me."

"Really?"

Swan links his hands behind his head and leans back.

"Your friend, the big one, will do whatever you ask of him, just like Brother Red will for me. Same for that other one, that timid boy you came with. And others, too. They wait for us. They look to us to make decisions. They follow. Why this loyalty? It's because of who we are. Everyone has a station. Yours is easy to see. The way you're thinking things out, because you know, in the end, you'll be the one to tell people what to do. You try to hold back, like you're not a leader, but you are. You recognize it in me too. Don't act like you don't. We're alike."

Swan resumes play, and the game speeds towards an inevitable close.

"Cole, I've been waiting. I need a protégé, someone to take over when I'm gone, to continue what I've created. I won't be here forever."

"You've known me for five minutes."

"All I need is five seconds."

"What if I'm not the person you think?" Cole says.

Swan smiles. "But you are," he says.

Cole watches his last checker leaped. The board is empty of black.

"And with that, our contest is done."

"That seemed too easy. Another game?" Cole says.

"Certainly. It's your funeral."

This time, Cole resolves to play quickly, to not analyze and predict. Sports has taught him that overthinking can diminish a player's skills. Sometimes, he knows, you must break from the plan and throw or run towards empty space. You just have to swing. You just have to go.

"You think this will change things? Playing wild?" Swan says. "I don't think it will."

"Maybe it will. Maybe it won't." Cole shrugs.

His unpredictability, his quick willingness to give up pieces to get pieces, frustrates Swan into mistakes. Swan's discipline turns sloppy; he tries to adopt the same approach as the game before, taking time to think through each move, but immediately after sliding a checker forward Cole responds, and Swan is then back to analyzing the board. Cole never lets him rest.

Soon, Cole has kinged two of his checkers to Swan's one.

Swan irritably studies the board. Announcing a break, he stands and stretches. His hands on his hips, he gazes across the pond. Cole's eyes follow: the boys of Level 2, working, following the rules.

"My mother died giving birth to me," Swan says. He smiles, and a brief fit of manic laughter escapes. He turns, facing Cole. "I don't know why I told you that, and I don't know why I laugh, honestly. Maybe it's because I killed my mom, and now I'm here." Squatting, his knees crack. He rises, and he resumes his observation of the boys, serfs in his empire. "She's the one who named me. From what I know about her I doubt she ever saw a swan. She was born and raised in the same tiny town where I lived, with not a lone swan in it. Maybe she saw one in a book. A pretty picture that stuck with her. I wonder sometimes. I wonder what she saw in her mind when she said that name.

"Now my father, I don't know what name he'd have given me, but I doubt it'd be Swan. My father was a farmer; he's the one who raised me. We grew onions, cucumbers, some cotton. You name it. I loved being out in the fields with him.

I loved seeing those neat rows of plants busting from the ground. My father explained soil to me, how it needed a guiding hand. You have to steer soil for it to give you what you want, he told me. He taught me that.

"One time, when we were tilling, we came across a young rattlesnake. It was just...there, in a place it shouldn't have been. He told me to stand back; a small snake could pack just as much venom as a big one. We had a weeding sack, and he snatched the snake up by its tail and dropped it in and spun the sack closed.

"I asked if we could keep it. He looked at me, curious, like he saw something he'd never seen before. I saw the snake twisting in the burlap.

"'We can keep it if we never give it a name,' he said.

"'Why?' I asked.

"'Because it's a snake,' my father said. 'It doesn't want a name.'

"We kept that snake in our barn, in a cage he made. It was more like a high-walled pen, lots of room to roam. We trapped mice and rats. Sometimes we would take our dinner to the barn, drop a mouse in the pen, and watch it hunt while we ate. I'd see it curl into an S and strike, see it sink its fangs into its prey. That moment, with the fangs sunk, how do you describe that? I watched it shed skins and grow big. It got as long as me. During the summer, my father sometimes set it loose in the barn. He'd padlock the door. Then we'd return a few days later and go back in together. Take a flashlight to peer in the dark places, and step lightly until we found it. He never used a stick or other tool. He just grabbed the snake by its tail. Put it back in its cage.

"He told me that in a few years, when I was quick enough and strong enough, he'd let me start handling the snake. One time, years later, I asked him if I was ready. He said, 'No, a little while longer.'

"When I first came here and I had to catch my own worms, I'd imagine holding that snake. That's what I thought about.

"It was one summer when I saw the tree. A hot, hot summer. Dusk. The sky was filled with all sorts of color."

Swan grins at the memory.

"I walked to the edge of the field where the woods began, mainly pines. I was barefoot, like now. I remember the soft, damp soil. It had rained earlier. I thought about stopping to check on the snake, but I didn't. I wish I had.

"We'll always wish for things, you know that, Cole?

"For all the time I've been here, I've watched my other self. The Boy, right? This is how we see them. What we call him in our minds. When my father died, The Boy took over the farm. He only grows one crop, sugarcane, and he doesn't treat the soil right. He sprays poisons and little green pellets. With every passing year the ground becomes more brittle. He talks about 'maximizing the land.' He drives a flashy car. And the first thing he did after my father died was go to the barn, take a shovel, and kill the snake.

"Cole, when I'm gone, I need somebody to take over this part of the shore, someone who keeps the snake alive, and feeds the snake mice, and keeps the mice in control. Order, Cole. Before me there was none. Now there's work and food and leisure and order. I am the father of Level 2, and I want a son to teach. I need someone who has power inside them."

Swan sits down. He rests his chin in a hand and looks at the checkerboard.

"Are you like your father, Cole?" he says.

All this time Cole has kept his eyes on Swan. Now he looks into the pond. He feels its light go into him. His words are the light. "No, I'm not."

"No?"

"My father," Cole says, "wants me to be someone I'm not."

"How can one hate their father?"

"You're wrong," Cole says. "I love my father, but he...misinterprets me." He pivots his attention back to the board. "Swan, we don't plan to stay."

"No?"

"We're going up."

"Up you say?"

"Yes."

"There's always the pond, you know, if you want to leave."

"We're not leaving like that."

"Cole, not thinking may have won you this game, but that approach only gets you so far. There is no escape. There's only here. Below, you know, is misery, and what awaits above is not pretty."

"What is above?"

Swan laughs. "I'll leave that mystery for the great explorers."

"You've never been past Level 2, have you?" Cole smiles, considering Swan, his purple shirt, the glittering gold chain.

"No, I guess I haven't," Swan says.

"Why?"

"That's for you to find out."

Swan slides his final checker, which Cole jumps.

"A tie," Cole says.

"Yes, I guess we'll have to agree that there is no winner, not yet."

41

Except for the standard group of boys viewing the pond and those moderating the viewing, all activity has stopped. The cavern is unusually still. Earlier, Red announced an immediate suspension of all workstations by order of Brother Swan. A surprise event would take place shortly, he said, a "reward for good work."

Idle boys mill about. They talk about jobs, worms. Most choose to sit and quietly wait near shore for their chance at the pond.

Cole finds Adam and Phillip. They stand by the abandoned washing station. Clothes lay about like debris left over from a disaster.

"Swan is dangerous." Cole speaks quietly.

"How do you mean?" Adam says.

"I think he's one of those persons," searching for the words, "who could hurt a lot of people, and he wouldn't feel bad about it. Tony was right. We need to get out of here."

"Where is Tony?"

"By the relics," Phillip says.

Cole sees Tony, engaged in some sly ploy no doubt, talking to a boy with twitchy eyes.

"The Armbands are a bunch of bullies. They push everyone around," Adam says.

"What do you think, Phillip?" Cole says.

"This place is kind of like a prison," Phillip says, "without bars."

"Look." Adam points with his chin.

Armbands, about fifteen or so, suddenly enter the cavern's arena of light. They are like large ships emerging from a dark horizon. The cavern goes silent. All eyes follow them as they clomp single file to the shore's edge. They stop near the rock and bell. Each Armband, Cole estimates, weighs as much as two half-starved boys. Their stony expressions reveal the empty space where a conscience should be. They are well-fed, and because they want to stay well-fed, they will follow any command, no matter how cruel. They are dangerous, Cole knows, because they are so simple. They enforce Swan's law. Together, they are a hammer, which they like being.

The Armbands sit. They cross their meaty legs, and for a while they do nothing but stare ahead, expressionless. Then, together, they raise their arms with open hands and slap their fleshy palms. The simultaneous clap is as loud as a gunshot. They do so again. And again. Soon, the clapping assumes a recognizable tempo.

The rhythm is familiar, but Cole can't place why.

Swan, exiting the relic shop, joins the Armbands. He has changed into jeans and a denim button down shirt. A tall, suede cowboy hat sits atop his head. He stands beside the rock and claps in tune and taps his foot: 1-2-3-4, 1-2-3-4. He clears his throat. Then, with a definite and resounding voice, he bellows, "Grab a partner, Do-si-do. When it stops we never know."

The square dance has begun.

Pairs of smiling boys skip to the center of the spacious field. More follow. And more.

It is obvious they have done this before,

The clapping grows louder, merging with Swan's words into one accelerating stream.

Boys sweep past. Cole steps right, left, trying to dodge them, but it's impossible. He is swept up, along with Adam and Phillip. Soon every able boy has joined the dance, propelled by Swan's mad words.

"Swing your partner, Do-si-do. Where we go we don't know."

The rowdy cavern rocks. The now crowded field swims with bodies. This is crazy, Cole thinks, absurd, but he is laughing. He feels free, for the first time since entering the tree. He locks arms with a black boy, skin as dark as moonrock, and releases into a spinning clover of dancers that includes Tony. His gecko eyes bulge like small white domes, and his teeth are ivory white. Then Tony is swung and disappears, swallowed in the melee. The exchange is so quick Cole isn't sure it happened.

It doesn't matter. Cole skips and kicks high his knees. The floor under him slides, and the clappers smile hideously as they fuel the dance. Boys stomp the ground, and mud is kicked overhead, spraying them. Legs are browned to the knees. The dance intensifies, getting faster. The swinging becomes more aggressive with each turn. Boys begin to smash one another and hurl each other like sweaty projectiles. Cole is no longer laughing; he pushes, lowering his shoulder, defending himself, snarling at the snarling faces that swirl around him. No one wants this to stop. They want to go farther. Swan's voice has become a growl, spewing nonsense. The dance is on the verge of igniting into a brawl, into chaos, and one punch is all it will take. This is meant to happen. Cole's hands scrunch into fists. It is what Swan and all the boys want. It is, Cole realizes, what he wants. He wants to hit someone. In the jaw. In their ribs. He wants to rage and feel that crack of bone. Grinning, his eyes searching, he feels the exciting, impending violence and readies to fight.

But the bell saves them. It saves them all.

42

The boy carries the unmistakable lethargy of having just left the pond. He is normal looking. Nothing about him stands out, except the gold bell that he lifts and rings. He does not speak. He proclaims nothing.

The dance has stopped.

Every boy in the cavern heads to the pond, but no one runs. They are in no hurry. Their sweat and rapid breathing subsides. The raw energy of the dance, at a boiling point a mere minute ago, quickly fizzes until flat and gone.

They gather by the divine rock, which Swan stands beside. He is handed the bell, which he holds against his hip. His guards, beside and behind him, scan the crowd.

"The pond has gone empty," Swan says. "It shows us nothing. The pond demands a sacrifice."

There is widespread murmuring. Cole tries to listen to the chatter, but too many conversations happen at once to comprehend any of them.

Swan speaks over the noise. "What then, brothers?!" He raises his free hand, the one not holding the bell, and looks up, acting woeful, as if desperate to solicit help from above. "What contest do my brothers choose—to see who leaves for a better world? What contest—so the pond will show us our lives again?!"

"Skill!" A boy from the center of the crowd jumps, his hand raised.

Swan points to him and snaps his fingers. "Brother Josiah suggests a game of skill," says Swan. "What say you, Level 2?"

"Brawn instead. Brawn is best!" This boy, in back, has a deep voice.

"A fine choice, too!" Swan executes another loud finger snap. "But is brawn best? Is brawn what we want?"

"A game of chance!" A boy near the front turns to the crowd. "Chance!" he implores.

"Rock Paper Scissors!" says another. "Best of five!"

"Brother Nelson says leave it to chance. Shall we leave it to chance, brothers? Send me your wish."

"Chance!"

"Yes, chance!"

"It seems that chance is what you crave, and chance will choose."

"Race!" Another boy from the back shouts. "Let them race!"

With these words a babbling quiet settles over the crowd.

The settling becomes a hush.

Then there is silence.

A low chant begins. "Race ... Race ... Race."

The chant builds. It loudens and hastens with enthusiasm as more and more add their voices. Cole watches the crowd change. He feels its growing and gleeful bloodlust. The boys are forming into a mob.

Soon the chant is deafening, thundering off the cavern walls.

"Okay!" Swan, smiling, tries to calm the crowd. "Okay!" He motions for quiet. When this fails he turns and, with a hand cupped over his mouth, speaks to the red-capped boy. Quickly, guards disperse and surround the crowd. They all adopt a similar stance: feet spread wide, an open hand wrapped over a firm fist.

Swan rings the bell. He does so once, and the chime mists into the crowd like a breathable tranquilizer. Slowly, the chant begins to break apart. The noise wanes. The mania recedes until Swan wields control again.

"Brothers, you have spoken! With sure and passionate voice you have spoken! Thus, we will race. And as elected leader of Level 2, I hereby decree race rules. Two boys. At a run. Three times around the pond. The first to finish three, he goes free. The boy to come in second, the pond gets him. As current champion, undefeated in eleven bouts, I give to you Level 2's own Brother Red, and as for runner two, well, he must be a Traveler, and that's for Travelers to choose."

43

Swan's brazen smile matches his outrageous cowboy hat.

"What if we refuse?" Cole says.

"One of you will run. If no one runs, then I'll call a vote. We'll pick, and we'll pick one of you, and whoever it is goes in the pond, willingly or by force. It's your choice. At least if you race there's a possibility, however slight, that you might win. Good luck, Cole."

Swan, followed by his entourage of guards, leaves for the pond. The other boys of Level 2 have already spread out, finding good spots to view the race.

"I'm the fastest runner," Cole says to Adam. "Swan's right. I have to run."

"Red's a bully. I should run. He's going to bash you."

"It's not a wrestling match, Adam."

"What makes you think there are any rules?"

While Cole and Adam argue, Phillip studies the pond. It approximates an oval. He gauges its turns and two long straightaways. For some reason he briefly thinks of Tony, but he can't find him.

Nearby, close to the rock, which will serve as the race's start and finish, Red stretches. He shakes out his legs and arms. He performs some jumping exercises, squatting low and leaping high. Then he bounces on his toes and shadow boxes.

His freakish muscles do not seem possible for a boy. He removes his red cap. A shaved, veiny head shines in the cavern's light.

Phillip stares, remembering that hair does not grow inside the tree.

"Just stick close. If you're close, you can win. Adrenaline will kick in. You can outrun him at the end," Adam says. He's conceded.

They've made the decision: Cole is running.

"Wait a second," Phillip says.

"Don't take the lead. Let him lead."

"Okay."

"Wait a second," Phillip says, louder.

Adam and Cole stop their back-and-forth.

"This is a long race," Phillip says. "In a long race I'm faster than either of you."

Then he explains why.

44

The crowd is a blur beside him. Some spit and jeer insults.

"You're dead, Traveler!"

"Good luck, chicken legs!"

But he doesn't let it bother him. He keeps a relaxed, even pace. The sand is firm beneath his feet.

Other times he hears Cole or Adam cheering him on, screaming to make their voices louder than any in the cavern. "Go, Phillip! Go!" One time he even hears Tony: "Bash that wanker, that bloody baldy!" The support sends a rush of pride through him.

They run side-by-side, him and Red.

They pass the rock.

One lap complete. Two to go.

What his opponent does not know is that at home Phillip did not just hike the woods. He knew the woods so well he ran them. He darted through the slim divides of trees, leapt fallen trunks and patches of muddy pond grass. He ran mile after mile, day after day, and when his shoes grew tight he often ran barefoot in cold and heat, and the bottoms of his feet toughened into leather.

He loves to run.

He runs as if life stems from his churning legs.

He senses Red thinking. Sweat glistens on the shaved head. A bluish vein near his temple throbs.

Red must take two strides to his every one. Phillip breaths smoothly, through his nose and out his mouth. His slim build has become even slimmer since entering the tree, and he feels weightless.

He is the better runner. He will win this race.

His synchronized legs and arms are like a metronome, and Phillip feels himself entering that zone running takes him to—where the world falls away and he disappears into memory.

He recalls his father playing catch with him. It is a sunny day; white clouds are splinters in an otherwise solid blue sky. The baseball thumps the leather of his mitt, and his dad, smiling, says, "Nice catch, son."

The image clicks to another.

His father's tired eyes are fixed in a state of paranoia as if nails are pounded into them. His hands shake so badly. Placing his own hand on his father's wrist, Phillip helps guide a fork into a steamed carrot.

The image clicks again.

He sees his mom. She looks at him so severely she carves into him.

Though he wishes otherwise, he must let the memory happen, as he has done hundreds of times before, because he cannot stop it. This is why he knows the memory is real: it won't leave him.

This is the secret he carries, what he tells no one.

He sits on a stool at the kitchen counter, and she stands across from him. A few feet is all that separates them. Phillip has just returned from school, his backpack still on his shoulders. He is hungry, and he hopes his mom will make him a snack, like his dad always does. His dad has gone away to war for the first time, and he misses him.

His mother stares directly at Phillip, and in her detached eyes rest what he has always noticed but never accepted. He is made to look down. He notices the strange design on the countertop: a sand dune, and all over the dune are razor blades.

She says, "From the moment you came out of me, I haven't wanted you. You're going to have to start taking care of yourself, because now that your dad's not here, I don't have to act anymore."

He was eight-years-old when she told him this, and since that day he has been watching after himself.

He feels Red close. Alerted, Phillip discovers Red has moved to his outside shoulder. He is now pinned between Red and the pond. Elbow to elbow, they round the second turn of lap two, and Red begins pushing, driving him towards the pond. Phillip realizes that he was wrong. Anything goes. Anything goes when it's life or death.

Phillip slows to let Red pass, but before Phillip can react Red slides his arm under Phillip's, plants his foot in front of Phillip's leg, and hip tosses him towards the pink water. Phillip somersaults in the air.

Pond, sand, pond.

He lands hard on his back, which knocks the wind from him.

A cheer erupts and fills the cavern, shaking it.

He looks down at his feet. A pane of water slides up the shore, shapes into a hook, and sweeps for his ankle. Phillip scurries backwards just in time. The water draws back and rejoins the pond as before.

Phillip locates Red, far ahead of him now. His sweaty head shining, he looks back, laughing.

Phillip is up quickly. He knows not to sprint. That will only tire him, and he'll have nothing left at the end. He must slowly make up distance and try to reach Red by the final straightaway.

Pay attention.

He brushes sand from his arms as he runs. He sets his eyes on Red's back and focuses on getting a little closer every third or fourth stride. Relax. He finds his new pace. Phillip enters the first long straightaway as Red rounds the third turn.

They think it's over. They don't know.

He is angry now, at himself for being so easily thrown to the ground and at a universe that he cannot control, all which causes his heart to ache. Sometimes his heart feels strangled, and it constricts the blood pumped through his veins.

He is angry at his closed, anxious heart.

So he runs.

The cavern is silent. His concentration makes him deaf. He follows the footprints in front of him. He bears down on the boy named Red.

The gap closes by small amounts. One time, Red peeks behind, and Phillip sees the strain on his face. It makes him smile the smile of revenge.

Going into lap three, he is about twenty feet behind.

He gains on the straightaway.

When they enter the second turn, the gap is fifteen.

Then ten.

At the fourth and last turn leading into the final straightaway, Phillip could reach out and touch Red. He could tap him on the shoulder.

Now, instead of silence, Phillip hears every sound, from whispers to screams. The crowd is manic, a fevered cacophony, faces twisted into shouting deformities that lean towards the racers. They look like gargoyles.

"You're done, Traveler!"

He hears Red's harried breathing.

They complete the turn. A straight sprint now. The rock, the finish line, is within sight.

Phillip readies to make his move; he will pass on the right, distant from the pond—wide, so Red can't touch him. But Phillip is wary. He knows Red won't let him by without a scrum.

Despite this, he is not ready for what comes next.

With no warning, Red stops and spins. Phillip brakes, backpedaling as Red reaches for him. Red gets his hands on Phillip's forearms, but Phillip shakes them off. Red lunges for him again and this time grabs ahold of Phillip's wrist, but Phillip twists free and scrambles to the side, away.

A group of boys blocks him. They push him in the back, and he trips and falls. Gets a mouthful of sand. A spectator shrieks in his ear: "Worm food!"

Red takes the opportunity and sprints to the finish, and Phillip chases.

He is able to catch up with about thirty yards to go. Again, Red readies to turn. Phillip sees it coming. The strategy is obvious: Red will wrestle him to the ground and pummel him, all the while creeping towards the finish until he can leap across it.

Phillip must find a way to pass. He will not be able to run around him. That is what Red expects. In order to win, he will have to surprise Red—and surprise himself.

Just as before, Red turns as Phillip nears. Red crouches, ready to pounce. And Phillip is about to react as before: run away and avoid contact.

But something changes within him. He doesn't flee. He stops and adopts a crouch as well. It is as if a pellet cracks open in his chest and delivers the courage to be free of the memory and the worry it causes, to know it is not his fault, and he can be a person who, up to now, he has never been.

They face one another, a standoff.

Just as Red leaps for him, Phillip attacks Red. Phillip is much taller, and he swings as hard as he can, and he watches with uninhibited, merciless hate as his arm unfolds towards its target, not knowing where or if his punch is going to land. His elbow locks. When his tight fist connects square against Red's nose, it leaves a dent that he feels on his knuckles.

Red staggers back, bent and head down, and Phillip does not hesitate. He charges forward, and when he is close he jams his knee upwards into the bottom of Red's jaw.

Red's teeth clack, and there is a snip.

The tip of Red's tongue arcs in the air. His scrunched face is crazed and howling as he falls backward.

With Red on the ground, hands cupped over his bloody mouth, Phillip runs past. He sees the piece of tongue in the sand. It doesn't even seem human, this small chunk of flesh. There is a moment when he glances back at Red, who knows he has lost and knows what that means.

Red scowls.

Phillip smiles.

He sprints, not taking any chances, checking behind him. But Red does not follow.

When Phillip passes the rock, he collapses. He rolls onto his back, and Adam and Cole mob him. They tousle his hair and slap him on the chest. They lift him on their shoulders and carry him like a king. He is the tallest he has ever been, and he feels his heart open wide. Adrenaline rushes through him, like new pathways have opened within his body. He is calm. He is joyful. Flying, almost. Free.

I was never a ghost. I was never a ghost.

The crowd begins chanting. "Red is dead! Red is dead!"

45

Red is dead. He most certainly is.

It wasn't pretty. It wasn't dignified. It was glorious.

At first Red refused.

But the boys said no.

"Red is dead," they calmly chanted.

"Red is dead," they demanded.

Red begged. He told Swan to pick another.

When Swan did not respond, he fumed. "Any one of these pigs!" He swept his arm in defiance. Of course, because of his chopped, swollen tongue, the words sounded more like, "Anone oft the pig!"

"Red is dead," the chant continued.

Swan smoothed back his wave of hair with both hands. He held up his arms for silence. The thick gold necklace shone like a crown. "What's fair," Swan said, "is fair." Then he drew a slow finger across his neck.

In the end it took five Armbands. Red kicked and bit and wrestled every step before being heaved into the pond.

When the capsule was ejected, a mob descended on it, shredding it into waxy flakes. Red's boneless body was carried atop a wave of eager hands and dumped without ceremony into the tunnel.

The worms did the rest.

Now Tony strolls around a Level 2 that is in disarray, un-recognizable from a few hours ago. Swan and the Armbands have taken refuge in the shadows, no longer in control. The workstations are inactive. The pond system has fallen apart.

A revolution.

Most of the boys have taken spaces near the pond, includ-ing Cole, Adam, and the Phillip. A few others sleep. Some eat worms. A lone boy plays with a rusty miniature battleship.

It makes Tony a bit sad: given the choice between a relic and a screen, most choose to stare at the screen.

No one has the stick. It remains right where it was left, in a special section of Relics devoted to Swan's personal items. Tony sees it leaning unnoticed against the cavern wall.

Tony chuckles. He discovers Red's cap half-buried in the mud, all that's left of the thug.

An uprising like this, he thinks, should result in more than one boy being thrown overboard. Tony recalls a story he read long ago. In the story a mutiny occurs, and a ship captain and those loyal to him are set adrift in a small rowboat. They fi-nally land on a Pacific island. At one point the enraged islanders hurl stones at the sailors.

It was a good story.

Tony scans the cavern and tries to find Swan, but he can't. Swan's no dummy. He knows his reign is probably over. He knows fifteen or so Armbands can't hold back a hundred boys. Best to lay low for a while, try and avoid getting killed.

Avoid hurled stones.

Oh well. Tony doesn't care. Swan might survive; he might not. He'll stay on the ship or get thrown in the row-boat, or out the rowboat. Maybe it's the worms for him. It matters nothing to Tony, because he is moving on.

He whistles a familiar tune as he approaches Relics. It's the tune he whistled on that special day, the day he stepped into the tree: "Happy Birthday."

Some birthday that was. A real winner.

There it is: the stick. He walks right up and snatches it. He also grabs his backpack and waist pouch. No one notices. No one objects. He doesn't have to bribe anyone.

Bunch of pondheads.

He's still whistling when he enters the tunnel.

46

Someone has carved into the handrail, "You're all going to Hell."

Adam glides over the stairs that lead to a bench inside the ga-zebo. The Boy sits here, wearing a heavy coat zipped to his jaw. The nearby playground goes unused. Swings hang from chains. Courts and fields are empty. The Boy stares beyond the pond to where a thick forest stands.

This time of year the forest is a scraggly nest of bare trunks and branches—except for one tree. It has an odd canopy of black leaves.

The leaves look scorched by fire.

On this drab afternoon, the landscape leeched of color, the leaves shine. They are like curious black lights, and the low sky is the ceiling of a metal gray room.

Adam joins The Boy's gaze.

Why have the leaves not fallen?

47

Glossy white walls. A polished concrete floor.

The shiny surfaces wipe out any hint of shadow. Sterile. Nothing can hide. A large stainless steel sink takes up one corner. Machines with green digital displays are wheeled into position. An array of surgical instruments, gleaming silver, is neatly arranged on a white cloth.

They could be weapons, Cole thinks.

A crisp sheet covers The Boy to his neck.

His eyes are closed, but the lids flutter, like The Boy is trying to open them so he can scan the stark room.

Or maybe he is dreaming.

What would he dream of at a time like this?

Cole floats above, as if he is a soul that has left a body, as if The Boy is dead and he is the departing soul.

48

The Boy sits against a tree.

His dark clothes merge with the wintry woods. The overcast completes his camouflage.

In his lap, in his right hand, is the gun.

He is still, watching the path.

Waiting? If so, for what?

Someone approaches. Phillip squints at the figure coming into focus. It is a girl. She is familiar, and Phillip tries to place why. Her hands are deep in her pockets, and a red scarf is wrapped around her neck. She walks with her eyes down, guarded against the cold.

The Boy slowly stands.

Phillip knows that girl.

The image shudders into dark water.

49

The canopy explodes. Small black birds fill the sky.

The tree is left bare.

They were not leaves.

The Boy rises from the bench and looks to where the startled birds flee. There must be hundreds. For a few seconds they spiral in sustained loops, their curves precise, as if drawn by a protractor, before the flock straightens into a V that wedges forward, flying away.

Leaving the gazebo, The Boy heads for the path leading towards the woods. Adam sees the worry starting to pool inside him, and he must rush to keep up.

When the worry becomes too much, The Boy breaks into a run.

50

A surgeon, a petite woman, stands beside the operating table. Her eyes are closed. Beneath her mask, her lips move, just barely— too disguised for Cole to determine what she is saying.

A nurse straightens the folded towel beneath The Boy's head. Her hands are gloved.

For a few seconds she stares down at The Boy, his jumpy eyelids.

Perhaps she has a son who looks like me, Cole imagines. Or a nephew.

She reaches across The Boy's chest.

She pulls back the sheet.

Her eyes round.

What she thinks at that moment will never be known by anyone except for her.

We have so many thoughts that we never share. They die with us.

The surgeon opens her eyes. "Let us begin," Cole sees her say. "Scalpel, please."

51

The Boy runs through a rug of brittle leaves. Crouched, he ducks and snaps low-hanging limbs.

Phillip chases.

Ahead, the dirty tent is half collapsed.

The Boy yanks open the flap. Inside, he paces in tangled, panicked circles.

He did not plan for this, or did he?

The Boy stops. "Okay," he says. He lifts his hand from his side, and he rests the gun against his cheek. "Okay."

Phillip wants to grab The Boy, as if an answer can be grabbed, as if it's that easy.

52

The Boy lowers to his knees, a few feet from Lily. He maintains this pose, watching her. He leans forward and places his hands on the cold ground.

Maybe he smells her shampoo: lavender, or pomegranate.

Blood spills from the side of her head and spreads into a red orb, darker than her scarf. Her hands are stuck in her pockets.

The Boy sits beside her. Reaching into a pocket, he frees one of her hands. He holds it, wanting, it seems, to find a place for it, then puts it back into the pocket. Beneath her other arm is the drawing she was working on in school.

The Boy slides the paper towards him.

53

His right arm is rotting.

The entire hand is black; the skin looks charred. His fingers resemble burnt peppers, and above the wrist the black skin transitions to aggressive red streaks that travel to his elbow.

Cole descends.

He gets so close that he can see the creases in each decaying knuckle.

He looks at his own hand, then back to The Boy's.

What they share cannot be undone.

54

The Boy shoves the gun into his backpack. He collects what little food is left. He grabs the notebook. He quickly rolls up his sleeping bag and slings it over his shoulder.

He takes a deep breath, scanning for anything he's missed. He reaches for the flap and slips outside.

He glances briefly towards the path.

Phillip rises above the treetops for a better view. He sees Adam, the other Adam, sitting next to the girl. Immediately, Phillip knows she is dead.

The Boy turns and heads deeper into the woods.

On the run.

Phillip hesitates, checking the path once more, before deciding to go after him, to stop him.

55

The Boy studies her drawing.

Adam peers over his shoulder.

Lily has sketched a forest. The sky is a dark scream, gray and black streaks rubbed into the paper. A full moon illuminates snow falling and gathering in deep drifts.

In the bottom left corner, small and intricate, is a boy. His clothes are tattered. He stares up at the moon. It seems he wants to go there, to outer space, but he knows he will never be able to, and he is angry at his limitations. He is stuck, and he knows it. He has the face and claws of a wolf.

56

A spotlight shines down on The Boy. His right arm is extended. It lays on a separate table, separate from the rest of him.

The petite woman is handed a saw. She presses a button with her thumb, and the circular blade spins into a blur.

Cole turns away.

57

A strange vapor has formed around Phillip.

When he moves, he feels remnants of air through which he runs.

He tries to catch The Boy.

Particles of one world shed from him as particles from another attach, and for a moment he smells the damp forest.

How can that be?

Phillip reaches for The Boy's shoulder.

He will yell at him, hit him.

But his lungs seize, and he tastes oxygen, the wet cold. His legs give out, and he is falling. His mouth gapes.

It's as if all the life in him is gone.

58

There are no black shapes.

The disruption has woken the boys. Wrenched from their trances, confused, they look to each other, from one to another, for an answer.

The pond has been newly fed. That is the agreement.

Adam does remember waking. He cannot recall rising. Sand is stuck to his knees, and he reaches down to brush them. It feels like something has torn inside him, like a rib has sheared off and is floating through his side and knifing him.

A small bun of Lily's brain spilled from the hole in her skull, the skull like a red drink that tipped over.

He turns his head, to turn away from this image, but he is again assaulted by what he sees: Phillip has fallen forward into the pond. His arms are covered to the elbows, his face submerged.

"Phillip!"

Adam rushes to his friend. He wraps his arms around Phillip's waist and pulls. His muscles lock and shake. But it is like trying to drag a ton of steel, like Phillip is stuck in cement.

Adam tries again, but his heels drag forward, and he must let go and backpedal to keep water from sliding over his feet and getting trapped himself.

With alarm he realizes Phillip might not be breathing. "Help me!"

Cole arrives. Other boys follow, awake now, frightened. They line up like a tug of war. Each secures his arms around the waist of the boy in front. Twice, the human chain attempts to pull Phillip free, but they cannot budge the pond.

More join, until every boy in the cavern is helping, and a line extends to the cavern wall.

Again and again they try.

They must rest. They plop to the ground in a collapsed heap of limbs.

"He's dying," Adam says. Phillip's arms are limp, his face sunk deeper into the water, almost past his ears. Adam holds up the dead weight. His whole body aches. "It has to be now," he tells Cole.

Cole says, "Everybody, on the count of three! As hard as you can!"

The boys of Level 2 reorganize. They dig in, into mud and sand. Cole counts. On three they pull—everyone, with one concentrated blast of energy—and Adam feels a surge behind him unlike any before, and a sound like ripping paper accompanies their falling backwards as Phillip is freed from the pond and dumped back onto land.

Adam stumbles and falls on Cole. Cole tumbles atop the boy behind him and so on like dominos. Staring at the darkness above, Adam has the thought that they have ripped off Phillip's face.

He rushes to his feet.

Unmoving, Phillip lies on his back. Two globules of pink slime snake from his forearms and meld into the pond.

But a portion of the pond remains.

Phillip's face is still attached, but what covers it resembles a lethal jellyfish. A thin layer of pond, light pink and opaque, is pressed over the contours of Phillip's face. Beneath are Phillip's eyes, his nose, a mouth—Adam sees them—but they are distorted. Tentacle-like straps wrap tight behind Phillip's head. It is a sick, scary mask.

Adam reaches, ready to try and tear the thing from Phillip's face, but Cole blocks him.

"It could latch onto you," he says.

"What do we do?" Adam says, frantic.

"Phillip's breathing. See? Look."

Cole's calm allows Adam to steady himself. He watches the shallow rise of Phillip's chest, its quick drop. His friend is so skinny. He sees every rib.

"The pond isn't killing him, yet," Cole says. "We have time."

Adam squats. Staring at Phillip, he reaches for his own ribs and touches the ridges beneath his skin. He explores these bones. They are a mountain range that has always been there. They are rising, as his muscles recede, exposing what was hidden. The pain in his side is gone; his floating rib has reattached. He smiles, almost laughing, on a tightrope and ready to step off into insanity. Try it out. See what it's like. Almost laughing, but not quite. That's what he's doing when he watches Cole walk away, straight for the bell, which glistens cruelly.

59

Cole picks up the bell and slams it hard against the rock. It clangs, discordant. He is surprised by how heavy it is. The gold is unblemished. He slams it again, and the handle cracks. He grabs the handle with both hands, presses down, and it snaps. He tosses aside the splintered wood. After finding a comfortable grip, he cocks his hand beside his ear, takes a few hopping steps, and hurls the bell as far as he can.

It feels good.

The bell sails almost to the opposite shore and smacks the water. For a second it sits on the surface. Then it sinks slowly, going under.

"We gave you a sacrifice! Now leave our friend alone!" Cole says.

He turns around. The gold bell, good as new, sits on the rock. It is not a replacement, he knows. It is the same bell.

He grabs it, smashes it again, throws it again.

"What more do you want?!"

Bell after bell.

"Why are we here?!"

"What is this place?!"

His arm tires. He struggles for breath, and the throws lessen in distance. The questions end. But Cole continues.

He wants a response. Not answers. Just a response. Acknowledgment.

Near his twentieth throw, at the moment the bell is swallowed by the water, the pond flattens and becomes still. The opalescent shine dims. The cavern darkens. It is as if early nightfall sets.

Cole sits in the sand, which sticks to his sweat.

Across from him, on the other side of the pond, sits Swan, wearing black sunglasses. For a moment they regard one another.

Transfixed and uneasy, the boys of Level 2 watch the water.

The calm is a precursor to what? Cole slouches forward. It feels like weights are pulling him down. What response has he compelled?

In the center of the pond a small black circle appears. It flaps at the edges and spreads evenly outwards. But the shape does not stop at its usual borders, its expected size. Instead, it continues expanding, stretching beyond what Cole thought possible, beyond what feels safe, until the entire pond is covered in lustrous black.

Awed, the boys gather around.

60

Though he can feel his limbs, he cannot move. He can't even twitch a finger, which he tries. This, Phillip suspects, has something to do with what covers his face. It dispenses some type of anesthesia that paralyzes his muscles.

His mask.

With his eyes open he sees nothing but pink jelly. He is not breathing. He is aware of this. The mask breathes for him, pushing air into his lungs, keeping him alive while at the same time tranquilizing him.

Phillip closes his eyes, to rest. Has he fallen in the pond? Is he losing his bones?

What if, with each breath, the pond is placing something within him? Do they think I'm dead?

The questions are nightmarish, but he does not panic. He is tranquil, knowing he is not in control.

He did not kill Lily. The Boy did.

I am not a killer.

He opens his eyes: more pink jelly.

His mind wandering, he remembers being lifted after defeating Red. How tall he felt. He recalls the worm vein, twisting it in his hands, and laughter. The pelican. Unexpectedly, though, the pleasant string of thoughts ends at the dark entrance to a cave.

He has never been here before. Where has his mind taken him? He hesitates, enters.

Inside, there is faint light, just enough to perceive the smooth surfaces and stone dome overhead. White, green, and gray have combined into one color. This is not a natural place. It has been carved and shaped by hands. Phillip has read about cave drawings left by ancient peoples, but the walls are bare. Who builds such a place and does not leave a sign? If he could, what would he draw, what image from his world?

In the center of the cave is a chair. Chunks of stone and small piles of powder are heaped around it. The chair was once a boulder, chiseled into this rough form. It is leaned back at a steep angle so that when Phillip sits he views the curved ceiling.

Above him, a light appears, one becoming many.

61

Minutes have passed with no change.

Cole stares into the pond. He tries to see beyond the black water and waits to be taken away like before.

They all do.

But no one is seized. This is no portal to home.

Boys glance at Cole.

He feels their eyes, and he knows what they are thinking: the pond is broken, and he is to blame. They will be stranded here for the rest of their lives with nothing to fill the time except for worms, grimy relics, and each other.

Murmurs begin.

"He did this."

"It's his fault."

He senses Adam, tense, beside him.

"Cole," Adam whispers.

Cole ignores him. "Come on," he says to the pond. Surely, there is more. There has to be.

Glances become glares.

"He broke it," a nearby boy says.

"He didn't do anything," Adam says.

"Then what do you call this?"

"Fix it!" An angry shout echoes across the cavern.

Staring at the black water, Cole's eyes tire. His body is sore, and he is hungry. He is always hungry here. Is this it? An empty and ruined pond. Boys unifying against him. Phillip dying, maybe dead. He feels foolish for believing they could be anything other than prisoners. Exhausted, stripped of any faith in himself and with no willingness to regain it, Cole says, "Please."

He speaks to no one person or thing. Rather, the word is cast into the void, like a message in a bottle tossed to the currents.

Seconds pass, and his eyes close. Sleep would feel so good, but he is pulled back. Something yanks him back.

A blip of pale light, low over the pond, glows briefly, silently, before dying.

Another takes its place.

"Look," a boy says, pointing.

More appear.

Disappear.

They arrive and depart in unpredictable patterns. They last for as long as a yawn. Each is like the tiny, fleeting glow of a firefly, and with each brief glow a small circle of light washes over the pond. Where light touches water, silver circles, as shiny as tin foil, are branded onto the pond's surface.

Light.

Circle.

Before long the black water is covered in silver polka dots. The circles are not static. They begin to seek each other and merge, and as they do they spread in size, like spoonfuls of batter dropped in a pan. Three become one. Five more join. This circle fuses into thirty others.

Boys smile, enchanted. They creep close to the pond's edge. Soon, every light has expired, and the circles have all combined. A seamless glassy surface remains, shining and smooth.

Curious images ripple on the surface. Watery at first, the images crisp into recognition: people. They look back with wild eyes. Who are these strangers, and where have they come from? It takes a while to understand. The images, Cole realizes, are themselves.

The pond is a mirror, and they are the strangers.

Cole views himself in the absolute present: half-starved and feral looking.

Boys gaze at their reflections. All are shown in conditions unrecognizable from when they first entered the tree. Some wave to make sure it is not an imposter. Others softly say their names, unsure if what they see is real. Eventually, after becoming convinced the image is valid, they view each other's reflections as well—these boys with whom they share a life. They see the civilization they have created, every boy housed in the cavern that is the reflection's backdrop.

Some laugh. Some are made sad. Most are too overwhelmed to react either way.

Across the pond, a straw-haired boy draws Cole's attention. Cole does not know his name. He is tall and long-limbed. He seems popular. In the past, Cole has seen other boys congregate around him. Hesitantly, the boy taps his toe on the surface. Satisfied, he steps forward. His other foot follows. He stands atop the pond. After a moment of pause, the boy begins walking cautiously towards the pond's center.

Boys gape as they watch his slow progress.

Cole dips his chin. His reflection tells him to not be afraid. "Go," it says.

When his foot meets the surface, his heel slips forward and he almost falls. He did not expect the mirror to be so slick.

He extends his arms, like wings, to steady himself. He takes small, choppy steps.

More boys follow. They gingerly test the surface, like thin ice they might fall through, and shuffle forward.

Cole stops to look back. He has travelled about ten yards, and in that time the pond has filled with boys. Most stare at their feet, navigating the slick surface with caution. Adam has adopted his own approach. He does not lift his feet; he stiffly slides them forward.

Cole bends his knees, lowering his center of gravity, and pushes with one of his legs, gliding. He does the same with his other leg.

Another boy near Cole tries as well, and he, too, begins to skate.

Soon, everyone joins in. Some skate with skill; they zigzag as if steering through a course. Others teeter and take choppy slip-steps. All move in the same direction. Around the rink they go.

They lean and build momentum. Their reflections shine below. Sometimes they watch themselves. *That is not The Boy. That is me, skating atop the mirrored pond.* How can this be? No answers are sought. Instead, they laugh and skate, joy splashed onto faces that have not expressed joy for far too long. Boys whirl and drift and fall on their butts and get back up and join the rotating current.

They have fun. They are allowed, during this brief spell, to be kids, as it should be. They play until their muscles tire, until the rink has been circled fifty times. Never once do they think of stopping.

But all good fun—as the saying goes.

The pond's surface begins to soften and turn sticky, and skating becomes difficult. Cole looks down to see his image gone psychedelic. The silver is awash in color. Reflections glob together. Pink light shines through the metallic surface, and boys scamper from the pond back to sand.

Winded, sweaty from their exercise, they stand onshore and watch the mirror melt, caving into the goo beneath. It doesn't take long for the pond to return to its normal state. It's as if what they remember never was. The boys are left looking at an undulating pink soup.

For those who continue to stare, black shapes form before them, enticing them. Most stay. They gather at the pond's edge. They are taken to the other world, where their stories continue to unfold.

The remaining few, like Cole, walk away, needing rest. He thinks of the pond's response to his questions and demands. Lights. Circles. Approaching the mud field, Cole recalls how the mirror beneath him was solid and how good and dependable it felt when sliding across its surface. It was as sure as anything he has ever known.

62

A tiny sting behind his right ear spreads to the size of a dime. Seconds later, at once, a hundred needles stab his stomach; they sink deep, and his neck locks. His feet turn hot. There is no order to how parts of him reawaken: behind a knee, near his hip. His fingers start to play piano. He tries to bend his elbow, and his lower arm rises like a drawbridge.

He remembers to breathe. A painful gasp scrapes his throat.

He grabs his face. Rubbing his eyes, he feels eyeballs beneath the lids. He licks his lips. The mask is gone.

"Phillip!" He hears Adam.

He coughs.

Adam helps him sit up. "You okay?" He gets thumped on the back.

"Phillip, say something," Cole says.

Phillip clears his dry throat. "Alive," he croaks.

"He's okay!" Adam says.

And Phillip is happy, his eyes shaking open, laughing at his confusion, at having survived whatever has occurred. His vision is fine; he sees what he should see. He is the same, of course he is. He remembers, in bits, the beauty of what he saw in the cave, but he cannot make sense of it, and this is funny too.

Lights. Circles.

Then he remembers.

The Boy. The gun. Lily.

For a moment he tries not to panic, but panic ravages through him. When this relents, he is left with dread, and he accepts it, because dread is normal. He cannot cast out what will always be in him.

What does Adam know? He assumes Adam isn't aware of anything, and Phillip is tempted to keep quiet, but that is not what a friend would do. He cannot keep secrets anymore. He steps back, creating distance.

"What's wrong?" Adam says.

"I'm sorry," Phillip says. He tells Adam everything.

The camp at the edge of the woods.

The gun in the backpack.

He tells him who killed Lily.

Finally, Phillip tells Adam that if he wants to kill him, he can. He would understand.

63

"They're not us," Cole says. "We're not there."

"You're my friend, Phillip. You're one of my only friends." Adam speaks in a blank, stunned way.

"We don't control what they do, Phillip. It's not your fault," Cole says.

"Okay," Phillip says.

"It's not," Cole says.

"But he's part of me."

"Why would he do that?" Adam says.

"I don't know. There was nothing—"

"Why?" Adam says, spiked with anger. "At least I could know that."

"We may never understand," Cole says. "Okay?"

"You're not sure why? Not even a little?"

Phillip shakes his head.

"Then the pond should show me." Adam stands. "I deserve that."

"Adam, it won't." Cole claws the ground. He squeezes fistfuls of sand between his fingers. "It doesn't care about you, or me. You don't deserve anything, good or bad, like no one here does. There's no deserving, just what happens."

Cole meets Adam's stare. Adam's appearance hardens, his features chiseling into an ax, and Cole gets ready to fight, but they stretch past that moment when such confrontations are decided, and Adam sits back down, facing the pond, resting his chin in his hands.

"I'm sorry, Adam," Phillip says.

Cole sees he is on the verge of crying.

"It's okay," Adam says.

Phillip wipes his eyes.

Cole sinks into the surrounding quiet. The cavern looks ransacked, clothes and tarps strewn about. Only a few boys move—slow, tired. It's like a game has just ended, and it's time for everyone to go home, but no one can. He searches for what needs to be said, to move them to whatever is next.

"I've never caught a fish." Adam's voice is friendly. His eyes do not stray from the pond. "You ever catch a fish, Cole?"

Cole feels a grin form, as if it's being drawn on. He and Adam have had this conversation before, at home. "Nope. Never," he says. Cole knows what Adam will say next. *Once a year*—

"Once a year my dad and I go to this bridge. I get excited. It's a good spot, people always there. I use the right bait. We go early, at dawn, like we should, but it doesn't matter. It's always the same: nothing. I go home empty. It got me think-ing. Why do I want to catch a fish? I mean, I've really thought about it."

"Yeah, what did you decide?"

"Well, I don't want to eat the fish. I don't like fish. So it's not for food. And I don't care about the *stuff*—tides, lures, different poles and all that. I don't even know what type of fish I'm fishing for. So that leaves me with this. This is what I decided. I want to catch a fish because it's a wild animal, and I think part of me is animal."

"What part? Your nose?"

"Funny. We're humans, but there's a part of us, a small part maybe, that's more animal, I think. And it's nice to feel that sometimes. To see it in something else, and know you're connected."

"You're part fish."

"Whatever, you know what I mean."

Cole does know, what's it's like to run as fast as he can, to watch the slow crawl of a cloud and feels its pull—to recognize that within him there is chaos, and it's the same, everywhere, in everything. He's told Adam all this.

"I also thought about something else, while we've been here," Adam says.

"What's that?"

"If there were no worms, would people eat each other?"

For a minute, Cole was home, talking to his friend, but that fantasy is gone. Level 2 has never looked more depressing or dangerous. The stink is awful. Idle boys, alone or in small groups, wait—as if stuck in a sinister painting, trapped in brushstrokes of glossy pink or menacing shadows. "There's no fire to cook meet," he says.

"What if there was wood, and it was dry. What if there was fire?"

"I think then...it would probably happen. But it would take a person, someone who could do it first."

"Then it would get established, right? Once he did, others would follow, and it would go on and on, if it could."

"I guess." Cole shrugs. "Yes, people would do that, I'd bet."

"And some would be prey. They'd get eaten."

"Some would have to."

"What would you be?"

Cole foresaw the question. He's read stories with similar situations, civilization crumbling, but they were stories. What would he do to survive? "I don't know. I really don't. I would fight, but I don't know if I could go beyond that."

"Me too. I'm not sure what I would do," Adam says.

We're animals, Cole thinks, not part animal. The tree provides just enough to keep the boys from slaughtering each other. Worms and water are needed, but it's the pond, too, making the dreary tedium bearable. "If there were fish in this pond, and we used the worms here," Cole says, "we should catch a whale."

"I'd eat whale," Adam says. "I'd eat the whole thing."

Their morbid laughter is long, him and Adam, his best friend, and as it winds down, Cole remembers Phillip, nearby, right next to him, so quiet he's gone undetected this whole time. "Hey, Phillip," he says, "ever catch a fish?" But when Cole turns, he sees that Phillip is not listening. Phillip's mind is elsewhere.

"Can I tell you both something?" Phillip says. He speaks towards the ground.

Cole says, "You can tell us anything," and he believes this. It will not matter what Phillip says. The truth is all that matters in this place. Maybe the truth is deserved. They have nothing else.

The friends are facing one another.

Phillip describes his father's hands, how they never rest, how they tremor and jump. There are pills, but they do little to help. He tells them about his mother, of her disregard. Her hate. He describes what it's like caring for himself and how it makes him scared and turn inward, how it feels to be unloved.

Cole says, "No, she loves you. She just doesn't say it." What he says is a reflex, because he can only think of his own mom, and he cannot understand a mom not loving her child.

But Phillip hangs his head. "No."

Cole knows that what Phillip says is true.

Then Adam reveals his secret: his first kiss. Under the gazebo, near the pond, they leaned towards one another. Lily's lips were red in the cold. The lips of a girl are special and different. He speaks with no embarrassment. He says it was beautiful. He uses that word.

And Cole and Phillip are enraptured because they have never kissed a girl.

"I miss her," Adam says.

Adam tells them that because he is black Lily's parents didn't want her to see him anymore.

"You're black?" Cole says.

They laugh.

It is Cole's turn.

His arm is rotting. He saw crinkly, black skin. There will be an operation. The Boy cut his hand coming back from the woods, and an infection is eating his flesh. Cole admits that he is terrified The Boy will die, and he will die in the tree like Peter.

Afterwards, the three friends hug. They slap each other on the back. In a strange way they feel like men. They gather themselves and move on.

"We need to talk about what we're going to do," Cole says.

The pond has returned to normal. Boys have begun to gather around. The remains of Red's capsule have disintegrated into sand, rejuvenating the shore. The bell gleams.

"Tony's gone. He took the stick," Phillip says.

"I know," Cole says. "There are no keys. No door. He just wanted to separate us."

"He's a snake," Adam says.

Cole thinks of Swan for a second. "He is."

"We knew that," Phillip says.

"We don't chase him. It doesn't matter. We eat, shower, pack, then go. Whatever happens," Cole says, "we keep going."

"To the top," Adam says.

"Okay," Phillip says.

"We keep going." Cole eyes the tunnel.

It is all one can do.

64

Mashburn is exhausted, and he is haunted. He cannot shake the image of his own reflection: how gaunt and pained he looked. The pond's transformation was not scary. In many ways it was gorgeous, but he has been left cold by it, and he has been stripped of any fear.

He is changed.

Swan must go.

He feels duped, because for too long he has labored under the rule of a boy who views him as a puppet.

He is ashamed, because he has let himself be held down.

He thinks of the place he grew up. A stinging lakeshore wind. Abandoned houses set on fire and left to crumble. The smell of fire was in the air, always. He was taught to rely on no one. Family? Like Dad, like Mom? There were people with those names, but they were just like everyone else: flat shapes, like stickers stuck on glass. He stole. He took what he could, when he could. He remembers running away from people who wanted to hurt him. Ducking behind cars and buildings. He remembers checking behind him, to the side, anticipating. He learned to stay silent and accept the way it was.

How many shirts has he washed? How many pants and pairs of underwear and for what?

He feels shame. It is the first time he has ever felt this. It is deeper than embarrassment, more painful. Stealing meant survival, and there was no shame in that. To steal was to fight. But here he has chosen not to fight. And why? For brief, desperate moments when he has watched a replacement living his life, so he can eat worms.

Mashburn looks at his hands, cracked by water and mud and toil.

So much time has been wasted.

Swan must go.

It is clear to him.

"Swan must go," he says.

"Swan must go!" louder.

Again.

Another boy joins him.

And other boys with no fear join them.

Soon, a new chant starts to warp the cavern.

65

Swan doesn't like sitting in the shadows, beyond the reach of the pond's light, but this is where he waits, thinking in the dark.

There is the tunnel or the pond. Head for the tunnel and start again or join the pond. Remaining at Level 2 is no longer an option. He knows this.

You cannot be made to feel the universe and not be changed. The boys of Level 2 have been filled with new thoughts, and these thoughts have replaced order. They have replaced him, the face of order. Therefore, he must leave.

They are ungrateful, sniveling mice, and they will regret their disloyalty. They are stupid.

But right now they are filled with fire.

What is that annoying chant?

He admires his stretch of beach, like nowhere else on Earth (or under Earth), yet the ground, in the shade, seems hard, less forgiving. Swan digs with his toes, and clumps of sand slide over the tops of his feet. The cavern possesses a precarious aura, like much thought is taking place, like many boys are contemplating the same dilemma.

That incessant chant is bothersome.

All the Armbands have left. They removed the strips of cloth from their biceps and fled. They want to survive.

Cowards.

He needs to make up his mind.

Tunnel. Pond. Tunnel.

Damn it all.

If he could return home, he would take a shovel, the same shovel used to destroy his snake, and kill his alternate self. He would smash its face, smash the nose and lips and teeth and eyes into a pie filling. He would drive the flashy car into a brown lake. He would rip up the sugarcane and cultivate the crops his father grew. He would catch another snake and raise it in the barn until it was long and big. He is old enough now.

Will the pond take him home? Should he try to go to Level 3?

But he is too late. They come before he can decide. The boys choose. He knew they would. A part of him always did.

When they grab his shoulders, he does not fight. He feels fingers in his hair, gets hit in the face. Scratched. Kicked. Voices jostle around him. It is so loud. He goes limp; he protects his mind, because that is what matters.

Damn it all.

They lift him, these mice. A hundred chattering mice fling him high into the air. His gold chain swings around his neck. A bed of hands keeps him levitated.

They say horrible things.

Above him is not a sky that extends outward. It is just the bottom of something he cannot see.

"Okay, I will go," he says amid their chanting. No one hears him, he knows.

"You're being silly," he says to the boys who speak his name. "It's so silly."

"Swan in the pond!"

"Swan in the pond!

"So silly," he says to himself. "And ungrateful! And stupid!"

When he plunges into the water, it coils around him like a snake, and he screams.

66

"Come with us," Cole says.

"We don't want that. We want a chance to rebuild."

"What is there to rebuild?"

"Our lives," Mashburn says. "They're still ours."

They sit by the shore's edge. Most of the boys have gone back to viewing. The pond emits a calm hum.

"Here?" Cole says.

"Even here. Our lives can be better than they were." Mashburn extends his hand to Phillip. "I never thought you'd win." He grins.

They shake.

"What should we expect?" Cole says.

Mashburn glances at the tunnel. "Cold. Try to keep dry, and there's a spot. You'll see, where you stop. You'll stop. Something big is there. You feel it."

"What is it?" Adam says.

"I don't know. No one here does. That's where we turn around and come back." Mashburn shakes his head as if trying to discard a frightening memory.

"What about people who have gone to Level 3?" Cole says.

"We've never seen them again."

The tunnel is behind Cole. He feels its unending stare, its pull. The future, he knows, depends on it.

"How many have gone?"

"Since I've been here?" Mashburn counts in his head. "One every few years. Five. Six, maybe."

"So few?" Adam says.

Mashburn nods.

"What else?" Cole says.

Mashburn's expression flickers with something like shyness. His eyes become skittish, moving about the cavern, settling on a spot past the pond, far away, to a place, Cole suspects, that exists only in Mashburn's mind. "There's a king. Geiger. As tall as a man. And berries. Not a lot, but you can eat them. Tart ones."

Adam raises his eyebrows, about to speak.

Cole stops him with a quick shake of his head. "Really? You're sure?" he says.

Mashburn shrugs. "I mean, that's how it's always been. That's what people say. We believe there is."

"You believe?"

"Yeah."

"Why?"

Mashburn says, "We just do. We know. It's like, well, we do. Some say they've heard sounds in the tunnel—from Level 3."

"What type of sounds?" Adam says.

"Sounds. Uncertain."

"But they won't go?" Cole says. "To Level 3?"

"That spot," Mashburn says. "The light changes. It's like the light knows too. Something there's not right. You have to be brave, I guess."

"Be brave," Cole repeats

67

Adam discovers a miniature baseball bat. He rummages through a collection of pocketknives and takes the most sturdy and sharpest. There is a flathead screwdriver, which he leaves. A blue water bottle. Two drumsticks. No drum.

These are all found in Swan's personal stash.

There will be more to carry this time—tarps, jackets, and weapons—and they will leave for Level 3 with more unknowns than answers.

They will depart with no guide leading them.

They will trudge to a spot where (they are told) they will feel great fear, not knowing why, and they will have to plunge into the shape of this fear.

They will experience cold.

They might meet a king. Eat berries.

No one says anything about escape, as if this would sound foolish, as if there is no such thing.

Amongst the clutter, Adam finds a thin silver chain, similar to what his father wears. He clasps it around his neck. If he wears the chain, he thinks, his father will be close to him and try his best to protect his son.

He misses his father, Jacob Bellflower. His father is a painter, but not just any painter. He specializes in bridges that span large bodies of water. Sometimes he is gone for weeks at a time in another state. He is an expert at knots and has no fear of heights. He dangles from harnesses high in the sky and applies color to iron. The best color for a bridge, he says, is a bright blue.

The sky. Adam would like to see it.

He misses his mom, Agnes Bellflower. She is a nurse, and the best thing about being a nurse, she jokes, is wearing pajamas to work. She makes chocolate chip waffles with an old, beat up waffle maker. She cooks them in bulk, plowing through three boxes of mix at a time and neatly storing the waffles in freezer bags. Every morning Adam pries free a waffle and toasts it.

Waffles.

Will the pond ever show his parents to him? What would they have said about Lily?

They would have said what they always do: treat people with respect and kindness. They would have said that Lily was a nice girl and very pretty. They would have let her come over so she and Adam could do homework together and share dinner and maybe watch a movie. They would have said that some people are ignorant and mean. It will always be this way. They would have consoled him. They would have prayed together for Lily and her family.

Then Adam realizes that his parents do not know he is gone. They do not know he is inside the tree. They have consoled another boy they think is their son, and for the first time he feels anger at having been replaced so easily, for having been taken away.

He grabs a handful of shoelaces to help make a spear. It feels like getting to Level 3 will involve more than stamina.

He wonders what Tony took besides the stick. Adam knows Tony travels light. He closes his eyes and imagines Tony moving up the tunnel at a quick pace, building distance between them. He keeps that picture in mind as he continues to collect whatever might prove helpful.

He comes across a pair of hockey skates, and it is like he has found buried treasure.

At the other side of the cavern, he sees Cole and Phillip return from the tunnel. Cole limps. Each carries a long, powerful worm around the neck. The worms are as long as jump ropes. They struggle to keep them under control.

They walk to the washing station. Phillip lifts his worm over his head, slides his hands just below the twisting, toothy mouth, and swings into a sharp rock again and again until the worm hangs limp from his arms, dead.

Next is Cole.

They call over to Adam.

Cole says that the worms are so big they could feast for days.

Adam carries the backpack by one strap, just like at school. This is so not like school. He laughs to himself as he goes to see his friends and eat.

So not like anything.

68

Its roar fills the tunnel. Boys from every level panic, fueled by wild thoughts of monsters and demons and other crazed fictions. The bear begins its long trek upwards. Its great size is a burden, and the tunnel drains its power. Growls change into lonely calls. Black fur matted with mud becomes a hot and leaden suit. What is left is an exhausted animal barely able to drag forward. Its tongue lathers grotesquely and swings from its mouth. Eyes whirling, it collapses. Right there. That spot. Boys gather and understand: the beast has gone as far as it can. They rush water and scrape away mud with their fingernails; they press the pads of its fantastic paws. It dies. Worms swarm and strip its bones clean.

"Phillip, you okay?"

"What?"

"You were dreaming."

Phillip sits up. He rubs his eyes.

"How long have you been awake?"

"Awhile. I can't sleep," Adam says.

Beside them Cole stays in a deep slumber. Earlier, they showered. Their gear is neatly packed.

"What did you dream about?"

"The Bear," Phillip says.

Adam smiles. "I forgot about that. What happened, in the dream?"

"I watched it die, for real, I think."

"You saw the past?"

Phillips nods. "It was sad. It suffered."

"If only you could see the future."

"Then it wouldn't be so exciting to think about."

"That's funny."

"Thanks."

"It just keeps getting better, doesn't it?"

Phillip realizes how much older he feels, how he has grown up.

"Are you ready?" Adam says.

"Yeah, I am."

"Me, too. I want to end this, one way or another."

Cole stirs. He begins to wake, moving away from his mind, spreading outward into limbs and eyes. Phillip watches him slowly being pulled from sleep—by something, back to here, this place where dreams can be real, and what is real feels like a dream.

Part III

Return

69

I should not still be here.

This is why.

I had made my decision. My time was done. I found the house. I knew that in the house was a mom, father, and son. I knocked on the door, and when Phillip's mother answered I explained to her the choice.

She looked at the tree, then me. She said to take her son, for all she cared. She called him an awful name. Then she slammed the door.

I was shaken. I expected otherwise.

Phillip has his mother to thank for the worms.

Then again, maybe it is better that he be far away from her, even if it is inside the tree.

She seems a hateful woman.

The tree moved. If I were to guess, I would say that I am in the high desert somewhere. The ground is hard scrub. Daytime, the temperature is scorching. Last night there was frost.

Some places I like better than others. It is too dry here. Whenever the wind blows, it whips up dirt and pebbles. It reminds me too much of home. I prefer places that are much different from where I used to live.

My way of trying to forget what I miss.

The tree sits near a cliff that overlooks a lunar valley filled with peach-colored and white rocks. A small batch of scraggly trees stays alive near where water collects. Miles and miles beyond this, at night, is a faintly lit line. The nebulous line can only be seen at night. During the day it is lost to haze and wind and shades of beige that muddle the horizon.

Is it a road?

The tree always settles in the solace of wilderness, a place where a rare child might venture, far from commotion. The other day a father and son hiked up to view the valley. They were both carrying walking sticks.

I floated above them, watching their slow progression.

While the father took in the view, the son peered into the tree's black opening. There was the moment: the son looked to his father, whose back was turned, and decided to be safe. He went to his father's side.

One time he glanced back.

How much longer will the tree stay here? It is not up to me. Nor do I decide where it goes. But since we arrived I have had a strange feeling. It is different than anything I have experienced before.

I think the tree is headed back to a place it has been, and this will form a loop, and my period as Keeper will end. I have served long enough.

That is how I see it, time circling forever, passing over beginnings and endings, which—except for their appearance—are the same beginnings and endings.

The next home I visit will be the one.

Phillip's mom just wasn't the right person.

70

He has sat in this exact spot many times before, and every time he has turned around and gone back the way he came. But now he is ready to go further. To Level 3. A boy becomes a man.

He feels fear, yes. It is deep and unwavering. He grips the stick to help steady his thoughts.

The clothes are stinking rags. He gags at their odor. He carried them in his backpack to keep them dry and fresh, but the moisture of the tunnel permeates everything. The sweat-shirt is heavy. The sleeves hang past his hands; he scrunches them to his elbows, but they fall. His corduroy pants are soaked. The socks and sneakers are like dumbbells.

He'd prefer to move about in underwear, but he must dress for cold.

He lays the stick by his feet. From a pocket of his jacket, he takes the leather gloves and puts them on, sliding his fingers into the slots.

He studies the tunnel, how it immediately and without explanation becomes enormous. Up to this point he has been forced to crawl on hands and knees through a narrow channel. In front of him, in one step, the tunnel becomes large enough for a train or bus. Here, the surface is unnaturally smooth.

Footprints, left by the few boys who have entered, never to be heard from again, mark the ground.

They are shallow footprints, as if those who made them were trying to tread lightly, silently. They are artifacts, as if those who made them were from a time long ago.

The light changes, too. Within the pink glow is a red tinge. Pink and red.

Magenta. That's the color.

Tony reaches into this different light and feels a bracing cold, like the light itself is cold.

He realizes he is nervously whistling.

Happy Birthday to me.
Happy Birthday to me.
Happy Birthday dear Tony.
Happy birthday to me.

He has always known how to whistle, even in his earliest memories. "Whistle your good mother a lovely song," his mom used to say.

And he would whistle whatever came to mind.

Happy Birthday to me.

The day he walked into the tree was nippy, but he did not wear a jacket. He remembers being cold and blowing into his hands. Hard patches of old snow tiled the ground. What led him to the woods that birthday morning? His mom was busy baking a chocolate cake. His dad helped, cracking eggs, gathering measuring cups, because they liked to cook together. The kitchen was warm. He could have licked frosting from the bowl.

Happy Birthday dear Tony.

He stops whistling. A frightening silence deadens the air. On second thought.

He removes his gloves and unzips his pouch. The cough drop. He takes it out and studies it.

"For Colds and Cough."

Discipline. The heck with it.

He untwists the ends of the wrapping and tosses the small square of paper over his shoulder. He places the cough drop on his tongue. Immediately, it begins to dissolve, and with this comes a punch of intense flavor unlike anything he expected.

When he sucks out the first lemony sip and swallows, he is forced to close his eyes—so delightful is the taste.

A minty mist powders his throat and nostrils.

He laughs, savoring the moment, moving the cough drop around his mouth with his tongue, hearing it click his teeth, thinking that discipline has its benefits, but so does just saying the heck with it all.

He resolves to head out once the cough drop is gone.

The heck with it.

71

Tony's whistling descends like a strange, eerie bird call, melodious and wicked.

"Happy Birthday, everyone," Cole says.

Adam and Phillip offer wry smiles.

Cole could say that walking into the tree birthed a new him. He could say that because no one ages there are no birthdays here. He could say that being inside the tree is like dying, which is the opposite of being born. He could propose that for all these reasons "Happy Birthday" carries a disturbed and painful significance, and only a creep would whistle the song.

The whistling ends. Its resonance is like a light drizzle of rain.

They are nibbling cubes of worm. Slowly, the temperature has fallen, but water still drips steadily. They sit on and shield themselves with blue tarps to try and stay dry. They wear the tarps like ponchos, over the pants and shirts taken from Level 2.

"Not hungry?" Adam says.

"Not really," Phillip says.

Adam offers the water bottle.

Phillip shakes his head.

"Cole?"

"Thanks," Cole reaches for the water. "What?"

"Your hand," Adam says.

Cole looks to where Adam stares.

A bright dot of white light blinks on his right pinkie.

Suddenly, there is a second. A third dot appears on his thumb.

"Oh no," Cole says.

Adam and Phillip look to him for guidance. Cole doesn't know what to do. A sudden nauseous knot in his stomach makes him bend forward, and a tingle spreads over the surface of his hand, which he feels go lame. There is an outbreak of more blinking dots. His fingers are quickly covered. His palm. Cole lifts his arm; he rotates his wrist. He yanks up the sleeve of his jacket, and the tingling dots climb. Hundreds of small white lights. Thousands. The blinking quickens. His hand glows. Below the elbow, he feels nothing but growing, watery warmth.

Then the first *pop* hits and a hot sting washes over the back of his forearm. He winces. Grits his teeth.

"Get back," he says.

"No," Adam, wide-eyed, mumbles.

"Get back!" Cole moves up the tunnel. His arm drags behind him. "Get away!"

Another cell explodes.

He cries out.

Like popcorn, he thinks. At a certain temperature, after a certain amount of time, a mass of kernels will rupture.

"Get away from me." His words slur. A series of pops stops his heart for a brief time, and he feels with relief its return. He crawls upwards, lurches into the mud. Is up again. Climb. Reach. He is light-headed now, his entire arm like a hot coal.

Adam and Phillip are gone. He is alone. His arm boils. He is covered in sweat. He will not survive.

Something in his shoulder cracks.
He only vaguely feels the eruption.

72

Cole's right arm, glowing faintly, floats down the tunnel towards them.

Ahead, Cole is motionless, on his side. His shoulder, where the arm severed, is a tangle of clotted blood.

The popping has stopped. The tunnel silent.

The ghostly arm glows soft white in the pink light.

Phillip and Adam move aside, press themselves into the tunnel wall to let it pass.

It drifts at eye-level.

They watch the arm. Its fading light and delicate fingers mesmerize. It is like a slowly sinking ship.

Far down the tunnel it glides, its light weakening until none remains, as if nothing at all ever existed.

73

Adam kneels. "Cole?"

The right sleeve of the jacket is empty, deflated. The shoulder is blotted with dark blood stains. There was an arm. Below the wrist was a hand.

He imagines the arm, wrapped in black plastic, at the bottom of a trash can.

Nothing indicates Cole has survived the amputation. He is pasty and absolutely still.

"Cole? Please."

Adam touches Cole's cheek. He places his hand near Cole's mouth. His eyes close in concentration. "Come on," he whispers.

Faintly, after a few seconds, he feels a weak breath brush his knuckles.

The relief is brief. From his mother, Adam knows that a wound is a nest for infection, and they are in a tunnel plagued by mud and worms. Phillip is close beside him.

The tunnel is silent except for the sporadic drip of water. It makes him want to scream.

"We have to help," Adam says.

There is instinct. Save him, instinct says. But there is only what can be done. Nothing else. Can he even affect the outcome? The other world determines death. Isn't that what

Tony said? He can make decisions and act and wait, and those actions will accumulate, and maybe they will matter, maybe not. They will become part of history. It will be what happened. At least he can provide his friend a witness, and Phillip will be his.

Let him live. Adam doesn't know to whom or what he prays. There are only words that he wants to come true. He tries to form a god, a person to speak to, but his mind stays black, a locked room with no windows, doors, or lights. That's all there is, him and the dark, as he makes the wish.

They easily remove Cole's coat. But when they peel off his shirt, the material sticks to the wound. The blood is the consistency of old grease.

Cole moans.

They lay him on a wet tarp. Everything is wet. Hopefully, the tarp will keep the worms away.

Adam sees that a surgeon has sawed off Cole's arm just below the shoulder. Excess skin is pulled taut over bone and muscle and is secured with large, thick stitches.

How have the stitches made it here?

Already the wound is seeping.

They rig a makeshift tent. Adam cuts one of the tarps in two. Using the miniature baseball bat and two drum sticks as posts, they drape the tarp over Cole.

They raid their backpacks. Shirts and underwear are torn into strips. Phillip wraps the pieces of cloth in the other half of the tarp to keep them dry.

Adam must clean the wound. Thankfully, the water bottle is full, and he trusts the water is safe. Conserving as much as he can, he squeezes the bottle and flushes away blood that has leaked and congealed.

When he is done, half the water has been used, but he sees the incision and every stitch. He uses a dry piece of cloth to dab and wipe the skin. He is not timid. Cole gives no indication that he feels anything.

He hands the spent cloth to Phillip, who gives him two more strips, which Adam uses to wrap the wound.

"Okay," he says, satisfied.

"What now?" Phillip says.

"We wait. Stay alive."

Days pass. How many Adam is not sure.

Cole is in and out of consciousness. He dunks into fever. A folded, wet shirt is pressed to his hot forehead. Adam does his best to tend to his friend, but conditions are impossible. Mud and grit find their way into every crack. Their improvised bandages quickly dampen and turn filthy. The shoddy tent constantly leans, falls over. The water bottle is soon empty. All he can do is keep the wound mostly free of muck.

Phillip stabs at worms that come prowling, but near camp they are hard to kill. It's as if they sense the danger. Phillip must travel down the tunnel to hunt. The worms he brings back are long and weighty.

Cole never opens his eyes. He sometimes babbles incoherently, or he might utter a lucid statement that makes no sense: "I am not proud of lemons," he says one time, which sends Adam and Phillip into a macabre spiral of laughter.

Adam talks to Cole, even if he may not hear him. He tells Cole to heal and that he loves him. He says that he will always be his friend no matter what.

Phillip tilts Cole's head and attempts to force his mouth open. Adam squeezes gritty water from a wet shirt, but most of the water misses. They do the same with a worm vein.

Cole's situation, Adam worries, is worsening.

Exhausted, both Adam and Phillip fall asleep. Adam wakes mortified to find a massive worm gnawing on Cole's neck. He screams and rips away the worm. With one angry bite and yank he severs it in two and flings the still squirming halves down the tunnel.

Blood covers his hands. He feels blood in and around his mouth. His body shrieks with adrenaline. He closes his eyes and lifts his hands to his face, and he smears warm blood over his cheeks and forehead and down onto his neck until he is covered in the red of worm.

"You all right?" Phillip says.

"Fine," Adam says.

Later, he sees Cole's wound has festered. Cole has not spoken for a long while. His breathing, which had grown stronger, is shallow. The fever rages. Adam inspects foul-smelling yellow puss that oozes.

Phillip scrunches his face.

Adam flops against the tunnel wall. He is spent, and he is slathered in mud and worm blood. His best friend is half-dead. "There's nothing more to do," he says to no one.

"We can't stop," Phillip says.

"We tried. This place is too tough."

"I have an idea," Phillip says. "You're not going to like it, but I have an idea."

Phillip disappears down the tunnel. While he is gone Adam watches Cole. Water drips, the sound tranquil. They have made it so far. They have climbed miles. It can't end like this, but of course it can. Anything can end in any way. He holds Cole's hand, which is so hot Adam is startled.

Adam jerks awake, unaware of how long he has been sleeping. More time passes, and Adam begins to worry. He is about to yell for Philip when he sees him, distant, crawling cumbersomely towards camp. In the dim light it appears as if Phillip has grown extra arms. Adam squints: Phillip wrestles with a worm. He goes to help.

Phillip is covered in mud. A red ring marks one cheek. The worm has to be over six feet long.

"Thought you were gone," Adam says.

They drag the worm back to Cole.

They discuss their plan.

Since Adam is stronger, they decide he will steer the head while Phillip grips the end. They sit on the tarp and shovel their heels into the mud, holding the worm like firemen wielding a live fire hose. One hand cupped tightly near the toothy mouth, Adam leads the worm to Cole's wound.

The worm rears, and they must pull and straighten it. Finally, it settles.

Adam gives the worm time to probe. Inches from the wound, it sways over rancid puss and gunky blood. The foreskin around the worm's mouth slowly curls back so that its teeth fully bare. An ugly smile. They are not the small and rounded nubs seen below Level 1. These are more like human teeth, his teeth, capable of chewing, ripping.

Adam studies the worm. There are no eyes, but it sees. There is no nose, but it smells.

When he thinks the worm is ready, Adam presses its mouth lightly to Cole's damaged flesh and gently loosens his grip.

Slowly, the teeth retract into a tubular gum line—a knife sliding into a scabbard—and the worm begins to suckle. Adam steers. It is like a gently pulsing vacuum. Infection is drawn from the wound and swallowed. A mild whir tickles through Adam's hands, and with horror he realizes it is a purr. It is the worm's pleasure. Soon, this purr is all he hears.

Minutes go by, and the red vein glows brighter.

Brighter.

Behind him, Phillip stays silent. They do not speak this whole time. It is comfortable: not speaking.

They re-dig their heels.

The brewing infection within Cole is matched only by the worm's appetite. It suckles without pause. Adam watches and guides the mouth over the wound.

A minute folds into another.

The worm becomes a cylinder of neon light.

The cramped tunnel turns red.

Adam's arms go tingly. His back and legs ache. His hands cramp.

The worm is warm, and this warmth climbs into his wrists. It travels up his forearms, past his elbows. It inches towards his shoulders, over his collarbone, and then it is like a hot needle pricks the artery pulsing within his neck. He closes his eyes.

If he gave up, no one could blame him.

The hot needle presses into his skin.

Willingly, he goes.

Like an injection of medicine, the warmth mainlines through him, and it makes all his pain disappear. For a moment he feels like he is floating. He is a bubble. If he could be like this all the time, he would not care where he was. He would not care about anything.

He imagines standing beneath a waterfall.

A pale blue deluge splashes over him. He turns his mouth up, and he gargles. The water is sugary. The water turns to blood. It does not matter. He drinks the blood. It is the blood of boys eaten by worms, boys whose bones give life to visions. Praise be to boys.

He bends his knees and jumps, jetting upwards towards faraway green lights. His arms are wings that he steers with, and the closer he gets to the lights the greater they shine. They have turned to every color of the rainbow. He reaches for them, his hands buzzing. His hands are hives of bees.

But he slows. His steering starts to fail. His turns become lazy. The power propelling him is fading, and he is sinking, and he knows: his dream is almost over. He has hit a high point from which he must fall, because nothing lasts forever. Nothing. He takes one final look at the colors before giving up, accepting the fall.

The descent is slow, lasting millions of years, and he lands softly, feet first, in a bed of mud.

He wakes with his eyes closed. The purr has stopped. Water drips around him. The worm is heavy and limp.

He opens his eyes.

For a lost moment he forgets where he is. Then he sees his friend.

Cole's wound has transformed. A clear film is sealed over the skin and stitches, and the swelling has disappeared. There is no more vile leakage. The skin is pink and nourished. Sheened. No stitches are torn.

Deep asleep, Cole breathes strong and steady. The fever, Adam can sense, has broken.

"It worked," Phillip says, marveling.

Adam remembers Phillip.

He stares at their work. The amputation sight is a grisly piece of art—the way each thick and precise stitch is like a dam holding back a flood of blood, how flaps of skin have been pulled and folded over sawed-through bone. Sometimes a surgeon has to be half butcher. Sometimes loss is part of saving a life.

The worm is dead weight in their arms. Its glow pulses. They lay it gently in the mud. There is the slightest bit of blood on its teeth.

"Go, worm," Adam says. "Shoo."

It stays there, unmoving, for a number of seconds, like a large fish that has been out of water. Then it whips its tail and burrows into the ground, free and beautiful in its own way.

74

The cough drop is gone. The last brisk bit of taste has died.

It is time.

Though dressed for cold, Tony has decided to go shoeless. He has lived so long without shoes that they would only slow him. If he has to break into a run, he doesn't want to be weighed down by a pair of muddy clodhoppers. He'd rather have cold toes than be delayed.

He makes sure not to step into another's footprint as he tentatively steps downward. Bad luck, he thinks. He uses the stick for balance. Then his other foot sets firmly in unspoiled mud.

He is officially standing on the other side, the Level 3 side, dwarfed by the expansive tunnel. He is made pensive and scared. Something lurks, he feels.

Geiger, berries, girls: this is the mantra he uses to calm and assure himself. To inspire.

And the mud is cool. Stiff. He exhales and sees his breath. He is again reminded of that chilly day long ago. Magenta fog.

What is the source of the cold?

His first step is soft and short. He looks ahead. Nothing stirs. His second is longer, and his foot sinks, deeper. The stick stakes into the mud.

The stick.

It is here, rediscovering the knobby end, that he has an epiphany.

No, he thinks. It couldn't be.

He laughs. Surely not.

But these thoughts are mere affectations that underscore his giddy certainty. He lifts the stick to both hands and studies its length, its slight twist and glossy bark. In particular he gazes at the knob. The smooth and bulbous knob.

He closes his eyes, taking himself back in time. Was it fated? He sometimes ponders this. Is every moment part of a predestined grid, or is there no plan, just a haphazard throw of confetti?

That day.

What led him to those empty woods?

Before he stepped into the tree, he looked up at its stark canopy, the few diamond-shaped leaves and its system of branches.

He recalls each branch. Each pattern. The maze of limbs.

The stick is not just a stick.

It is a branch.

The branch belongs to the tree.

What Tony does next is not planned. He runs. He does not know why, nor does he know what he will do with his discovery. But he runs nonetheless because surely the stick must mean something larger. Surely, it must. How could it not? So he runs. The tunnel consumes him. The high, wide space leaves him feeling exposed to attack, but he does not slow. He will run the entire way to Level 3. He will not stop, not when the cold deepens, not as his lungs burn or his hamstrings crumble, not even when he sees that what lives in the tunnel is real and worth the fear it instills—and how it explains the chill and light.

He runs.
He has a piece of the tree, after all.

75

Adam: "Alligator attack."

Cole: "Lawnmower accident."

They wait for Phillip.

"A ninja did it."

Adam offers Phillip a high-five. "Nice one."

"Or maybe," Cole says, "I can say I had to have my arm amputated because my alternate me, Cole 2, cut his hand in the woods and got infected with flesh-eating bacteria."

"That sounds too crazy. No one will believe you," Phillip says.

Cole is sitting up, propped against the tunnel wall. In his left hand he holds a muffin-sized piece of worm, which he periodically takes small bites from.

Since waking, a day ago perhaps, he has experienced a gradual resurgence. He eats, naps. Cole and Phillip tend to him. His shoulder aches, but at least the throbbing has stopped. With every passing hour he feels stronger. His mind is clear. He chews slowly, to give his famished body time to recover. He doesn't want to throw it all up. The banter with his friends fills him with good spirits, but the cheer is blunted by his new reality: he has one arm.

You need two to crawl.

This is a physically strenuous world, and he is not sure he can handle its demands. His body, in a way, has yet to catch up. He has accepted the loss of his arm, but he still feels it. His biceps. Elbow. Each finger. His severed nerves and brain continue to sense what has been part of him his entire life, even though it is no longer there. His nerves are waiting for his arm to return.

"You okay?" Adam says.

Cole realizes he has been gazing at his stump. It is wrapped in fresh strips of cloth. Part of his identity is being the quarterback. Even if he does somehow get out of this place, he'll never throw another touchdown. That part of him is gone, and he had not realized how much he enjoyed it. "You may have to go without me. You know that, right?"

"No, I don't," Adam says. He rips free a chunk of worm. Swallows.

Cole stares at Adam staring angrily back.

"We made a promise," Adam says. "Right, Phillip?"

"Right," Phillip says, softly.

"Friends don't go back on a promise, Cole."

"I lost my arm."

"So."

"So?"

"It doesn't matter."

"Yes, it does."

"No, it doesn't."

"How can it not?"

"Because there's three of us. You're not alone. If it was just you, okay, but Phillip is here. I'm here. We're going to help. And you're coming with us."

"What if I don't want to?"

"That's dumb. What are you going to do, go back to Level 2? Eat worms forever and stare at a pond?"

"I don't have to do that."

"No?"

"No." Cole looks back down the tunnel. "I don't have to do that. I'm tired." Suddenly, deeply, he is tired. "My shoulder hurts." He fans the phantom fingers of his right hand. He senses what he knows is not there. How is that possible? "That boy who walked in the pond. Why do you think he chose that?"

"Only he knows," Adam says. "He must have been in pain, for a long time."

"I wonder if he would take it back, or whether it was the right thing."

"Cole," Adam says, "I won't let you get tossed into a tunnel. I won't watch you get eaten by worms. You could have died, but you didn't. You're alive for a reason."

"Yeah, what's that?"

"To be here now, with us."

Cole notices the silver chain around Adam's neck. "Where did you get that?"

"Found it in Swan's stuff."

"The person who it belonged to is probably dead," Cole says.

"Please, Cole," Phillip says. "You and Adam, you're my friends. This place made you my friends. I thought the tree would be different. I didn't know. I wanted to leave home. But I didn't know. What's in here is wrong, and we have to see what's above us, and we have to do it together. If we don't, then none of this will mean anything. We'll join all the rest. We'll be nothing."

"What if there *is* nothing?"

"Then we know. Then we can decide," Phillip says.

"We have to find out," Adam says.

Cole coughs, which tugs his stitches, and the pain is like a hundred hornets. He wipes sweat from his forehead with the back of his hand. "I still feel my arm," he says. "I know it's not there, but it is. It's strong, like a current. I guess you have to lose something for a while before you stop feeling it. Maybe it never stops. Maybe you carry it forever. Or you have it without knowing. It's there, but you don't know it's there. You can't see it. You learn not to listen."

76

Running saves him.

If he had not been running he would have been walking, and if he had been walking he would have stopped, and the ensuing spill of fear into his limbs would have left him frozen and defenseless. He would have turned and tried to flee. Perhaps he might have tripped, blundered to his feet, and offered some pitiful clawing defense and yelping.

The creature would have eaten him.

Instead, when he sees it, he has no time to respond. He is on it too quickly to do anything but continue running, which he does, faster, right past as it wakes. It did not sense his approach. He dashes through raw cold and red light. Throbbing light. The space between him and *it* is but a few inches because of its size, its circumference.

Awake and aware now that Tony has sped past, its screech sends a surge of cold through the tunnel. This rattles a chill deep into Tony's bones, and he feels his marrow. Every hair on his body turns icy. He runs as fast as he can, as fast as he has ever run in his life.

He does not turn around. He does nothing that might slow him down. If he is caught, it will not be because he is not running as fast as he can.

Thank god he is not wearing a pair of muddy shoes. He knew he made the right choice. He pumps his arms, the stick like a long baton clasped in one hand. The backpack bounces on his shoulders.

Behind him, he hears it slugging after him.

He understands now why the tunnel is so massive. Why it is frigid. The red light.

"Oy," he says, panting.

77

"I can't crawl with one arm."

"You won't have to. Get on."

Cole's left arm locks around Adam's neck, and he balances his legs along Adam's sides as if in stirrups. The extra weight makes Adam's hands and knees sink deep, and rather than try to pull them completely free from the mud he slurs forward.

Phillip follows. He adapts to Adam's pace by slowing his crawl.

Adam begins a count, planting a hand on each number. "One. Two. Three. Four. One. Two. Three. Four."

They grind up the tunnel.

Phillip keeps track. Like a machine, Adam makes it to four-hundred and thirty-six before needing to rest.

Cole slides from him.

Adam squeezes pain from his fists. He rubs his neck and shoulders.

They cannot find the water bottle, so they spread a tarp. It is noticeably cooler.

Phillip offers to try and carry Cole.

"Be my guest," Adam says.

"Let me try on my own," Cole says.

"You can't," Adam says, firm. "You need our help."

With his head down, Phillip adopts Adam's count. Cole is heavier than he thought. He stiffens his back and plods forward. After a while, he dips to his forearms and shimmies. His back arches painfully. His hands and knees and feet are numb from cold. Eventually, he must stop and let Cole slide free.

"I'm sorry, Adam," Phillip says. "That's as far as I can go." His arms shake, rubbery.

"You did it. We're here," Adam says.

"What?" Phillip looks up.

"This is it," Cole says. "This is the place."

It doesn't seem possible. Before him, a few feet away, the tunnel expands, abrupt and startling. Phillip thinks of a subway tunnel.

Ahead, the light changes from deep pink to red. It is the entrance to a haunted house. A demon's lair. Swampy coils of red-pink smoke turn slowly like sinister Ferris wheels. Up to this point, the narrow confines of the tunnel had become familiar. He had grown used to the crawl. It had come to feel secure. But this. The tunnel's huge expansion provides more space for the unknown to exist within.

Adam and Cole, too, stare ahead, taken aback, and Phillip senses their worry.

A far-away screech erupts and echoes toward them.

"What was that?" Cole says.

Mashburn mentioned boys hearing unidentifiable sounds. Phillip extends his arm across the threshold, where the drop-off into the tunnel occurs, and the cold wraps around his skin. At first it feels good, so different than the journey up to this point. But then he shivers. He must pull his arm back.

"That rat."

Phillip turns.

Adam holds a wrapper between his fingers. "This was mine. He took it."

Phillip sees it is a cough drop wrapper.

"That sucks," Cole says. "No pun intended."

"I knew I had one left. He must have gone through our pockets. I could be enjoying a cough drop right now."

"Don't forget my stick," Phillip reminds Adam.

"I'm going to get that guy," Adam says. "I mean, really get him."

"What does that mean?" Cole laughs.

Phillip chuckles, too.

"You don't want to know what it means," Adam says. "Anyone who gets to know what that means never again wants to know what that means."

"Oh, yeah."

"Yeah."

They are all laughing now. Their cheer extends for a short while. Then it ends, and they are left with their lives. The climb.

"At least we don't have to carry you anymore."

Adam is right. The tunnel ahead is big enough so they can all walk. An adult elephant could easily fit.

"Maybe a herd of elephants lives here," Phillip says, riffing off his thoughts.

"Or giant spiders," Cole adds.

"I hate spiders," Adam says.

"I know you do. That's why I said it, tough guy."

"Me too," Phillip says.

"Especially the ones with hairy legs," Adam says. "Especially those."

Phillip agrees, nodding. He does not want to encounter a hairy-legged spider the size of an elephant.

"I'm ready when you are," Cole says. He shimmies to the ledge, sitting. His feet dangle.

Phillip looks at Adam, surveying the tunnel and trying, Phillip knows, to do what is impossible: foresee what awaits.

"I'll go first," Adam says.

They step down into the tunnel, as cold as a refrigerator.

As he puts on his jacket, Phillip notices fresh footprints. Tony's. He points them out to Cole and Adam. After a few feet, the stride lengthens, like Tony started running. He wonders why.

Why would he run?

Trekking into the expanse is like entering a new realm: walking on a strange moon. The tunnel's floor and walls are smooth. Their warm breath vines into smoke. The red light is a filter that bloodies all they see. When Phillip glances behind him, it seems as if the tunnel closes and all that has happened is now irrelevant. It feels like they're on their own in a way they've never been before.

78

They snack on the last of their worm.

Earlier, Adam removed his jacket and shirt and laid down shivering in the mud, waiting for a worm to come nosing. Cole spied the still ground. Because the worms have become bigger and hard to handle, Phillip had a spear ready—the small bat with a pocket knife tied to the tip—but no worms appeared. In fact, they've not seen one since entering this part of the tunnel.

Soon they will be out of food.

Their clothes are heavy with damp. They cough, bent over.

His shoulder is healing well; the stump feels like a strong weld. Already he notices more dexterity in the fingers of his left hand. He squeezes the worm as hard as he can, releases. He is getting strong.

He thinks of his sports-obsessed father and how he must be reacting. No doubt he is plotting some type of training regimen to transform The Boy into the first one-armed major league pitcher. Or an Olympic javelin thrower. He's probably devised a weight lifting program and imposed a 500 pitches per day quota. Something crazy like that.

His father tries to push further into his thoughts, into the room of his mind, but Cole purges him. He's not interested in listening to another speech about defeating the opponent and how winners have more fun than losers. Cole doesn't want to hear of how when his father played football…

There, he is gone.

He savors his last bite of worm. Food is food when you're hungry. As he chews he stares down the tunnel.

Movement.

He squints and notices a change in the light, something manipulating it.

There, again.

The temperature seems to drop by a few degrees, like from a biting wind, but there is no wind. Only still cold. He notices tiny ice crystals in the mud. Coils of vapor rotate slowly. Cole shakes the sting from his numb fingertips.

"Guys," he says. "Something's there."

79

"What is that?" Phillip whispers.

A hulking presence waits in the distance. It breathes. He senses that. It is shielded by a shell of red light that glows from some source within.

They are being watched.

This is when they find out if this is hell.

A tangy and metallic taste rises in Phillip's throat. He gets light-headed. Sweat webs his body as he swallows and regains firm footing. Cole and Adam don't notice.

The nausea passes.

But he feels something inside him. He cannot explain what. The strange taste remains on his tongue.

"Get the weapons," Adam says quietly.

Phillip slips off his backpack. They have three short spears, the tips jerry-rigged with pocket knives tied with multiple shoelaces wound tight. The small knives are attached to the ends of a miniature baseball bat and two drum sticks. Adam takes the bat. Phillip and Cole get a drum stick each.

Adam unpacks a pair of hockey skates from his backpack. There is a moment of surreal contrast: there might be no other item that appears as out-of-place in this world. Adam slides one of the skates over his free hand, the blade glinting.

He hands the other to Phillip, who regards Adam.

With his bladed hand and spear, his muddied face and clothes, Adam looks like a maniac.

Phillip slides the second skate over his own fist.

Two maniacs and a recently crippled boy.

"Stay behind me," Adam says. "I have a bad feeling. I don't think we're about to make a new friend."

Friend, Phillip thinks, his eyes fixed ahead. His squeezes the handle of his spear.

80

He takes one cautious step forward. His plan is to patiently get an idea of what they are dealing with. He is halfway into his second step when the plan falls apart.

Instead, the mud and cold and light come alive, combining. They are parts, Adam realizes. Together they form a beast. His knees weaken, but they do not buckle. Before him, the tunnel uncoils—expanding—and slides towards him. It is a worm. Its girth fills the tunnel, and Adam hears the mud pressed beneath its weight being smoothed.

"Oh my god." It must be thirty feet long. Then the vein and its gallons of glowing blood shoot a flare of red light that turns his vision kaleidoscopic.

He blindly stumbles forward, angry now. He scowls. *Fight.* He isn't about to wither and get steamrolled. He knows how leverage works and its importance. *Push.*

"Let's go!"

They charge.

Adam sprints up a slight incline into what is now bitter cold. The mud beneath his feet is firm. He hears Phillip and Cole close behind and to each side.

"Get ready!"

The collision almost shatters him. He tastes blood in his mouth. Pain floods his nose. He spits. Luckily, he is bounced upward and not on his back.

He comes down dizzy. His skate clinks teeth, and his spear jabs easily and deeply into worm flesh, the consistency of stiff jelly. The worm lets out a splitting hiss, and Adam rips free the spear while punching unrelentingly with the skate. His head clears. He stabs and slashes. Both hands, one after another. The immediacy and intensity of the fighting is a fast slideshow: a giant surprising eye; teeth like beaks; Phillip atop the worm, thrusting his spear downward; Cole, his face marked with sweat and mud, beside him.

They attack viciously, not like boys, more like insects, as if they are fighting the tree itself, all its pain and frustrations and uncertainties.

Someone has managed to nick the vein, because ankle-high puddles have formed. Cold blood merges with mud into a ruddy, chilled sludge. It splashes on them as they fight. The fierce red light weakens to a smolder. Minutes into the battle, Adam feels hopeful. Just stay away from the teeth, he tells himself.

81

The worm lashes its tail.

Phillip is flung and lands hard on his side. Adam is knocked backwards, and the spear falls apart.

Cole grabs the pocket knife from the ground, the blade bent to snapping.

"Watch out!" Adam warns.

Cole, who has turned to check on Phillip, sidesteps just in time. The teeth miss him by inches. Like a pendulum, the worm swings back for another pass, and Cole jabs at the mouth engineered like a grinder: three circular rows of teeth. The drumstick snaps. The pocket knife is swallowed. He retreats and joins Adam and Phillip.

The boys step out of range to regroup.

The worm is the color of white corn. Kernels of skin form its armor. Wounded, it studies them. Every few seconds a reeking, raspy breath exits its mouth, which is the size of a car tire. One cycloptic eye roves. The lidless eye is solid black, mounted above the mouth like a periscope.

Cole stares into the eye. It is a giant pupil, as big as a softball.

The worm is as tall as him.

With only a little spear and a pair of hockey skates, they are in trouble. There is nowhere to hide, and their weapons are insufficient. They either kill or get shredded into meat.

How many boys have been caught? Cole wonders.

How many has the grinder got?

Did they thrash and scream?

What were their final thoughts?

"Guys," Phillip says.

The worm's teeth are triangular and serrated.

"Guys," Phillip says again, something unusual in his voice.

Cole turns. Beside him, Adam does the same.

Phillip is holding up his hand. The palm and fingers are pink. His side is splayed with pink.

82

He landed on the pocket knife, which stabbed into the fold just below his ribcage. When he rolled, the knife dislodged. He pressed his hand to his side, to where he felt pain.

Now it is unmistakable.

He is bleeding the pond.

He thinks back to the mask on his face, the pond sending itself into him. How he was paralyzed. He thought he was losing his bones. Now, though, he understands. He was not being attacked. He was being prepared.

"I feel all right," he says.

Adam and Phillip share the same dumbstruck expression.

"This is okay. I'm sure. This is meant to happen."

One spear remains, the tip pink.

Phillip offers it to Cole. "You need to throw it, Cole. You're the one. You need to aim for its eye."

83

The monstrous eye sways. Cole holds the spear firmly, but tries to keep his body light. Gripping too tightly, he knows, can hamper the flight.

How many times, with his other arm, has he thrown at a target? How many times has he hit? How often has he missed?

The tiny spear feels right in his hand, like it belongs. He is strong. He wraps his fingers around the smooth wood.

The pink glow at the spear's tip is like a small cupola of blown glass.

Adam and Phillip step aside.

He does not hesitate, and he feels no tension. What unfolds is as natural as a hawk gliding on trails of wind.

Him. The eye.

You don't aim. You just throw.

"Time to go away," Cole says.

He steps forward with his right foot aimed as his left arm rears back, rotates forward, the shoulder its fulcrum, the elbow and forearm acting in concert, an even and coordinated assemblage of parts, his foot planting and wrist simultaneously whipping—the spear, released.

*   *   *

The spear arcs through the lean air. Pink light washes across the tunnel.

There is never any doubt.

When the spear connects, dead center, there is a *squish*, and the blade sinks to the shaft.

Enraged and hissing, the worm thrashes. It bashes the sides of the tunnel, and the tunnel shakes. They step back. Despite the thrashing, the spear stays stuck, and the worm tires. Blinded, huffing, it lumbers side to side. Each hiss is less fierce than the previous. It grits its hundreds of teeth and sweeps its mouth, attacking boys that aren't there, and slams the wall. It crumples in the mud. It lifts its head, drowsy. Lays back down.

After a weak shake, it goes still.

By himself, Cole walks to the worm. He stares at the big eye. Veins of pink lightning spread outward from the spear's tip. The eye looks like a ball of static electricity.

He notices the pink bolts slowly widening, the spear filling the giant eye with pond water.

Adam and Phillip join him. They stand to each side. Together, they watch the eye become a gaseous pink planet.

When the eye is full, the pond begins flooding into the rest of the worm. This happens quickly, as if a gate has opened. The cylindrical body is like a measuring cup. ¼. ½. ¾.

The pink glow intensifies and warms the tunnel.

It is a warm embrace. Cole thinks of his mom.

84

A transfer is occurring. The spear is the conduit. This world to which Phillip has traveled courses through him, and his veins thrum. All this time he has had the pond inside, its power coaxed from him by the need to kill the worm.

Prepared as its vessel.

As the pond leaves him, Phillip feels its departing. His limbs loosen and become syrupy. For a moment he feels so relaxed and cleansed.

The worm is entirely pink now and shines like the pond itself, but when it can accept no more, when it is full to the brim, it begins to melt, like a lump of ice cream in summer heat.

The eye dislodges. It plops in the mud. Then a thick, fleshy chunk slides off the worm's side and sloshes across the tunnel floor. There is a repulsive stench. The sour-smelling slop sinks and disappears into the muck.

They step back. They hold their noises.

This quick liquefaction takes a few minutes, and the boys watch—granted access, however briefly, to a life and death previously beyond comprehension.

The creature is gone. Nothing remains, not even a smudge. Phillip stares up the tunnel. The ancient smell of mud returns. It is oddly comfortable.

"You okay?" Cole says.

"Yeah." Phillip checks his side and sees that he has healed. There is no blood, no pond. He wishes there was a scar, as proof.

"The pond saved us," Adam says.

The light has changed from red to soft pink. Though he can see his breath, Phillip is not cold.

"We saved ourselves," Cole says.

"But the pond helped. Why did it?" Adam says.

They are bathed in light. Each is alive.

"It wants us to keep going," Phillip says. "It helped us get farther. That's all."

Cole says, "We don't know what's next."

"What's waiting for us might be worse," Phillip says.

"Or better," Adam says.

"Or the same," Cole says.

"Do you think there are any more?" Adam looks up the tunnel, but he appears calm, as if he fears nothing and never will again.

"If there are, we're done for," says Cole.

"That was it," Phillip says.

"Why are you so sure?" Adam says.

"Because we killed the beast." Phillip says this simply, surely, as if this lone fact should suffice. "A nightmare has one monster. Behind all the scares, there's only one."

Water begins to drip.

We are the one. We are the monster.

Sometimes Phillip thinks about what his dad saw, or what he did, that left him so scared and lost, what he cannot shake loose from his mind. He reaches down and scoops mud into one of his hands. He squeezes. Mud meshes between his fingers like ropey brains.

The monster may be gone for now, but nothing has changed. The tunnel: this is where they are. The pond helped them, but only so they can climb deeper. When a nightmare ends, you're supposed to wake. But what if you already are? Then you walk. Your feet sink. You head towards the unknown. You live in this dream. You hope for better. Beyond the beast is anyone's guess.

85

This must be an elaborate joke.

There is a pond. Water trickles down the cavern walls. Looking up is like seeing a cloudy night. A rock. Bell. It is the same. Colder but the same. The only difference is that there are no boys. None.

There is nothing.

He scans for succulent plants and tart red berries. He spins, looking for the Pond of Lost Girls. He waits for a pane of sunlight to warm his face, roughed with mud, but the only light comes from the pond, which moves in one steady and familiar undulation. There is no meat, never will be.

He is exhausted, having run the entire distance between Levels 2 and 3.

He has run all this way.

For what?

He watches his breath smoke around him. He is starving.

Bonkers. A crazed laugh. He grits his teeth. *I'm a punch-line*.

He walks across the sand and stops, inches from the pond. He yanks down his pants, readies to pee. See how it likes that. In response the pond inches towards his feet, and he must scurry away as urine sprays his legs.

"Piss on you!" Tony says.

What good is the stick?

He must be missing something.

"King Geiger!"

He had believed.

"I have a stick, not just a stick. A piece of the tree itself, sir!"

The emptiness and silence intimidates. He feels lost. He is so used to seeing the caverns populated with boys that he has the spooky sense of having woken in an abandoned city—abandoned for reasons unknown. He keeps expecting someone to jump from a hiding place and give him a good scare.

"Hello! Anybody!"

He follows the shore and decides to circle the pond. He scans the floor beneath him: a faint set of large footprints in the sand. They are Geiger's. They must be. He hikes swiftly, jabbing the footprints with the sharp end of the stick.

At the other end of the pond, far from the tunnel, is a shady, private beach. He must skip along a narrow edge of sand to reach it. This peninsula, surrounded on three sides by water, is like a tiny island. Here, the footprints continue, but they turn from the pond and disappear into the dark, towards a wall of the cavern. Tony follows carefully, cautious. Ahead, the steep wall approaches, a dead end. But as he gets close he realizes that there is an opening in the rock: a cave.

He must bend to enter. A sudden wave of trepidation causes weakness, and his legs shake.

Inside, the ceiling is high, and he unsteadily stands. His eyes adjust. The radiance of the pond is enough to provide a smoldered light that mimics the glowing log of a half-extinguished fire.

He squints.

Before him, sitting against the far wall, is a boy. His legs extended, he is almost as tall as a man. Long black hair falls over his face.

"Geiger," Tony whispers. "Is it you?" He takes a wary step forward. "Sir, I have a stick. See? A special stick. It is part of the tree."

He kneels. He holds the stick in upturned hands and extends his arms. His head is bowed. "A stick meant for a king," he says, just as he imagined, just as he practiced.

"King Geiger?"

Geiger doesn't move.

Tony scoots forward on his knees.

When he is close enough, he sees what the dimness has hid up to this point, and a soul-crushing pall forms over him.

There is nothing but a skeleton, wearing stiff jeans and a ratty gray t-shirt. Behind the skeleton, scraped into the smooth rock, in a boy's script: "Geiger wuz here."

Why would he spell 'was' in such an idiotic way?

A myth. That's all it was. And a silly one at that.

Tony stands. He flips the stick so that the knobbed end is up. He grips with both hands, rears back, and swings.

Geiger's skull is sent tumbling across the ground. It bounces and rolls clumsily before coming to rest on its neck. The black hair looks like a wig.

"Putz," Tony says.

From there he walks straight out of the cave to the sand— and further, to the pond's edge.

Discipline is for fools.

He kneels, just as he did for Geiger, for the skeleton.

At least the pond will give him something in return. For years and years he has denied himself. No more. The black shape comes, even for him, and he submits.

86

Tony floats beside them.

The Man holds her hand as they walk an inclined path. The path is hardscaped with pebbles and leads to a raised observation area that overlooks a field dotted with tall, shady trees. He pays for three large leaves of lettuce and a leafy twig, which he hands the girl. She is seven or maybe eight-years-old.

That giraffe's name is Maya, a zookeeper says. She just became a mama.

A baby giraffe lopes in the distance, near a far fence.

Maya, as tall as a house, approaches with a slow gait and stops.

The girl laughs, giddy, as the giraffe extends its long purple tongue and snatches the lettuce. For the twig, it must wrap its tongue around each leaf and yank.

Hold on, The Man says, smiling wide.

The leaf stems snap, one after the other, until the twig is bare.

They walk to the kangaroos next, followed by big cats—sleeping lions, lurking panthers—then rhinos, an ostrich, sloths, otters, and animals with odd, unfamiliar names, which the girl reads off display cards: bonobos, capybara, the rock hyrax. Animals from all over the world.

Lemurs leap and swing from ropes. Lorikeets fly to her shoulder and lap juice from a small plastic cup that she grasps tightly. Feet away from a Silverback gorilla, they marvel at the size of its head and massive arms. They count twenty-two alligators sunning themselves.

All the while The Man watches, encourages, smiles, teaches.

They have lunch outside, sitting on a bench in the shade. The Man has brought peanut butter and jelly sandwiches, applesauce, and chocolate chip cookies. They share water from a thermos.

Near the end of lunch, the man says, Stay here. I'll be right back. Don't go anywhere, okay?

The girl nods.

The Man leaves.

The girl sits alone on the bench. Another man, wearing a wide-brimmed straw hat, walks by, glancing at her. She puts her head down. Swings her legs. When the man is past, she looks up again.

Where has he gone? He shouldn't have left her.

Then The Man returns—carrying a tall vanilla ice cream cone and a fistful of napkins.

Thank you, Daddy, she says.

You're welcome. You're the best kid I know. I love you.

I love you too.

They sit on the bench, the girl enjoying the ice cream.

A piece of vanilla dots her nose, which he wipes.

Afterwards, they continue to explore the zoo.

They pass under a sign that says, "Komodo Dragons: Turn Left."

They turn. The gardens on either side are beautiful. Tall stalks of bamboo move in a light breeze. Flowers, large to petite, are every brand of color.

Dragons aren't real, the girl says. I mean the type that breathe fire.

Maybe they live where we can't see them. Maybe there are still places that haven't been seen. What do you think about that?

They walk for a bit.

I like that idea, she finally says.

Why?

The girl stops, searching for her answer. Well, because it means there's mystery.

That's a great word, The Man says. Mystery.

There are things that haven't been discovered.

That's right, he says, nodding.

The girl does not notice her father smiling. She is thinking quietly, it seems, of things undiscovered.

Later that day, exiting the zoo, the sky is on the cusp of sunset. The girl takes her father's hand when he offers it. They head for home.

When does a boy become a man?

Oy.

87

"Oy, friends."

Tony sits, legs crossed, in the sand. Arranged before him in a semi-circle are his few possessions: a small, sequin-covered lizard, a pocket mirror, a red rubber ball, and the comb. He is wearing gloves. The stick lays beside him. He faces the pond, too far away to view.

"Found out I'm a father. Went to the zoo. Saw an anteater!"

Adam bends down and picks up the stick. He hands it to Phillip.

"Of course," Tony says. He smiles. "Sorry about that. Have it. Won't do much good. Nothing here, you know. Just a few skeletons. There. Another over there. Geiger's in the cave, bones. Figure they starved. No worms to eat. Surprised you got past the big fella."

"Cole killed it," Phillip says.

"Did you? My goodness, have you always had one arm? Oh well. One. Two. What does it matter?"

"I should kill you," Adam says. "We should."

"Really? Go ahead. Do I care? No. I don't, Mr. Adam. Have at it."

Tony's concession defuses their anger.

"Geez, you all look a complete mess. Take a shower. You'll find it to be freezing! Your wee will shrink!"

"You've lost it," Cole says.

"Have I?"

"I think so."

"Well, Cole, perhaps you're right. What do you think, Phillip? Adam?"

They don't respond.

"I'll take your silence as confirmation. I don't necessarily disagree. I've lost something. Discipline, definitely. I had your cough drop by the way, Adam. It was wonderful. I'm sorry for being a thief. So, discipline, yes, I've lost. Sanity. That's the question. I don't know. I figure we all go a little crazy in here. How can you not? By the way, if you haven't figured it out, there are no berries! No king! The place is a real skunk!"

Cole sits down. He sighs.

"Yes, sit, please. Where are my manners? Join me."

Phillip and Adam follow.

The four sit together, just like in the pit.

The cavern is still and wickedly cold. It wouldn't surprise Phillip if it started to snow.

"My how we've changed since we first met," Tony says.

"You're staying?" Cole says.

"For a bit," Tony says. He looks at the pond. "Still going all the way, are you?"

"Why not come with us?"

Adam gives Cole a nasty look.

"It's okay, Adam. I'm not coming with you. I understand your anger. I'm sorry. I've been a lout. I admit it. But for a very long time I came to believe in something that wasn't true.

I became obsessed, and it led me here, to this. I'm regretful, but, well, what else can I say but that? I could babble forever, I suppose, and never explain anything in a way I would even understand. Thank you for the offer, Cole, but I must decline. I'm staying here."

"Here?"

"Yes, here."

"How will you survive?" Phillip says.

Tony shrugs.

"No one else has survived," Phillip says.

"That's true," Tony says. "It seems that way." He nods.

"Well, we're going," Adam says.

"I know you are," Tony says. "To the end of the tunnel. And I wish you good fortune. I really do. I wish I could tell you what to expect, but I can't. These skeletons around here might know, but because they are here and not somewhere else, I think that says something about the possibility of escape. I wish it were otherwise. I wish I could feel more hopeful about your chances. There I go jabbering again. Then again, what do I know? Look at me. A big dupe, just another fool."

They don't say any more, tired.

They fall asleep. They sleep for a long time. Phillip is first to wake. He stretches, sits up, tries to warm his hands.

He sees Tony, knee deep in the pond. Tony has stripped to his underwear but, oddly, is wearing gloves. In his hands he holds his relics: the ball, comb, mirror, and lizard. Not the stick, though. He has left it on the sand. At first Phillip believes he is dreaming, but the chill lets him know he is not. His teeth chatter for a few seconds before settling.

Tony notices Phillip. "Oy!" he says.

This rouses Cole and Adam. Groggy, they notice Tony and are instantly alert.

"Wakey wakey," Tony says. "Eggs and bakey." He cackles. That cackle. He takes a step forward, and another. "Good luck, boys," he says. "I'm headed out. Taking my things with me. Oy!"

Phillip holds back a rush of tears. "Tony!"

"Yes, Phillip." Tony stops. The water is up to his waist.

Phillip stands. He thinks of what he wants to tell Tony, but decides against it, or perhaps he doesn't know what to say. "Goodbye," he says.

"Yes, goodbye to you all. And by the way, the stick—it is part of the tree. It is a branch," Tony says.

Then he waves, departing, walking into the deep waters.

88

At the kitchen table his father sits across from The Boy.
Each has a piece of notebook paper and a pencil.
With his left hand, The Boy writes his name again and again.

Cole
Cole
Cole
Cole

The writing is like a first grader's—strained and misshapen.
His father, too, writes awkwardly with his left hand.
Cole sits next to The Boy on the bench seat.
The Boy feels his presence. He stops writing.
They nod to each other.
I've been thinking, Cole's father says.
The Boy and Cole look up.
We should take those pennants down and paint your room something new. Those pennants are old anyway, and they've been up since you were a baby. I put them up, and it's time to put them away.
Anything?
Your choice.
What about pink?

Pink walls?
Yeah.
Well, geez, okay.
I was just kidding.
Funny.
The Boy begins on the alphabet, lower case.

a b c d e f

He stops. I'm sorry, he says.
Sorry? About what?
The Boy scribbles on his paper.
The father gently takes The Boy's pencil and lays it on the table.
He holds what he believes is his son's hand.
Cole is tempted to place his hand atop theirs, but he doesn't.
Cole, all I care about is that you're here. When you were sick,
I wanted to help, but I couldn't. The day your mother and I brought
you home, that was the best day. We didn't think we could have a
child. But then you came. It was like you were delivered to us. I
love you. I haven't said that enough in the past.
The Boy nods.
Do you ever want to know about them, Cole? It's okay. You
can tell me.
Not really.
You're sure?
If they wanted me to know them, they would have found me.
His father peers at The Boy's writing.
Sometimes, Cole, it's not just about wanting. It's about what
you can handle, what you're able to do. When someone isn't able,
you can't be angry. Okay? You understand?
Yes, The Boy says.
Let's take a break. That's good work.
The Boy says, Do you want to watch a ball game or something?

Do you?

I don't know. Maybe.

How about we go to the library? I know that's always been mom's thing, but I can read, too, you know.

You can?

I can read. I'm a fabulous reader.

Cole's father sees The Boy looking at his sheet of paper.

Here. He slides it across the table.

Cole.
Adam.
Phillip.
Tony.

What made you write this? The Boy says.

It's the same question Cole wants to ask.

I don't know. Who are Phillip and Tony? They friends of yours that I've met?

No. I don't think so.

The names just came to me.

Cole thinks of the treeman. Roots, Adam said. We live in the dark, digging through the ground, searching for water, an extension of some unseen thing. Cole thinks of how we sense worlds different from our own, even if we are not aware of doing so. These worlds are all around us. They're real. They fill the empty spaces. He is sure of this.

89

The train clacks across the plain, stretching flat to the horizon. A morsel of sun feeds light to the sky, deep purples and blues at this early hour.

The boy sits alone in an empty train car. He stares out the open door.

He must have cut his hair with the pocket knife. Roughly shorn tufts, stick up like a messy patch of thorns. Dirt smudges his face. He is drowsy.

Where is he going? Or is not knowing the point?

His notebook is open in his lap.

Phillip walks over, sits next to him.

The Boy flips the page and writes. He then holds up the notebook: "I sense you," it says.

He turns the page back to what he was writing.

He lays the notebook on the plywood floor and taps the words with the eraser of the pencil.

Read, he says.

My name is Phillip Strong, and I attend school with the girl who died, who I accidentally killed. I didn't mean to kill her. I had been living in the woods for a week or so, near the edge of the path that leads to the park. I ran away from home, and I was playing with a gun when it went off. The gun is my father's, a veteran. I took it without asking. Please forgive me, and please do not place any blame on him. This is my fault, and I made a horrible decision. I swear I didn't mean to hurt the girl. I wish I knew her name. I only saw her a few times at school, and she seemed very nice. I am so sorry. I would never hurt anybody on purpose. I am not capable of that. I am a quiet person, and I am filled with sadness about what happened. I should never have left home, and now I feel I can never come back.

Sincerely,

Phillip Strong

How quickly the sky can change. Orange and pinks have joined the mosaic. The train clacks rhythmically beneath. Clack-clack. Clack-clack. The Boy, Phillip knows, has no specific destination. The train will take him where it does, and that will have to suffice.

Where the sun rises, he will be.

90

The suspension bridge stretches over a mile, like a giant mechanical arm extended. Adam has never seen such a magnificent structure. It traverses a choppy bay and carries an unceasing parade of vehicles across it.

The Boy and Adam's father sit on the balcony of the hotel room, admiring the bridge. A city teems around them.

I was painting that pole today. Did you see me?

Yeah. I looked through the binoculars.

Do you like the color?

Orange? I guess.

They do it so people will see it. That way they pay attention when they're driving on the bridge, instead of getting lazy and looking at the view.

Who pays for the hotel?

The people who want their bridge painted.

How long will it take?

About ten weeks, I think. Where's your mom with that pizza? I'm starving.

Patience. Isn't that what you always say?

You're right. When are you flying home? Sunday?

I think.

A surge of wind plows over them, through Adam. Here, the wind's whistle never stops.

Dad.

Yes, Adam.

Do you think I loved her?

He is a big man, with a wild, bushy beard, and his work has made him muscled. Orange paint flecks his hands. The edges of his mouth turn down as he reflects. Yes, I do, he says.

Why?

Do you love us, me and Mom?

Yes.

Then you feel love. You know what it is. If you say you love someone, I have no reason to doubt it.

Would it have lasted?

I don't know. But just because people part doesn't mean love wasn't real.

But I'll always love you no matter what.

It's different between a parent and a child.

All the time?

Not always, but usually.

Why do you think that?

A parent helps brings a child into the world. You didn't ask to be born. And this world is beautiful, but hard. There is a good hand and a bad hand. And when a child feels pain, a parent who loves their child feels pain too. The parent helped cause it. I brought you here; I helped create you. I knew that the bad hand would touch you.

Sometimes, when I'm up high, I stop and look far away. I think of the people below me, thousands I'll never meet, and there are billions on this planet, and it may take me a week to paint one pole of a bridge. I will cover a little every day. That is my task. I do it again and again. Sometimes up there I feel so small.

But then I come home, down to the ground, and I talk to you and your mom. That's when I feel big. That's the good. That's love and friendship. They mark your place.

268

91

It is hard to watch, but I must.

They slog forward. What light remains lowers towards brooding dark. The tunnel narrows, and when they crawl their backs scrape mud. For days they head up steep grades. They go without food. Grow weak. Their cheeks are hollow. They collapse and fall asleep, then wake in rushes of paranoia, seeking each other to confirm everyone is still alive. They spread the tarp and catch water. They fold the tarp and harness the water into a crevice that they pour and drink from. The water is muddy and cold. They don't speak because there is nothing to say. Their hands are numb from wet and chill, and they squeeze and rub their hands, puff air into them.

Shivers rock through them. Their knees and elbows are raw, the skin worn and bloody. Every yard is a struggle.

Cole has the thought that the tunnel is endless. It goes on and on, upwards to nowhere. They will never reach anything. Their stamina will not matter. Their desire for an answer will only prolong their pain. This odyssey will be their second terrible mistake. The first: falling into the tree. The second: trying to escape.

Darkness falling now, the last length of pink haze diminishing, the final light—when, at last, the tunnel stops.

Just like that. No announcement. Nothing special.

There is no hatch. No door.

Only mud. A wall.

An end.

Adam thumps the mud with his forearm. Cole weakly scraps away a clump of mud with his hand.

Phillip watches.

There is nothing behind the wall except more mud.

This is it.

They sit on a tarp, hold another one over them, and listen to plops of water drip overhead.

So cold.

The boys descend into a cryogenic state, their minds stalled. There are no options except to go back, which no one wants.

Hours pass. A day.

They sit huddled. Stay silent.

Nap. Wake.

There is nothing.

They made it to the finish, and it is an empty box.

Phillip tries to think of something to share and crack the silence. He cannot.

Hopelessness has smashed their will.

With no warning the tarp they sit on slides backward. In an instant they are yanked from their groggy inertia. The tarp moves a few feet, and they lean and claw the ground to keep themselves from skidding further. Panicked, their fingers dig like the blade of a plow.

They stop.

Their hearts thump, skin tingling.

Safe.

Together, they have awoken. It is time to make a decision: move or die.

Looking over his shoulder, down the tunnel, Adam is the first to have the idea.

Cole follows his gaze. Then Phillip.

They share the same crazed thought.

And they have nothing to lose.

Locking eyes, giggling to themselves, they silently agree. As a group, they have surrendered to a wild vision, and the allure of that vision rests in not knowing what will happen.

They turn around. For the first time since arriving in the tree all three face down the tunnel. Below them, like newly formed fog, is the ponds' pink light creeping from each cavern. They sit cross-legged, in a line, centered on the tarp. Phillip is first, Cole in the middle, Adam at the end. The other tarp, which they held overhead, is tossed behind along with their remaining possessions.

They are taking nothing with them.

They count with simultaneous nods of their heads.

One. Two. Three.

Swimming their arms, they propel themselves like they are on a sled.

Slowly, they gain speed, and eventually the tarp slides without the need to push.

Their momentum gathers.

They skate over the mud—faster, faster.

And they reenter the pink light of Level 3, which streams brighter the deeper they descend, moving swiftly now, the speed filling them with wild urges to whoop and smile, and when they pierce the light it becomes streaked with white, like the trail of a comet, like wild brush strokes of paint, and soon they are careening down the tunnel with such abandon that the pink light and walls form one solid blur, and they rocket forward, the tarp sounding like skis over packed, icy snow, almost to the entrance of Level 3 now, where Tony rests, Tony,

who stole Phillip's stick, who led them from the pit, who de-
duced what they all now know—the stick is a piece of the
tree—close now to where the skeletons of Geiger and boys un-
named lie, abandoned, boys who had homes and friends and
parents, boys who came before, and they punch through the
light of Level 3 and soon are upon the grave of the Great
White Worm, the place where Cole launched the spear, tipped
with a pink spearhead of pond, and then they are launched
airborne for a stretch, into where the tunnel shrinks, past the
cough drop wrapper, past where Cole's arm vanished, to where
Adam and Phillip used a worm to help mend his wound, and
it takes little time before they are wrapped in the powerful rays
of Level 2, approaching the arched entryway where Armbands
grabbed them, closer, closer, and they see two boys hunting
worms, and they yell to get out of the way, which the boys do,
leaping to the side, and they crash through an explosion of
light near the tunnel entrance, past Mash and Swan and Red
and the race and square dance and checkers and the massive
mirror that showed them their own feral reflections, a civilization of diverse boys snatched from their lives in the world
above, and Adam wonders what Mash and the rest are making
of their new world, their chance at reconstruction, but they are
moving too fast to see, the sled humming, and the bright light
of Level 2's entrance forces them to close their eyes as they
zoom like a shrieking wind, passing where Adam kissed Lily,
and Phillip first saw the campsite on the wood's edge, and
Cole came to know something was deeply wrong, and they
bump along, gripping the tarp over slick, wet mud that sloshes
in places, sending sprays of dirty water in their faces and hair,
like they are sailing in rough seas, and Phillip imagines it is the
ocean's spray and he tastes make believe saltwater on his lips,
which he has never tasted, but it is fun to imagine, and why
not imagine as they skid high up the tunnel wall around the

curve, halfway between Level 1 and 2, where Peter died, where bright dots of white popped like oil popping in a pan, and Adam was brought to think poetically of snow, and they are boring through the darkness now, as black as night, unable to see anything, the tarp steady, and this is where Phillip twisted a worm vein into a Cat's Cradle and Cole thought of carrot cake and Tony said, "Periwinkle Blue," and the continents were listed, and a pelican briefly captured their imaginations, and the darkness recedes, replaced by a pinhead of light appearing far ahead quickly growing until bursting pink again, and again they are storming through brightness when ahead they see the light grow, spreading, as they approach the entrance to Level 1, and they see the bones, and Cole screams to hold on seconds before smashing The Bear to smithereens, the bones rattling outside the entrance to Level 1, where they first saw themselves in the pond, where Adam dispatched Helmut and his gang, and Tayib chose to go away, where Phillip, in the moonlight, saw Midnight, and Cole watched himself bleed, and Adam sat next to Lily, drawing her picture of a snowy world home to a wolf boy, and they are retracing the path of the first crawl, where brash beliefs were humbled and fear was overcome and where they caught and ate their first worms, and where Cole, frustrated, hit his best friend, which he vows he will never do again, never, and never again, they know, will they climb up this tunnel, never again.

I pray they are right.

92

Feldstein reads the definition for "marsupial," a word he sort of knows. Kangaroos are marsupials. They carry their young in pouches. Then he flips ahead: "vital." Flips back: "tender." He likes to randomly jump around the book. For a word he is familiar with, he composes a definition out loud to see how it compares with the dictionary description, or he tries to list synonyms that might match any that are provided. He'll use the word in a sentence to capture its meaning.

For a word he does not know, he reads the definition a few times and repeats it in his head. Words he has learned today: jai alai, hummus.

Jai alai: a court game in which players use a long hand-shaped basket strapped to the wrist to propel a ball against a wall.

Hummus: a creamy dip originating from the Middle East, made from pureed chickpeas, etc.

Tayib, he remembers, was from the Middle East. Did Tayib eat hummus?

He looks back to the book. Tender. He says, "Sensitive, soft. The meat is tender. The worm is tender."

He reads in pink light emitted by the tunnel, draped under an old yellow raincoat. Somehow, over many years, the book has remained in good condition. The corners are worn, and the paper has swollen because of the damp. Ink has smudged. But the pages still turn. The words can be read.

Someday he would like to play jai alai. He would like for his leg to be normal. He wishes a lot of things would happen that never will.

The pit. The heat, mud, and wet. It's taken some getting used to. The cavern of Level 1, despite its drawbacks, had become cozy in many ways, cooler and roomy, but he has no intention of going back anytime soon. He just wants to be alone, him and his book.

He finds the word "history." Some words are only allotted one line. "History," though, has a long series of elaborations below it. It is a complex word, which is why he often comes back to it. Every second that passes becomes part of history. Time and events form its basis. Feldstein thinks about how the word applies to this place, where boys do not age. He thinks of his own history, all that has occurred here and in the world above.

Sadly, on the other side, life has been hard, and he is old. There is much loneliness. No family, few friends. He limps around an old, small house. The lights are kept off, so it is always dark. He watches game shows. Sometimes, peeling back a window blind, he stares outside at a world that doesn't care. It is why he has viewed the pond less in recent years.

Suddenly, the pink light streaming from the tunnel flickers, and he is distracted from his thoughts. The glow has always been constant; thus, the change gets his attention.

He stands and hobbles to where the tunnel carves a circle in the wall. When he looks up, he is confused. The flickering intensifies. He squints.

Something is coming down the tunnel.

He watches, listens. A growing and constant scraping sound worries him. Louder. Unaware of what is happening, he should hide, but the pit is small, and he cannot turn away. The tunnel darkens further, a jumbled and large black shape approaching. Then he sees faces. They are barreling towards him, muddy faces fixed with white, wide circles for eyes.

He dives out of the way, just in time, and the book falls from his hand, into the mud.

93

They jettison from the tunnel, and the tarp falls away beneath them.

For a brief, pleasant moment they are flying unbound, as if thrust into the weightlessness of outer space, before smashing into the far wall of the pit.

The impact is momentous.

Adam expects every one of his bones to break. He is certain he will die; he will die in the pit, where his journey began.

He grips the silver chain.

But it does not take long for him to realize that he was wrong. His bones have not turned to powder, and he is not dead. In fact, the opposite has happened. The boys have destroyed the wall instead of it destroying them.

The wall has given way. Chunks of earth float around him, dreamlike. They have smashed *through*.

Tumbling within fresh air and sunlight, Adam greedily inhales; bright rays make him squint and heat the mud on his skin. The sky is striking blue. The sky. It is as if they have jumped out of a plane and are crashing earthward. To his right, Cole cartwheels beside him. Phillip is ahead, somersaulting wildly. They fall towards a tan, barren hillside below.

Though they did not die before, they might now.

He hits the tough ground and bounces, rolling out of control, bumping up spumes of dust and pebble. Down the long hillside.

It hurts. He tries to gain control over his limbs, tries to slow, but it is futile. Momentum carries him. Over a rocky ledge he flies, and he crashes through a thorny bush that lifts a leg of his jeans and momentarily leaves a barbed strand wrapped around his calf. It finally sheds after numerous rolls. He digs his fingers, but the ground is so rocky that it grinds his nails. He gives up trying to stop and just tucks his shoulder, preparing for each collision. 25? 50? It doesn't matter how many times he mashes the ground. Each distance covered is farther from the tree.

At last he feels a leveling off. The plummet slows, and he clatters to a stop on his stomach. Dirt in his mouth, he spits.

One of his eyes bobbles before righting itself. His calf stings like it's recently been on fire. He rolls onto his back and takes time to admire above him. A cloud, shaped like a big, puffy sheep, drifts past.

It morphs into a swordfish.

He lays there for a while. The arid, scrubby land is still. Sunlight is like blades of glass. They are in some barren place far from home.

Maybe they are in North America.

Asia.

Maybe neither.

He groans, turns his head.

Cole is standing, limping around as he digs for something stuck in his ear, but he seems okay.

Phillip sits up, mouth agape. His hair is sideways, and he's somehow lost his shirt. Next to him rests the stick.

They are scratched and bloodied and wrecked with dirt, and the mud from the tunnel stiffens over them like something baked.

When they notice each other, Cole is the first to start laughing.

Then Phillip.

Finally Adam.

They share this teetering laughter until a shrill sound grabs their attention. It is the sound of wind whistling and gathering. They look back to the way they came.

High up, embedded in the steep cliffside, is a dark gouge—where they busted out.

Above, atop the cliff, is the tree.

The sound: loose winds circle the tree and whip up the surrounding sun-blasted and parched topsoil so that each strengthening rotation darkens with collected grains of dirt. Quickly, the winds take one firm shape, and it loudens. The whistling changes to a roar. Adam observes the tightening and quickening, watches with awe how it gyres into a twister that snakes upwards to the sky.

He looks back to the opening in the cliff. The Boys: they could escape.

"Hey!" he says, waving his arms.

But it is too late.

The cliffside begins to crack, and the crack stretches into a gaping fissure. The earth beneath the tree, an entire layer of the cliff, is taken along.

The tornado rises and disappears skyward. The tree vanishes.

It is elsewhere now. Along with the ponds. And the boys.

Left behind, the cliff looks as it has stood for thousands upon thousands of years, as it did before the tree and as it will long after, as if nothing extraordinary has occurred.

Adam is thankful that he has escaped, and relief soars through him, but he knows others, decent boys who never sought trouble, remain caged in a tortured world.

"They couldn't have made it," Phillip says. "They didn't have time."

"I wonder where it went." Adam gazes at the repaired cliff and sky above, which show no evidence of the tree's former presence. "I just wonder where it went. That's all," he says, wistful.

"I think I know," Cole says.

Before Cole can elaborate, a weak moan startles them. At first Adam thinks it is an animal of some sort, but then he hears the sound again and knows it is human. They all make this recognition. Another boy? They look for its source, scanning the perimeter, but find nothing.

They stay silent and still.

They hear it again.

"There." Phillip points.

Their eyes turn in one direction.

It is not a boy.

A short old man, his eyeglasses askew, lies crumpled about twenty feet away.

They rush to him. He is as motionless as the landscape, as still as a pile of rags.

The three boys stand over him. The man wears underwear and nothing else. His eyes remain closed as he moans again. His bald, wrinkled scalp shines with perspiration. Except for being dazed, he appears okay, unbloodied at least.

"Who is it?" Phillip asks quietly, not wanting to disturb the man.

Adam examines the familiar face, but he cannot place where he has seen him before. He then scans downward, and his discovery jogs his memory: below one knee is a distinctly deformed foot and shin.

"Feldstein," Adam says, "is that you?"

94

They sit in shade at the bottom of the cliff. The sun has moved west from its highest point directly overhead. The air is less strained by light and heat. A distant rumble regresses towards them, finally arriving in a soft shake. Phillip looks for a storm cloud but sees none.

"We've aged," Cole says.

Phillip checks his watch. "It's working." 4:37. He smiles at the unexpected ticking of the second's hand. How does the little motor keep time to such precise measure? He notices that the month and day have updated. He remembers sitting in the muck of the pit and revealing the date and year to Tony. He now takes that date, the day he walked into the tree, and counts forward. "We've been gone twenty-two days," he says, "according to this."

"Twenty-two," Adam says. He repeats the number, then does so again as if he needs convincing. "I'm twenty-two days older. It feels longer than that."

"How long were you in the tree?" Cole asks Feldstein.

Feldstein's stare extends to the horizon, where the mountains are dyed a deeper shade of beige and the sky is cobalt blue. "Huh?" he says, blankly turning to Cole. He adjusts his glasses.

Cole asks again.

"Over 60 years, I think," says Feldstein.

Phillip wants to say he is sorry.

"What are we supposed to do?" Feldstein rubs his lumpy foot. "I mean, what do we do?" A hint of panic tins his voice.

Though an old man, he's still a kid, Phillip thinks. *We're all kids.*

"We go home," Cole says. "We take back our lives."

"Really?" Feldstein hastily removes his glasses and squints hard at Cole, even though he is only a few feet away. "And how do we do that?"

"I don't know," Cole says, "but I think we'll know when we get there."

"How do we get there?" Adam says. "Where are we, anyway? Do you have any idea where we are?"

"None," Cole says.

"We need water."

"You always head down to find water."

"We have to find a road."

"But what if we don't like our life?!" Feldstein's slams his fist to the ground.

The outburst catches Phillip by surprise.

"I've watched the pond. I know. I didn't ask for this. I didn't plan to leave. You wanted to leave, not me."

Phillip realizes that for Feldstein the tree was home. His prison was home.

Cole says, "It's your life. You can make different decisions. You can try to change it."

"You say that like it's so easy," Feldstein responds, "but it's not. You're just a kid anyways. What do you know?"

Later that night, Phillip wakes shivering. The cold has settled deep inside him. He sees Feldstein at the edge of camp, sitting alone and staring above them. There are stars stacked on stars. Phillip scrapes up a handful of dirt and watches it leak between his fingers. How long had that ground remained undisturbed?

Earlier, Adam lent Feldstein his jacket, and he is wrapped in it. The temperature has dropped to some range that feels near freezing, and moonlit frost has been applied to every angle.

Phillip considers joining him, but he decides to allow Feldstein his privacy. It is awhile, though, before he can fall back asleep, and during this time he twice witnesses Feldstein brush away tears with the back of his hand.

95

In the morning the old man is gone.

They call for Feldstein, but there is no response. Their voices echo across the wide valley. The name: it drifts around them—disbanding—until joining what little wind blows, and they know not to call anymore. The stunning sunrise, their first in twenty-three days, is a painting overhead. It is as if the sky has been knifed, and rare colors contained only in the sky spill forth. There is nothing to gather. No schedule. The ragtag clothes hang from their skinny bodies.

In the early morning they start walking. It doesn't take long for Cole and Phillip to have their jackets tied around their waists. Adam, bare-chested, wears his shirt as a head wrap. They do not talk of Feldstein or where he might be. They do not talk at all. They descend further into the valley and find themselves in a gorge, tall sandstone walls on either side. The stone is brittle. They follow a dry, narrow riverbed—a trail of pebbles and bedraggled weeds—that eventually exits the gorge and ends: a flat, vast expanse of scrubland, low mountains in the distance. They continue headlong.

A mile or two later they encounter a two-lane road. The concrete is cracked. Slats of faded white split the road down its center. It seems flawlessly straight, not a curve noticeable.

Cole is first to step on the pavement, so different than mud or dirt. Someone's hands helped build this, he thinks, someone's strong back and machines that dug, poured, and smoothed.

People. It will take them to people.

Adam follows Cole onto the road. "It's as hard as steel," he says. He stomps his feet.

Cole crouches and places his palm on the warm surface. When he lifts his hand, tiny pebbles are stuck to his fingers, which he scrapes clean on his jeans. "Which way?" he asks Phillip.

Phillip rests on one knee, using the stick for balance. He checks left. Right. There is little to distinguish either direction. Both offer the same pieces rearranged in different patterns—distant mountains, a few cacti, the pitiless pale light that has dried the ground to dust. He points with the stick. "Left," he says.

They walk with heads bowed while the sun beats them. They watch for vehicles, but none approach. There is no shade. The asphalt becomes a hotplate. They wish they had shoes. Cole, goofy with fatigue, says, "My arm is all alone."

In the distance heat rises from the road, and they see a small building, a weathered wooden shack.

"Is that real?" Cole says.

They stop and wait for the shack to disappear or transform, but it does not.

"Real," Phillip says. "I think."

"How do we know this isn't just another world, a version of what we left?"

Adam's question settles over them like fog, like doom. Up to this point, they had assumed they had escaped.

"Level 4," Phillip says.

The thought that they are not free seizes Cole, and his stomach sickens with doubt. Have they merely found a new dimension of the tree? What might await inside the shack, a cackling Tony there to greet them? Oy! Or will they open the door only to find an ancient pool of quicksand? The possibility shakes him, but he toughens himself against the fear and delirium he feels.

He says, "If this was a different world, and that shack was here, we would walk to it. No matter what this place is, there's the road. It leads somewhere. That's the only option."

They are too tired to argue, too tired to run or even hurry. They trod, eyes fixed ahead.

Cole hopes the shack won't vanish. Conversely, he prays it is not a trap.

As they get closer, the wind picks up. It is like a moat of wind. They must squint and shield their eyes when it gusts.

A dust devil whips past.

In front a tumbleweed leaps the road. It rolls and bounces madly.

They stop to watch.

They leave the road and enter a lot that is more dirt than gravel.

Mott's Store. The faded sign hangs by small chains over the front door. Hand-painted red letters were once neatly stenciled over a white background. Paint has peeled free. It looks like a small, dilapidated house that someone decided to turn into a store. Two steps scored from roughly cut two-by-fours lead to a covered porch. The posts lean. The building appears abandoned and made long ago by a crew of unskilled carpenters.

A bang from inside, like a gunshot, startles them. They duck and stay down, let the sound pass, then rise slowly.

Tense, they approach the door. Cole reaches with his left arm and grabs the worn brass knob. The door sticks, and he must yank hard to free it. A tiny bell rings as the door creaks open, and a tall, elderly man shakily unfolds from a stool behind the counter. He puts down a hammer. He is stooped and thin. He is older than Feldstein by many years, at the end of a long life. His eyebrows are wiry nests.

They enter.

There are three narrow aisles offering a sparse assortment of items, from canned peas to twine, all covered in a layer of dust. There is no logic to the arrangement. A 500-piece cat puzzle is junked in the same tray as a box of ancient mac-n-cheese. A taxidermied fruit bat looks down from a far corner. The floor is covered by thin, linty carpet the color of mop water.

"Please, help us," Cole says.

The man offers no response. He stares at the door, which smacks closed.

"Excuse me," Adam says, loud. He waves his hands.

Is the man deaf and blind?

The man keeps eyeing the door. He walks around the counter and down the center aisle. He takes short, slow steps. Cole and Phillip move aside, but Adam stays, saying, "Hey, mister," thinking the man will stop and acknowledge him. But the man does not. "Mister."

He walks right through Adam.

His body goes through Adam's body.

It happens with such ease.

The man opens the door and firmly wedges it shut, testing it. "Darn wind," he says. Using a different aisle, he walks back to his spot on the stool and picks up the hammer. Beside it is a box of nails. The man takes one, holds it steady, pinched between his fingers, and taps it into the counter. Then he rears back, lifting the hammer overhead, and smashes the nail flat.

Cole no longer worries of whether they have returned to the right world. He is sure they have. Where else would a man repeatedly hammer nails into a wooden counter for no other reason than to fill time? To say, I exist.

But there is one problem.

"We're ghosts," says Cole.

96

They sit on the front porch. Gaps between the wooden planks are wide enough to fit their fingers through. Their backs lean against the store. Nothing is level or flush. Warm gusts creak the warped wood, and the sign twists above them. They listen to the man hammer. He has adopted a slow pace, a nail every now and again. They have gotten used to the sound and no longer flinch.

No customers have stopped. No cars or trucks have motored past.

Whereas the tree was dark and confined, their new surroundings are defined by endless space—a mammoth sky and humpbacked mountains and miles long wraps of wind that swirl and whine.

They have shoplifted a bottle of water and a packet of crackers. Most everything else in the store required a can opener. It's easy to shoplift when you are invisible to others. It makes what you take invisible too.

This is the only conclusion they can come to.

This is part of being a ghost.

The man didn't even look up when the bell over the door dinged as they exited. "Darn wind," he muttered.

Cole twists off the cap, and Phillip rips at the crackers. The anticipation of tasting clean water and food other than worm makes their hands shake.

"Hurry up," Adam says.

Cole tips the bottle to his lips. The bottle glugs. Water streams through his body but does not stop where it should and splashes across the porch. The water puddles around him.

Adam starts giggling. "You sprung a leak," he says.

Cole eyes the bottle like it is cursed.

They look at Phillip.

Phillip takes a cracker. When he bites off a piece and swallows, the cracker falls straight out the back of his throat.

"Awesome," Adam says, his shoulders shaking with laughter. "Just awesome."

Cole stares at the useless water bottle. "The last thing I ate was a little bit of worm. That was days ago. We haven't drank anything since we escaped."

"We should be passed out or dead," Adam says.

"I guess ghosts don't need food or water to survive." Phillip watches a vulture land by the porch.

"Thank you, ghost expert." Adam is still agitated. "But at least we can be hungry and thirsty and miserable."

"Forever starving," Cole says.

The vulture steps closer, probing the boys.

"He probably senses us," Phillip says.

"Great." Adam chuckles. "The vulture knows we're here. He's wondering if we're dead." He tosses the bird a cracker. It squawks once before snatching it. "At least it'll enjoy it."

Phillip watches the bird flap into the broad maw of sky. The farther it flies the smaller it becomes. Eventually, there is just a black dot bobbing. Then that goes away. His eyes simply cannot cover the distance.

Phillip knows the bird is out there. It's just too far away for him to see it.

"What I don't understand is the stick," Adam says. "It's part of the tree. It should be magical. It should shoot lightning or summon fairies, but all it does is sit there."

"Fairies?" Phillip says.

"Fairies. I was being spontaneous."

Though he doesn't say so, Phillip has had similar thoughts. He has held the stick and wondered what dormant powers are waiting to be unlocked. Special words he must say. He has pondered if the stick is meant only for his hands, since he found it, and he has repeatedly asked himself the most obvious question. What are they meant to do—Cole, Adam, and himself—and what role does the stick play?

"Remember when I said I knew where the tree was going?" Cole says.

"Yeah." Adam and Phillip speak at the same time.

"I think it's going back home, to where we fell in."

"Why?" Phillip says.

"Because we have the stick, and we escaped, and that's where we're going. We're supposed to meet it."

"We are so far from anything that makes sense." Adam shakes his head.

"At least we're on the right continent," Phillip says. "I think."

"Is that a truck?" Adam's sits up.

A vehicle shimmers in the wavy, distant heat.

"Maybe it will stop," Cole says. "We'll catch a ride."

They watch its slow approach. A bleak pattering of rain falls, only to stop seconds later. They look back down the road. Nothing.

The vehicle was a mirage.

Perhaps the rain was as well.

Phillip's eyes narrow. He focuses on a muscular slope of distant mountaintop. It's as if a giant creature is the mountain, resting and waiting for the moment to rise on hind legs and reveal itself. "I can sense him. The Boy. Out there. Do you sense yours?"

A few silent seconds pass.

"Yes," Cole says.

Adam turns and looks down the road, which extends to a black tip on the horizon. "That way," he says. "Over there." He indicates a direction different from Phillip's gaze.

The point is clear. The friends will remain together for now. Eventually, though, they will have to part.

Phillip knows there is nothing he can say, no protest to mount. In order to reclaim their lives, to no longer be ghosts, each must find the boy who has replaced him. To do this, Cole and Adam will head home. Phillip, on the other hand, will travel to where The Boy leads him, and this means venturing far away from where Lily was killed.

Phillip smiles sickly. He recognizes the irony. When at last he no longer feels like a ghost, he is a ghost. When finally he has friends, he must leave them.

The sun's fiery rim dips under the horizon. The sky looks mauled. If there is a God, Phillip thinks, his eyes heavy with exhaustion. If there is then He is hard to understand, and maybe that's because the answers are not there. There are no answers to be had.

That night the boys don't mean to, but they fall asleep on the stiff porch. The intermittent sound of hammering nails lasts late into the night.

97

The following morning, inside the store, they take turns walking through the man. At first they are hesitant, but their unease lessens with each try.

When Phillip slowly crosses, he feels, for a fleeting moment, like he is fully flesh and not ghost. For a magnificent second his skin tingles and colors flash across his eyes. All the circuitry of his mind connects. In this moment he senses The Boy, and Phillip understands that he is part of him. He is a missing piece. Without The Boy he is a ghost.

Waiting to go again, the effects of the previous turn still stirring within him, Phillip decides that had he been home, he might have done the same. He might have run away. He might have taken the gun. He might have accidentally killed Lily.

There is no telling.

We think we know, Phillip mulls. We make a show of knowing, but we are imperfect. Good and bad. Sensible and reckless. Life is unpredictable, and that makes us unpredictable—even to ourselves.

We know close to nothing.

"Hey, Phillip. Watch."

Goofing around, Cole and Adam attempt to pass through each other, but when they do they smack foreheads and fall over. A ghost cannot traverse another ghost—nor wood, metal, or stone.

Only flesh and bone.

As Cole falls he bumps into a shelf, and a can of pinto beans clacks to the floor.

The can rolls to Phillip. He picks it up and puts it back. Phillip looks at the old man, to see if he has noticed, but the man is too focused on his nails.

It is hard to be near him. Phillip feels like a reluctant spy. It is difficult to not be acknowledged, to have words go unheard and actions register no response, to have to walk through this same person to feel complete, which is to be alive.

To be a ghost is to be in conflict.

98

Lunchtime, the man pries open a can of corn. Rather than watch him eat, they head out front. They sit down, legs hanging over the edge of the porch.

Nothing has changed since morning except the position of the sun. High now. White. The wind never lulls. The land is worn bare.

"This is like an outpost," Adam says. "A hideout."

"Not quite the world," Cole says, spacy.

"It's not a bad place to be right now, considering." Phillip leans forward on his hands.

"Why do you think no one has come?" Cole says. "You'd think there would have been at least one car by now." He scans the empty road.

Phillip shrugs.

"Want to know what I think?" Adam's voice is scratchy. The dry air.

"Sure," Cole says.

"Sometimes a new road is built. Then no one uses the old one. I think this place was built for the old road."

"Things get discarded. This place. The man. That's what you're saying," Cole says.

"Is that what we are? A new road came. Now we're forgotten," Phillip says.

"Something like that," Adam says.

Cole says, "I can't even remember what it was like being me, the old me. I don't know if I can be that person again. I don't know if I am that person."

"We all have a nature," Adam says.

"But we've changed," Phillip says.

"Our core doesn't," Adam says. "Who we are doesn't. At least I don't think it does."

"Even if we're ghosts? Even inside the tree?" Phillip says.

"That's the point. You're Phillip. I'm Adam. He's Cole. It never changes."

Cole smiles.

"What?" Adam says.

"Would you rather be a ghost forever or be stuck inside the tree?"

"That's a creepy question," Adam says.

"Neither," Phillip says.

"That's not an answer." Cole shakes his head.

"I'd have to be a ghost a little while longer to choose," Adam says. He stares at a flimsy cloud. He waits for it to move. It never does.

"It comes down to the pond," Phillip says. "How much you like watching. It can be addicting."

"The pond's a distraction," Adam says.

"But it was powerful. Look at Feldstein. He didn't want to leave. That was his life," Cole says.

"But what type of life?"

"A life. Just different," Phillip says.

"Tony would have rather been a ghost. He'd rather be here," Cole says.

"Can you imagine if he had come with us?"

"I wish everyone had escaped," Adam says. "Even him."

"There'd be hundreds of us. Hundreds of ghosts squinting in the sun," Cole remarks.

"Some would be very old," Phillip says.

"But they'd ask the same questions. And most would try to find home," Cole says.

"Because no one wants to be forgotten," Phillip says.

Adam sits up straight. He arches his back. He has always been tallest, the one centered in the back row of every team and class picture. "I had a dream last night," he says. "At least I thought it was at first. But after I woke up I realized it was a memory. An old memory. Something I hadn't thought about in a long time. But I can think of it now, and it's like it happened yesterday. If I close my eyes and recall it, it's like I'm there. It's real. My point is, just because something is forgotten doesn't mean it can't be found again."

He doesn't tell Cole and Phillip any more, and they don't ask. To their credit, they let him keep the memory for himself.

99

Behind the store are two junked cars. They sit side by side. One is an old forest green station wagon missing tires and spotted with ulcers of orange rust. The other, a little two-door hatchback, has no windows or motor. They take turns behind the steering wheels and act like they are racing one another. They imagine courses: perilous mountain roads, crowded city streets. They screech through hairpin turns and keep the pedals floored. Sometimes one will pretend to crash, and he screams like he is dying.

Cole is best at this, perhaps because he has been so close to real death.

Even though it is just a game, Phillip wants to win every time. But on Phillip's last turn, when Cole asks if he can win, Phillip says okay. He agrees to be the one who dies.

That's what friends do.

100

They find an old shovel in the back of the station wagon. They talk about digging a hole big enough so all three can lay in it and watch the few thin clouds that wisp overhead, but the ground is too hard to dig. All they manage are small chips in the earth.

They knock around for something else to do.

Adam picks up a rock. He tosses it in his hand. It is bleached white and round, about the size of his palm. Cole expects him to throw it, but Adam places it on the ground.

It shines like a bone.

Without any discussion, they begin to build a mound of white rocks that they gather.

They must scour the desiccate land. They use their shirts as marsupial pouches to carry the rocks through the wind and whipping dust. Cole hands Adam rocks, which Adam hauls. They work the entire morning and continue into the hottest part of afternoon. They never break. The rocks become scarcer, and they must explore farther perimeters across tough terrain to acquire them. They negotiate long distances. But they do not stop. They cannot. Each rock placed on the stone effigy tells them in primitive tones to build further and bigger. Build something. Leave something. The voice is in the wind.

The mound grows, now to their waists. Their shirts stretch. They do not speak.

The failing light determines when they stop. It is getting too dark to see no matter how hard they squint. By the time they are done the mound is head-high and just as long, and purple twilight emblazons them in its song, which they dance to, high-stepping around the mound and howling wild animal sounds into space, their calls travelling as night falls, the product of their hard work dully glowing like a giant white eye in the moonlight.

Their calls are heard only by themselves, though, because they are ghosts.

They sit by their creation.

At night the wind dies, and the desert comes alive. Red eyes flash in the dark, but it is too dark to see anything else. So they guess what the eyes belong to. That was a coyote. A mole. From far away they hear a lonely howl, and once a rattle shakes the air like a maraca.

"Snake," Cole says.

They make up scary stories. Ghosts tell ghost stories.

Cole goes last. It is a story he thought of long ago, which he has never told anyone.

His story is about a paralyzed man whose spine is replaced with a snake. The man suddenly is given the power to walk again, but as a trade-off he adopts traits of the venomous snake. He grows fangs and turns sluggish in the cold. His skin becomes diamond-backed with scaly flecks of mint and brown. In crowds he must resist the urge to feel threatened and strike. He is conflicted: he likes feeling dangerous, but he misses being normal.

Cole's story is voted winner.

101

The man lives in a small room in back. A short hallway connects the room to the store. There is an old television, and that night the man clicks on the TV and feebly turns a knob, trying every channel, staring as if waiting for something to materialize, but nothing does, just static. He turns it off.

He falls asleep on the couch. There is no proper bed, nor is there space for one, and Adam covers the man with a thin checkered blanket. He looks around. Cole and Phillip doze on the floor. The bare room seems stripped of any personal effects. Then his eye catches it: a wallet-sized school photo lying on a dusty shelf. The bookcase is empty except for the photo.

Adam picks up the photograph and stares at the boy. He examines his features—a gap-toothed smile, freckled cheeks. Cataloguing all the boys inside the tree and comparing them to the photo, Adam tries to find a match, but the face remains unfamiliar.

Every nail represents a lost boy.

The boy is the wolf in Lily's drawing.

He puts back the photo. No, it is no clue.

He realizes he is trying to discover connections where none exist. He is trying to make sense of randomness.

He finds a place on the floor.

Sleep comes quickly.

Standing at the edge of high tide. A low, gray sky and rough, churning ocean. At their feet sloshes a tide pool. Two nurse sharks feed on a school of silver fish. His mother points. A dorsal fin, rising, sluicing through. He watches with an intense, silent interest peeked by fear. One time a shark is so close to shore it thrashes its tail, spraying water and sand, to get back to deeper ocean. Without thinking, he reaches out to touch the fin, but he cannot. It is too far. It disappears beneath the water.

In the middle of the night, Adam wakes with a desperate thirst. He recalls his dream, which he recognizes as another memory. He is dreaming memories.

He wants his old life back, its routine and certainty.

He aches for it.

102

The next morning, beyond comprehension, an eighteen-wheeler stops at the store. The truck, gleaming white, is three times the size of the little shack and appears as indestructible as the store seems teetering on the verge of collapse. Its powerful engine whirs to a stop as dust settles. While the driver is inside, Cole, Adam, and Phillip climb into the cab and wait.

They wait for a long time. They watch the land around slowly fill with sunlight.

"A new day," Cole says.

Any more words might jinx them. Phillip notices how they all have their hands folded in their laps. They look straight ahead, at the road that will, with luck, lead them out.

When the man finally returns, he has crackers and water. *Ghost diet*, Phillip thinks. A minute later the truck rumbles onto the road. The instrument panel on the dash is covered with an array of gauges and dials and clocks set to different time zones.

With yearning, they watch him eat and drink. The truck gathers speed. The great weight of the truck is its own momentum. Huge tires hum beneath, and the shack—and its old man—are left behind.

For an hour they drive the lonely road with little to differentiate one mile from the next, and it seems the perfect time for conversation, but Cole, Adam, and Phillip have nothing to say. They do not speak because they are scared, Phillip knows. They share the same fear and are afraid that speaking of it may make it come alive.

Their unspoken fear is that the truck will drive forever, and it will never leave this wasteland, and they will remain hungry, roaming ghosts for all eternity. So they stay quiet. Instead, their eyes reach for what they hope: a new beginning, a path home. They anticipate that moment when their hope is made real.

Then they see it ahead. Distant and artificial at first, it nears and sharpens until undeniable, and the possibility of timeless imprisonment is washed away.

The new road.

It is upon them like a flashflood. Unprepared, the boys grip their seats as the driver sweeps the truck into a busy current of vehicles. After a quick jostling for position, the truck settles into the right lane.

People swirl in every direction.

Phillip cranes his neck and peers at drivers and passengers sharing the road. Each face is like a reintroduction. Each holds a life, from young to old. With each new face Phillip is drawn back to the world he was separated from for twenty-two days. This world is home to his history, and it feels like this history has resumed. He stays glued to the window until fatigue overwhelms him, and he can look no more.

With his cheek pressed to the glass, he closes his eyes.

They travel together across borders. They stop at a weighing station, and the line of trucks extends for a mile. The man drives for long stretches. Sometimes he pulls into a parking lot and will take a short nap or go to a restaurant and have a sit-down meal. At night he sleeps in a twin bed set up behind the cab.

The boys take turns sleeping during the day.

The truck is unloaded, reloaded. Cardboard boxes stacked on pallets are moved by forklifts.

They drive.

They cover land scorched and choked to a pie crust, cruise over green hills, grind past mountains. They see ruined cities. Forgotten towns. Metallic skyscrapers rising and new homes, each one a dream. Everything torn down and constructed and taken away and taken back. Bridges and birds and slow ships and broken boats and sign after sign listing the miles and places ahead. They encounter sleet and rain. Sunrise and heavy nights. Wind, gusting and soft. No snow though.

Not yet.

Phillip likes the rain most.

The driver, small and quiet, delicate almost, safely stays in the right lane, pegged to the speed limit, and never says anything. He makes no phone calls, writes no letters.

Every morning he shaves with a razor.

Instead, they listen to audio books read aloud by strangers, one after the other. They are all mysteries, written by the same author. The stories tell of people who vanish and the search to locate them. A woman disappears because of an accident. A man vanishes because he wants to. The last story involves a young girl. In the end she is found, stowed in a cabin and rescued.

There was never any doubt she would be.

If only every ending was happy.

At a truck stop, as the man gases up, the boys decide it is time to leave. Adam and Cole need to get off the Interstate and head east. Phillip senses that he must backtrack and then go northwest.

They step down from the truck and huddle in the rain and cold.

"It's kind of like Level 3," says Adam.

They steal clothes from a store selling an array of on-the-road merchandise. Jeans, flannel shirts, and rain jackets. New socks and underwear. Boots. Nothing for kids. They take the smallest adult sizes available and roll up the sleeves and pants legs.

It is simple. They enter the store, put on the baggy clothes, the shoes, and walk out. A security alarm beeps, but the clerk sees nothing.

Next door is a diner, and they enter for the warmth.

The diner is mostly empty. A single waitress and a cook.

Phillip sees the man who has driven them all this way, alone at a corner booth and sipping coffee. They head to the booth and sit across from him. Within his still calm, the man is observing with deep and furtive glances those few people inside the diner. Phillip places the stick beneath the table.

The truck driver seems to enjoy this life of solitude, watching the world, but it is hard not to wonder: where is his family? Has he, like a character in a mystery, vanished on purpose?

The man downs his coffee and leaves cash on the table. He tips his cap to the waitress as he passes the counter; she offers a tired smile in response. The moment feels rehearsed, as if it has taken place thousands of times before.

It has.

Then, surprisingly, the man turns—looking back to the booth. Phillip freezes, as do Cole and Adam. It is clear the man is trying to see. He just doesn't know what. He squints, as if it is dark and he is attempting to peer through the dark. He holds his gaze, but after a few seconds Phillip begins to relax. They are too well-cloaked. They cannot be seen.

Phillip thinks of what would happen if the man did see them, whether he would be changed.

"He's his son," Adam says, staring at the man.

"What?" Cole says.

"His son," Adam repeats. "That's why he stopped at the store. He drove the old road to see his dad. To check on him. I saw a photo when he was young. I didn't know then, but now I do. I see the boy in his face."

The old man, Mott, is not alone. He has his son, and the son has his father. They are not ghosts.

The door of the diner closes silently behind the driver. Outside, he does not hurry through the rain. He walks the same as if it was a sunny day. He seems unbothered by it.

The truck pulls away.

They don't know his name.

They cannot remember what he looks like.

They never learn what he hauls over the roads, what gets delivered and ends up in people's homes. What they never come to know, and the vague feeling of separation that results, is fitting, because of its contrast with what is to come.

This place is where they will part ways, this diner on a small edge of a world made up of innumerable small edges, and the parting will hurt.

The waitress delivers a slice of pie to a nearby table.

A fork breaks the crust, and steam curls from the baked apples.

A bell rings.

Initially, the boys are terrified.

The cook slides a plate under a heat lamp. An omelet and toasted hash browns. "Order up," he says.

They relax, laughing.

A clock hangs in the corner. 9:39.

Phillip checks his watch. The exact same time.

At 9:39 p.m. the diner is a slow ballet.

Phillip watches longingly.

"What are you going to do?" Cole asks.

"I'm going to find him," Phillip says.

"Then what?"

"Bring us home."

"Do you think anybody knows?" Adam says.

Phillip looks up. "That he killed her?"

"Yes."

"I'm not sure."

"What do you think will happen?" Adam says.

Phillip shrugs. "It was an accident. "You believe that, right?"

"Yes," Adam says.

Cole gazes out the window. The rain has remained steady. "I've been waiting to see other ghosts."

"Me too," Phillip says.

"Maybe we can't see them." Adam joins Cole. He peers outside for ghosts, too.

"Maybe we're the only ones," Cole says.

"Or maybe we see them. We just don't know they're ghosts." Phillip considers who in the diner might be a legitimate suspect. The waitress, who skims across the floor like she's on skates, is a definite possibility.

"Yeah, maybe that's it," Cole says.

"I'm going to miss you." Adam leaves the window to look at Phillip.

"I'm going to miss both of you," says Phillip. He feels the blush rising on his neck.

"Is there a chance you won't come back?" Cole says.

"I hadn't thought about that."

"Come home, even if you don't want to, okay?" Adam says.

"Okay."

"We're like brothers." Adam reaches across the table and places his hand on Phillip's shoulder. Cole does the same for the other.

Having a good friend is like having a family. A family can save you. "Thanks," he says.

Cole and Adam remove their hands.

The soft drumming of the rain is hypnotic.

"You have to take the stick," Phillip says.

"We know," Cole says.

9:47 p.m.

103

I do not know what to do.

Boys have escaped.

Saying this is as odd as the thought of hitting myself with a hammer.

Escape is still unimaginable to me. Even after it has occurred, I have a hard time believing it.

And I am back in the same woods where I first saw Cole, Adam, and Phillip, where I first spoke their names. The tree has returned to the edge of this familiar forest—as I foresaw—and it feels like everything is converging.

I am so worried.

Not much time has passed since I was last here, but the seasons have changed. It is colder. Early winter. The wet floor of red leaves has turned dark brown. The first snow, I sense, has not yet fallen—but is about to.

It cannot be a coincidence: me returning to where the escaped boys first fell into the black shape.

The vampire cape. The puddle of ink, as Cole would say.

Perhaps I should wait for Adam and Cole, to see if they are able to get back, to see if the stick does have magic in its smooth wood.

But I am tired. I have been Keeper for too long.

I have served loyally. It is time I get to salvage my life. Not the life I left, I know. I know that my son is already a man and does not need me as he once did.

It is time for me to leave and choose someone to take my place so I may become parent to their child.

I want to be a mom again.

The stress of this decision is difficult.

I think I have the right person. She is a nice woman and will, after she serves as Keeper, make a fine mother to a different child.

I just hope my plan turns out better than last time.

I just hope the child understands that sometimes our allegiances must change.

104

They are almost home. They have stowed away in the bed of a pick-up, the back of a station wagon, hiked through torrents of rain. At a small airport they boarded a full flight and slept in the aisle; the only time Cole woke was when a food cart rolled over him. The end of their journey is near. It is afternoon, chilly and overcast. Cole is not sure what day of the week. He could care less.

Their tired legs stride, determined. They follow the sloped sidewalk leading to their street. Familiar landmarks invigorate them: there is the steep hill, the stop sign, the bright yellow mailbox. They could walk with their eyes closed. Unseen dogs bark from fenced backyards. A bicyclist approaches, a stern-faced woman Cole has seen before, and they don't move. She rides right through them, one and then the other. Startled, the woman turns to look behind her to see if anything is there.

They smile.

The heavy sky looks pregnant with snow.

Leftovers from Halloween are scattered about like flak from an explosion: a few pumpkins rotting on porches, fake spider webs the size of fishing nets drooping over doorways, a skeleton hand reaching up from the ground, plastic gravestones.

And two ghosts.

Approaching the park, Adam slows. The pathway where Lily died is empty. A ribbon of crime scene tape has blown and twisted into the edge of the woods. Bouquets of now dead flowers, left by well-wishers, are bunched into a decaying memorial.

Further ahead is the pond, dark-watered and on the verge of freezing. The faded roof of the gazebo is small and far away.

"Do you want to stop?" Cole says.

Adam takes time to think. "No," he says. "I'll come back on my own."

Patches of grass are browned from the cold. Trees are bare and spindly-limbed. Dead leaves wait to be raked.

Their street.

They turn

Close now.

"Are you nervous?" Cole says.

"I'm happy. I don't know what will happen, but I'm happy right now. Nothing matters anymore, you know?"

"Yeah. I understand."

"We're almost there."

Their steps quicken. They round a bend, and at the end of a long street, nestled in a cul-de-sac, are their houses.

But something is wrong. The front door of Cole's house is open.

He sees her: Mom.

There is another woman on the porch. They are speaking.

In their yard is the tree.

"Mom!"

She does not hear Cole. She cannot. He is a ghost. Even though he is her son, he is a ghost.

But the woman on the porch turns. Her face twists in surprise. Somehow, she has heard.

She turns back to his mom.

What is she saying?

He sprints towards his house, Adam behind him.

Cole does not know what is occurring, but whatever it is must stop. He feels his mother slipping away, about to leave him right at the moment he has returned.

"Mom!" Without his arm, it is difficult to run. He must slow down to stay balanced, then sprint again. He does not look away. He is afraid that if he does she will disappear.

There are dangerous things in this world, and sometimes, without knowing or caring, they can take away what a person loves most.

105

I hear Cole yell.

A boy actually sees me.

"You were saying, about a choice," Helena says. She pulls her sweater tight around her.

"You're right...I'm sorry."

Her black hair is as silken as a cat's.

"Your choice," I say.

"Right."

"Would you sacrifice yourself for another?"

"Excuse me?"

"For someone you love."

A lesser person would claim confusion or try to shut the door, but Helena looks me straight in the eye. "Of course I would."

"It would mean you would lose this person, forever. You would never get them back."

"But they would live on."

"But you would not, not as before."

"That doesn't matter."

"You might suffer."

"I'd suffer more if I didn't."

"Then your answer would be yes."

"Yes."

"Thank you."

"For what?"

"For saying yes." I glance over my shoulder. "I don't think I have the right home."

"Are you sure?" Helena tries to be pleasant, but I'm certain she sees my worry, and maybe she is now concerned about her own well-being. Perhaps she thinks an unstable person has shown up on her doorstep, some follower of an extreme religion.

"Sorry to trouble you."

I have introduced myself, provided her my full name and where I am from. I have told her that she has a choice, but I have not revealed what that choice is.

I step back.

She has not peered down this whole time. If she did, she would see my feet do not touch the ground.

"Excuse me." Cole's mom reaches, and I watch her hand lightly touch my arm. "I don't know why I need to tell you this, but this is the first time I've ever noticed that tree." She looks over my shoulder, behind me. "How is that?" She laughs at the craziness of this.

Another yell from Cole lets me know he's close.

"Well," I say, "it's strange what we sometimes notice when we take the time to look. Goodbye."

You're busy, I tell her, from my mind to hers. *You need to go.*

"Yes, goodbye. I need to take care of a few things. Nice meeting you." Glancing at the tree one last time, Helena shuts the door. I wait until the door closes completely.

Then I turn.

Cole and Adam are almost to the edge of the front yard.

I shut my eyes. I feel the tree stir.

I am lifted and taken away.

106

Perplexed, they stand on the front lawn. They look about, first at the sky, then the ground. A circle of flattened grass, each blade quickly rising upright, is the only remnant left by the tree.

Then the remnant is gone.

There is silence and stillness. It's as if nature is holding its breath.

Cole says, "It was right here."

"Let's go," Adam says. He knows this feeling of frustration. During a football game, this is when he tells Cole to just follow his block, and everyone understands to stay out of his way. This is when he pounds his opponent backwards, and the flagstick pushes ahead. Play after play, they do the same. Run right. The yards pile up.

Adam leads. They march to the backyard and into the adjoining woods.

Twigs crack beneath their feet. Adam loves the smell of wet leaves layering the ground. He uses the stick to help guide him. They move persistently, one yard after another.

He follows the broken path they took weeks ago, when they became bored. They were just looking for something to do, not knowing what would occur and how they would be snatched and have to claw their way back home, but there are no black birds to pursue this time and point the way. Adam goes by memory and must repeatedly stop to verify their direction. Whenever they think they are lost, a landmark will appear.

They step over a fallen log.

A moss-laden stone.

They recognize the strange bend of light through a forked branch.

Adam did not realize how far they hiked the first time. He is sweating through his clothes.

But they are getting close. He feels it. The woods thin. Then, at last, his hand on a low-hanging branch, he pushes aside a bundle of dormant vine, and he and Cole exit the snarl and step into the clearing.

They look right.

Jutting from the edge of the forest is the tree. And in the middle of the clearing is the woman, the same woman.

She walks towards them. Her feet do not touch the ground.

They wait for her.

Adam wraps both hands around the stick, should he have to swing it.

107

"My name is Lee," I say. I didn't know how nervous I would be.

"Who are you?" Cole says.

"I'm not here to hurt you."

"Why were you talking to my mom?"

"Because I thought I was meant to, but I was wrong. You both arrived, and I realized I was wrong."

"If you're not here to hurt us, why are you here?" Adam says.

I begin to feel the cold. I have not felt cold or heat since becoming Keeper.

"I was taken from my family, just like you, 11 years ago."

"Don't interfere with us."

"I will not, Adam."

"How do you know my name?"

I think about his question and justified anger. How do I answer when there is no answer? I have had 11 years to prepare for such a conversation, yet I feel useless because the truth is inadequate, as it so often is. He wants to understand *why*, and so do I, but we never will. All I can say is what I know to be true: "I know everyone's name, yours and Cole's, and all the boys inside the tree. I know your mother's names: Helena and Agnes. And not just names. I know what happened to

Swan and Tayib and Tony and Lily, which I am sorry about. If I close my eyes and let my mind glide I can even see Phillip, travelling, trying to find his other self. I do not know how or why I can do this. And Cole, I saw you throw the spear that killed the worm, and I watched you, Adam, squash Helmut and his gang. I know how brave you both have been. I know how you have missed home—and your parents. I was a parent once too, but I had to make a tough choice, which is why I am here and not with my son."

I tell them of the choice and how one becomes Keeper.

They listen, and when they realize that I have been a witness to all their travels, they begin to tear, because this confirms that everything that has happened has been real.

Up to now, they were not sure. They still carried a little piece of doubt.

I want to hug them, as a mom would her sons, but I will not impose my own urges. After all, I am a stranger, and they are boys that have been tormented. They must decide if they will trust me. So I wait. The cold gathers around us, and I soon sense in them a want to be comforted. I extend my arms, and they step forward. I hug both at the same time. We lean into each other. Adam is taller than me.

"Everything will be okay," I say, looking behind them at the woods.

The feeling that arises clamps around my heart with such force that I never want to let go. I stay quiet for as long as I can. When I speak, I still hold them.

"Don't be scared," I say. "Turn around."

They carefully observe one another.

Tentative, Adam waves.

Awkward, Adam waves back. He tightly grips the stick, as reassurance that this is happening, something firm to hold onto in a moment that seems liquid.

The pairs of boys step forward. They stand face-to-face. Cole and Cole and Adam and Adam. They are close enough to shake hands, but they do not.

It begins to flurry. Small flakes of snow.

"You can see me," Cole says.

"Of course I can. You're me."

"But we're different," says Adam. "Aren't we?"

"In the end, we're the same," Adam says.

"I don't want to be a ghost anymore," Cole says.

"Me either," Adam says.

"We know. That's why we came."

"We saw you out the window, from Cole's room. You went into the woods. We followed you," Adam explains.

"We knew you'd come back," Cole says.

"How?"

Cole places his hand on his own chest. He spreads his fingers. "I could feel it."

Does his heart beat in rhythm with mine? Cole thinks.

The snow has picked up, a steady stream now.

"I just want to tell you that I like you, Cole. I'm glad I'm you. And I'm sorry I cut our hand."

"It's no one's fault."

"Me too, Adam. I like being you. I'm also glad you two are friends. That makes us friends."

"Do you know where we've been?" Adam asks.

"No, but I dreamed it was somewhere dark," Cole says.

"It was."

"And scary."

"It was."

"But now you're home," Adam says.

"I love the snow." His eyes closed, Adam leans back his head and lets the cold flakes patter his face.

"I do too," Adam says.

They remain silent while a blanket of white gathers around them.

Cole has not felt the chill until now. The clothes he wears are tattered from the long trip and too thin for the weather. He shifts his feet. His hair has lengthened since I first saw him.

"So what do we do?" Adam says. He is also cold. He blows into his right hand, the stick in his left.

"What do we do?" Adam repeats.

A period of time, not short, not long, passes. It is an indefinite span. The snow accumulates, and no words are exchanged. Nothing needs to be said. There are simply nods of agreement.

They count together. Their voices commune. On three, each steps forward, and there is a moment—legs scissored, hearts juxtaposed—where they share the same bodies but are still separate, and it is like a human octopus forming. But it is just a speck of time, a fragment of a second, before they bond, and then only two remain, Cole and Adam.

Best friends, home now.

It is how a story should end.

108

Adam sees it clearly: a notch low on one of the main branches where a limb snapped off.

Was it wind? The weight of a swinging body? What broke the branch, and did this, the breaking, make the black shape and the realm beyond? Did it form the ponds and giant worms and rocks and bells? Can a broken branch create a haunted world, a tree that travels?

One accident cracks the core, and good intentions don't stand a chance. The door opens and can't be closed.

There is a hand that crafts it all, or there is no reason. If there is none, if there is nothing, it does not matter. What matters is healing. What matters is now.

Because the past can never be fully unraveled.

The future is the next breath, nothing else.

Adam says, "I hope Phillip is okay."

He has always been tallest, the one able to reach the high shelf, and with ease Adam places the knobbed end of the stick into the notch.

He holds it there; his strong arm stays locked in place; he gives time for the wound to fuse; he lets go.

The limb stays.

And despite the cold and snow countless buds twist from the tree's smooth wood. Emerging slowly at first, they spill forth. It is lovely. It is lovely. Tiny buds unfurl into soft, bright leaves and dispense the few hard olive ones, which fall to the ground and accumulate near the tree's black fold. And as new leaves grow bountiful, reaching for higher air, a rich canopy having formed, the opening in the trunk, too, momentarily changes from black to watery pink, as if an opal has been made fluid, and the ghosts of those boys inside the tree are released to the world, hundreds of black winged shapes shooting in varied directions, to be reunited and joined with their other halves, to reclaim the lives lost, to live again in what is left.

I am released, too.

109

Phillip finds The Boy huddled under the quilt, dirty and soiled by his travels. He is alone and wedged into the shelter of a freeway overpass. The roads are empty. The land around is barren too except for endless plains buried by snow and the wire fences that go for miles. The Boy looks discarded, as if he's been crumpled up like a piece of paper and tossed aside.

Phillip does not know what state this is. Kansas, perhaps? He hasn't been paying attention. Just walking. Walking for days and days.

Inexplicably, a small, short-lived tornado touched down hours ago. Then was gone.

He turns to the woman.

"There," he says.

When they wake The Boy, he is not startled. He sits up and moves aside the quilt. He is gaunt and filthy, but he looks at them clear-eyed. Cheerful. Resilient.

"You found me," he says.

Phillip nods.

"Who are you?" The Boy looks to the woman.

"My name is Lee."

The Boy stands. He faces Phillip.

"She's going to help us," Phillip says.

"Thank you," the Boy says to Lee.

Lee smiles, backs away a few steps.

The Boy says to Phillip, "I'm sorry."

"It was an accident."

"I never wanted to hurt anybody."

"I believe you," Phillip says.

"Do you know why?"

"Because we've been hurt."

"No one wants that."

"It can make you someone you never had to be."

"But we don't have to stay that."

"No. We can change."

"Have you changed?"

"Yes."

"How?"

"The memory doesn't hurt me anymore." His calm never wavers.

"Why?"

"I've been running, and I finally won a race. I felt what that's like."

"You're not what I expected."

"What did you expect?"

"I didn't expect anyone. I thought I would be alone. I thought I would die soon."

"I thought that once."

"You don't anymore?"

"Not since I've been gone. I made friends."

"We have friends?"

Phillip says, "Good friends."

"And Lee."

"Yes."

"Is she going to be our mother?"

"Yes."

"I never…"

"It's alright."

Dusk. The stars are coming out. They are plentiful.

"I think I'm ready," The Boy says.

"It's time then?"

"I'm tired of being by myself."

"Then it's time," Phillip says.

"Do you think we'll be okay?"

"Yes, everything will be okay."

"No matter what."

"That's right. No matter."

The Boy closes his eyes. He whispers to himself, something Phillip cannot hear.

It sounds like a wish.

Phillip remembers walking into the tree and how, upon entering, he felt the slow heartbeat of a different world. When he steps forward, the feeling is similar, except this time the heartbeat is his own. He melds with his own heart, becoming synchronous and whole, and they are together—The Boy and him and Lee—truly, for the first time. They are a family, however oddly pieced, no longer ghosts, for they have trust between them.

This new world is wondrous, one of promises made and promises that will keep. It is a world where the possibility of love is real, and love is the promise. It is a place where a once anxious heart beats calmly, and a quiet wish drifts overhead.

110

My feet hurt. It has been so long since I have walked on solid ground. With each step I feel my bones as I never have before. It's as if my bones were taken, and new ones are growing. The pain makes me smile, because this confirms that my life has begun again.

Night comes quickly, and we follow a long, straight gravel road that leads to a barn; its silhouette stands maybe a half mile away. This is where we hope to sleep. The barn is a square with a triangle placed on top.

A silo is a cylinder.

The moon is a circle.

Shapes are everywhere.

It is a mild night of soft wind. A thin layer of glowing snow melts around us. Already, I sense how my hair has grown longer. I cannot wait to shower and run a brush through the knots and frizz. I may stroke my hair 1000 times.

For a second I think of Tayib.

Phillip is kind. I knew this, but he has proven so. Already he has told me "Thank you" a number of times. Once he said it to the sky.

At one point during our walk we stopped to look at an oil drill on the horizon. He said it was a giant metal bird pecking the ground for seeds.

I asked if it was a flightless bird.

It flies, he said, but not how we think of flying.

Is it flying right now?

He smiled. Yes, he said. There's lots of ways to fly.

He is a smart young man and has quiet strength in him. I no longer think of him as a boy.

We are headed back to where Phillip's parents and Adam and Cole reside. It will take many days. We will depend upon the kindness of others to help us. We will cross bridges. Eventually, we will reach our destination.

When we arrive, we will go to the police station. Outside the station, I will hug Phillip and tell him that I love him, and I will say that, no matter what, everything will be okay.

Because it will be.

I will watch him open the door. I will turn away as the door closes.

He will talk to the police. He will lie, without knowing he is telling lies. He will say that he accidentally killed Lily. He ran away because he was scared. He came back to face what he did, because it is the right thing to do.

He will not mention Red's tongue.

The giant worm.

Or the pond.

How could he?

He will hand over the gun—the weapon that fired and resulted in tragedy.

We found the gun with The Boy's possessions. It still had a clip of bullets in it. I removed the clip and held it in my palm; it was as heavy as an egg. When I closed my eyes, I saw everything. I saw how The Boy had aimed and slowly squeezed the trigger. He did so with empty calm. He did so with hate in his heart.

Lily's death was no accident.

I threw the clip of bullets as far as I could, in the snow.

I have not told Phillip. I never will. I never want him to know that inside of him is a liar. Inside him is a murderer. But that does not make him one. If it had been someone besides Lily walking that path, maybe The Boy would have acted differently. If it had been a sunny day, would he have raised the gun? A decision is stored in a prism, and the prism is filled with light that goes back through time to the very beginning of time. Sometimes there is no good guy. Sometimes there is no bad guy. Sometimes both are the same. All of us have people inside who, if we met them, we might not like. We look in the mirror. We see one person. We fool ourselves.

There will be some type of trial—or not. What will happen, whatever decisions are made, will not reflect the truth, because no one would believe that a tree can travel and snatch boys or that we have alternate versions of ourselves that can act differently than whom we see ourselves to be.

To be.

It is upsetting to think that if one tree exists then others probably do too. Maybe there is a cave or an abandoned building. Maybe there is a new red car, in a lot full of new cars, waiting to be bought by an unfortunate owner. It is upsetting to know that some might disappear and never come back. It is tough to think about people in need when we are trying to lead happy lives.

But we must.

Phillip could spend the rest of his life in jail, or he may walk free. For some stories the ending is like an open claw. Will it close? The ending is now, with Phillip sleeping in a bed of hay, cradled in a claw, as we all are.

Still, I will not let Phillip drift away from me. He has returned once, and I believe he will again, and I will be there.

I think of his last name: Strong.

I will also find Li.

When I look into puddles, I can still see my son—so not all my powers have left me, which means magic in some form, however potent, is still alive. A door, somewhere, is open. The black fold of the trunk may have a slight tear, or the joint where branch and trunk meet has not fully sealed.

I will not go back to reclaim my life. Yes, I will take time to see my son, and I will finally be able to tell him how proud I am of the man he has become, but that life is not mine anymore. That is not why I will go to see Li.

There are two of me.

There must be only one.

Before I knock on the door, I will make sure only Li is home. When she sees me, after the initial shock, after realizing I am not levitating, she will laugh and throw her arms outwards. We will go inside. We will sit on a comfy couch, and I will speak for a long time to a woman who looks like me but who is not me. We will catch up and talk of the many years spent as Keepers. We will laugh. We may cry. We both know that, in the end, we must do what is best and what is right.

I do not know what will happen when Li and I join. I might become whole again, or I will merge into Li and become a small part of her, or we will form a brand new person.

Whatever happens, the circle must close with us.

It is deepest night now.

Phillip is asleep beside me.

We have found refuge. Outside the open barn doors, stars cover an immense sky that seems to stretch the edges of Earth.

Sometimes I think about how we presume the sky will always look as it does, forgetting that every star has a lifespan, too. Even stars will disappear, just as new ones will be born.

Even the lights in the sky will change.

No, I will not reclaim my old life. That life is not mine anymore. It simply did not turn out the way, years ago, I presumed it would.

It does not matter. This is my second chance.

I do not know how much longer I will live, how long my light will be.

In many ways, being a ghost was easy.

This life is hard, but it is the one we are given.

It is hard to put into words. It is hard to explain just how scary and beautiful stars are.

Matt Lany lives in Jacksonville Beach, Florida. For more information about *The Tree* and other works by the author, please contact matthewlany@gmail.com.